Great Expectations!

Sasha and Alan have known each other forever.
Everyone assumes these two will marry.
Their parents expect it.

Lee and David both land the jobs of their
dreams at a new television station.
But they're supposed to be married.
Management expects it.

Nick comforts his brother's jilted fiancée as best
he can. And then he's proposing marriage.
Rachel's expecting!

Three delightfully arranged marriages by

KAREN YOUNG
GINA WILKINS
MARGOT DALTON

D0838230

RITA and *Romantic Times* award winner **Karen Young** is known for her groundbreaking stories in romance fiction. She is the author of more than seventeen novels published by MIRA, Harlequin and Silhouette Books, and is highly acclaimed as a "spellbinding storyteller." Karen and her husband, the parents of three grown daughters, recently moved to Jackson, Mississippi, from Louisiana, which means that Karen—a native Mississippian—has come home.

Gina Wilkins is the proud author of more than fifty books for Harlequin and Silhouette Books. She is a three-time recipient of the Maggie Award for Excellence, sponsored by Georgia Romance Writers, has won several *Romantic Times* awards, and frequently appears on the Waldenbooks, B. Dalton and *USA Today* bestseller lists. Gina particularly enjoys speaking at schools, where she emphasizes literacy, goal-setting and motivation. A lifelong resident of central Arkansas, she credits her successful career in romance to her long, happy marriage and her three "extraordinary" children.

Margot Dalton has been writing since she was able to read, and completed her first book at the astonishing age of eleven! She has now written more than thirty contemporary romance novels, and received a *Romantic Times* Reviewer's Choice Award for her Superromance novel, *Daniel and the Lion*. Her novel, *Another Woman*, was recently made into a television movie aired by CBS. A native of Alberta, Canada, where she was brought up on a ranch that had been operated by her family since 1883, she and her husband have recently moved back to their home province, where they now intend to stay!

Marriage
FOR KEEPS
KAREN YOUNG
GINA WILKINS
MARGOT DALTON

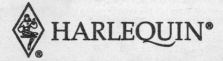

HARLEQUIN®

TORONTO • NEW YORK • LONDON
AMSTERDAM • PARIS • SYDNEY • HAMBURG
STOCKHOLM • ATHENS • TOKYO • MILAN • MADRID
PRAGUE • WARSAW • BUDAPEST • AUCKLAND

If you purchased this book without a cover you should be aware that this book is stolen property. It was reported as "unsold and destroyed" to the publisher, and neither the author nor the publisher has received any payment for this "stripped book."

ISBN 0-373-83407-1

MARRIAGE FOR KEEPS

Copyright © 1999 by Harlequin Books S.A.

The publisher acknowledges the copyright holders of the individual works as follows:

JILTED!
Copyright © 1999 by Karen Stone
BORN TO WED
Copyright © 1999 by Gina Wilkins
TO HIRE AND TO HOLD
Copyright © 1999 by Dalton Enterprises Ltd.

All rights reserved. Except for use in any review, the reproduction or utilization of this work in whole or in part in any form by any electronic, mechanical or other means, now known or hereafter invented, including xerography, photocopying and recording, or in any information storage or retrieval system, is forbidden without the written permission of the publisher, Harlequin Enterprises Limited, 225 Duncan Mill Road, Don Mills, Ontario, Canada M3B 3K9.

All characters in this book have no existence outside the imagination of the author and have no relation whatsoever to anyone bearing the same name or names. They are not even distantly inspired by any individual known or unknown to the author, and all incidents are pure invention.

This edition published by arrangement with Harlequin Books S.A.

® and TM are trademarks of the publisher. Trademarks indicated with ® are registered in the United States Patent and Trademark Office, the Canadian Trade Marks Office and in other countries.

Look us up on-line at: http://www.romance.net

Printed in U.S.A.

Table of Contents

JILTED!
by Karen Young

Chapter One

RACHEL WINTHROP HATED to be late. But after checking her watch for the tenth time in two minutes, she faced the inevitable. Tonight there was no getting around it. She would be late. For the groom's dinner. Awkward, to say the least, considering that she was the bride. She tossed her evening bag aside and sat down in disgust.

Where are you, Mother?

Growing up with a mother who was never *not* late may have conditioned another person to a life of perpetual tardiness, but her own character had developed in the opposite direction and she was simply unable to casually dismiss the importance of getting to an appointment on time. Miranda had promised to be at Rachel's front door tonight at seven sharp. But it wasn't going to happen.

Admittedly, it had been incredibly dumb to agree to wait for her mother to drive with her to the restaurant where Jared's family were hosting the dinner. When it suited her, Miranda Perkins was a stickler for protocol (punctuality being the exception) and she'd insisted to Rachel that they should appear together, mother and daughter. Along with Paige, of course, Rachel's eleven-year-old stepsister, who'd been chosen as flower girl in the wedding.

Miranda would have a perfectly logical excuse. She couldn't find her earrings, she'd had an unexpected phone call, a neighbor dropped by to borrow a cup of sugar and stayed for coffee, the dress she planned to wear was at the dry cleaners and she had to go get it because it was absolutely the only dress she could possibly wear. Rachel had heard every excuse under the sun and yet, cockeyed optimist that she was, she'd still expected that even Miranda would acknowledge the importance of tonight's occasion and, for once, be on time. Was that too much to expect?

Apparently, yes.

She leaped up from the sofa as the doorbell rang. Thank God, she thought, with a final glance at her watch. If they rushed, they'd make it to the restaurant only fifteen minutes past the appointed dinner hour. Snatching up her purse, she opened the door, ready to dash with her mother back to the car to try and make up at least some of the time they'd lost. But it wasn't Miranda at the door; it was Rachel's future brother-in-law.

Nick Preston greeted her with an unsmiling nod. "Hello, Rachel."

"Nick?" She glanced beyond his shoulder as if by some fluke he might have accompanied her mother, but there was no one behind him. It was not Miranda's Mercedes-Benz sedan parked in Rachel's driveway, but Nick's sleek black sporty thing. She couldn't remember the name of it.

"I was expecting my mother," she explained, sending another anxious glance down the street. Nothing except a UPS delivery van.

"I've just spoken to Miranda on the phone."

"Really?" Rachel said with surprise. "I tried calling her myself, but I couldn't reach her. I assumed she was on her way." Her expression changed as a thought struck her. "She's all right, isn't she? She's not—"

"She's fine." He took a deep breath. "I need to come inside, Rachel."

Her confusion mounted, but she stepped back without comment. In the lowering dusk of the June evening, his features seemed unusually solemn. Even grim.

Although they were brothers, Nick was nothing like Jared, her fiancé. He didn't smile as readily as Jared, he wasn't as quick with a comeback. He didn't light up a room the way his brother did, reaching out to people, effortlessly charming

everyone regardless of age—kids and adults
alike. No, Nick was more measured in his re-
sponses, slower to thaw, cautious when speaking.
And his storm-gray eyes were nothing like the
clear blue of Jared's. But oddly, Nick's eyes had
always had a most peculiar effect on her. There
was something about his gaze when it was directly focused on hers. As it was right now.

"Maybe we ought to go into your living room
and sit down," he said, glancing toward the cozy
little area she called her sitting room. In the bro-
chure which described the condo she'd purchased
a couple of years before, it wasn't the square
footage that had been played up to prospective
buyers, but the proximity to Houston's central
business district. She worked long hours as an
architect and her clients were scattered in all di-
rections from the center of the city. So she'd
traded off the relative spaciousness of a suburban
house for the convenience of being close to her
office.

"We don't have time to sit down, Nick. By
the time we get to the restaurant, we'll be at least
half an hour late. What on earth was Mother
thinking? If she had a problem, I could have
driven myself, it's no big deal. Why did she send
you?"

"Miranda didn't send me," Nick said, shoving

his hands into his pants pockets. "It was my idea to come over."

"But why?"

He glanced at the sofa. "Maybe we should sit down."

She released an exasperated laugh. "There's no time to sit, Nick. I've got to get to the restaurant. And in case you've forgotten, as Jared's best man, so do you."

Nick drove his fingers through his hair, muttering something.

"What *is* it?"

With a direct look at her, he spoke flatly. "A change of plans."

It was the look in his eyes more than anything else that made Rachel sit down suddenly. And once she did, Nick hitched at the creases in his pants and also sat. As she stared at him, a tiny thread of concern wove its way from her stomach up to lodge in her throat. Her heart began to beat heavily.

"In what way, Nick?"

"The groom's dinner has been canceled."

"Canceled?"

"Yeah, so you don't have to worry about being late. I've already talked to your mother. She and Paige are probably back home by now."

Rachel regarded him with confusion. "The

dinner was canceled and nobody called me? But why? I don't understand. Why didn't Jared call? Where is he?"

"Jared is on his way to Hawaii," Nick said, spacing the words evenly between his teeth.

"Hawaii?" She gave a short laugh. "Don't be ridiculous. That's not funny, Nick."

"Tell me about it," Nick said. After a beat, he drew in a deep breath. "This is a helluva thing to have to tell you, Rachel, but there's no need for a groom's dinner because there's not going to be a wedding. Jared…" Nick's tone was suddenly harsh with disgust. "My dear *brother* has changed his mind about marrying you, Rachel. And as his best man, I'm elected to tell you."

"No," she murmured, shaking her head.

"I'm sorry, Rachel. I know it's a shock."

"A shock," she repeated dully.

"I hated coming here like this," Nick said, springing up from the sofa with a tortured expression. "If Jared had to do something so rotten, he should at least have had the decency to tell you himself." He was pacing now. "He called me from the airport, can you believe that? He and—I mean, he must have known this was coming. A man just doesn't back out of a wedding— *boom!*—like that." He drew in a harsh breath. "I

thought he'd lost his mind, to tell you the truth.
I refused to take him seriously at first.''

"Who is it?"

He slowed, then stopped, looking at her.
"What?"

"Who was with him at the airport? You said
he and somebody. Who is it?" She was on her
feet now, too.

"Ah, Rachel, that's not important. He—"

She stopped him with an upraised hand.
"Don't you think I at least deserve to know
who's taking my place?"

"Denise Curtis."

"The paralegal at his office?"

"Yeah."

"They're going together to Hawaii?"

Nick was raking fingers through his hair again.
"That's what he said."

"It's not business?" The instant the words left
her mouth, a short laugh exploded. "Listen to
me! How could it be business? Jared was supposed to be getting married tomorrow. He—"

"I don't know what to say, Rachel," Nick
muttered, looking miserable.

"I take it they're…involved?"

"I guess so."

"You guess? He didn't explain why he was
going with Denise Curtis to Hawaii the day be-

fore he was supposed to be at the church getting married to me?''

''He says he's marrying her.''

She looked quickly at him. ''What?''

''He said they're getting married as soon as they can get the license. In Hawaii.''

''In Hawaii.''

''That's what he said.'' With a curse, he went to stand behind her as she stared out into the night. ''Look, Rachel, he's my brother and he's done some pretty unseemly things before, but this is the lowest, bar none. I wish I could think of something to say that would take some of the sting out of it. I wish I didn't even have to claim him as a relative at this moment. I wish I had his stupid neck in my hands right now. I swear I'd choke him.''

Rachel stared straight ahead, hardly listening. ''If he was so unhappy, why didn't I see it?''

Nick remained silent.

''And if he didn't have enough character to tell me to my face, why didn't I see that?''

He gave a wordless shrug.

She lifted one shoulder in dismay, looking at him. ''I guess I should be glad he's marrying Denise instead of me, right?''

''Yeah. You really should.''

She turned quickly, feeling her eyes filling and

her mouth begin to tremble. Pressure was building inside her head and she didn't know how long she could stand here without falling apart.

"I...I think I'd like to be alone now, Nick."

"Rachel—"

"Please. Just go."

"Rachel, I don't think—"

He was cut off by the shrill ring of the phone. Neither of them moved for a moment except to look at it. Rachel waited rigidly for the answering machine to click in. When it did, she closed her eyes as Miranda's voice broke the stillness in the room.

"Rachel, sweetheart, it's me. I know you're there, love, so pick up. I'm not hanging up until you do. Nick's there, isn't he? He insisted on being the one to tell you—he's such a gentleman. Too bad his sleazy brother doesn't have one-tenth of Nick's character or his backbone or his brains or his—"

Rachel snatched up the receiver. "Mother, please...I'm...I'm trying to take this all in. I just don't want to talk about it right now, okay?"

"Is Nick still there?"

Rachel closed her eyes. "Yes, he's still here."

"Good. Cry on his shoulder. It'll make you feel better. He's twice the man that jerk Jared is."

"I really have to go, Mother."

"Paige is here and she wants to say something."

Before Rachel could object, the young girl was already talking. "Hi, Rachel. I think you are *so* lucky that you found out what a stinker Jared is before you married him forever and ever. 'Cause I know you don't approve of divorce and look how awful it could be if you'd married him and had babies and *then* he did this." Paige took a quick breath. "Like, my parents have this really cheesy attitude about kids and all and if it weren't for Mama Miranda, who isn't even my real mother, I'd be in deep trouble and maybe even in an orphanage. And on top of that, I have you as my sister. So, thank goodness Jared won't be the father of your children because he's bad news!"

"Yes, I am thankful for that, Paige," Rachel said weakly.

"Rachel?" It was Miranda's voice again.

"I'm hanging up now, Mother."

"One more thing, darling…"

"What, Mama?" Her voice rose, threatening to shatter.

There was real concern in Miranda's tone. "Do you want me to come over and be with you, Rachel? I love you, baby, and I know this is *so* painful. Paige and I are only forty minutes away."

Rachel managed a shaky smile. "It's okay, Mother. Really." She drew in an unsteady breath. "We'll have to make a bunch of phone calls, otherwise how will people know n-not to c-come? Maybe you could do that for me?"

"Actually, Nick has taken care of that. The words were hardly out of Jared's mouth when Nick got the guest list and divided it up. His sister and Abigail are handling it." Abigail was Miranda's sister, Rachel's aunt, down from Dallas for the wedding.

"This is so humiliating," Rachel whispered, pressing fingers to her mouth.

"Not for you!" Miranda said fiercely. "Jared's the villain in all this. Now you just let Nick pour you a glass of wine and then ask him to run you a nice tub of water. Take a long, bubbly soak. Be sure to use the aromatherapy bath salts I gave you, you know the pretty pot I got from that masseuse in Montrose? It's called Tranquillity and it really works, you'll see. This whole fiasco will look a lot better in the morning, trust me."

Rachel stood for a moment, marveling that somehow this woman—so different from herself—had given birth to her. "Okay, Mother. 'Bye."

She hung up, but didn't move. Beside her, Nick radiated a mix of concern and chagrin and outrage. With her hand still on the receiver, she said, "You're to pour me a glass of wine, Nick, then let me cry on your shoulder. After that, I'm to get into an aromatherapy bubble bath, which you've thoughtfully run for me, and soak my cares away. It'll all look just fine in the morning." On the verge of hysteria, she looked up into Nick's eyes.

"Miranda's an incredible lady," he said, trying not to smile.

"She doesn't exactly hold to traditional philosophy about…things," Rachel said dryly.

"She's definitely one of a kind."

"She's been married four times, did you know that?"

"I did, actually. She mentioned it once when we talked at the grand opening of the Windstar."

"Really?" For a moment, Rachel was distracted. She hadn't noticed her mother and Nick together that night. She knew Miranda liked Nick. In fact, a couple of times she'd sensed that Miranda would have preferred Nick over Jared as a son-in-law. She brushed at a speck of something on her dress. "Only one of her husbands died, the first. He was my father. She divorced everyone else.''

''She mentioned that.''

Rachel wrapped her arms around herself protectively. ''She's ready to blow this away with the same casual attitude that she uses to rationalize her failed marriages. To her way of thinking, I should just wash that man right out of my hair in the Tranquillity bubble bath you're supposed to fix for me.''

''I'd be happy to do that.''

She felt like crying again. Miranda could be right. Why couldn't she have fallen in love with Nick? She regarded him in silence for a moment. The lean, chiseled angles of his face were blunted by his concern. The artist in her had always admired the sheer masculinity of Nick's features. Although the two Preston brothers were similar types, Jared was more conventionally handsome. Rachel once had the fanciful thought that Nick had been created as a rough prototype and then after the edges were smoothed and the harshness around the eyes and jaw and chin were eased, Jared was the finished product.

''Let's take Miranda's advice,'' Nick suggested. ''Do you have any wine on hand?''

With a sigh, she made a move to get it, but he stopped her. With a hand on her arm, he urged her toward the sofa and she found herself sitting down. "Just tell me where it is and I'll get two glasses and be back in a jiff."

"There's some chardonnay in the fridge."

Without another word, he disappeared. Nick was not a man who wasted words. It was one of many facets of his personality that Rachel found appealing. Jared had introduced Nick before the engagement, guessing that their respective professions would be a common bond and he'd been right. Nick was a successful building contractor, fully established in Houston. He'd been a good referral source for her and she'd been happy to return the favor. As time passed, they'd worked on several projects together, the Windstar Hotel being the first. The latest was an ambitious office building which had been designed by the architectural firm where Rachel worked. The project was Rachel's and she would be on the job with Nick as soon as she returned from her honeymoon. At least, that had been the plan. Now, with her wedding and honeymoon canceled, it appeared that she would have no reason not to be on the job Monday morning.

Tears welled up again and she fumbled for a tissue from a drawer of the end table. She still couldn't believe this had happened. Worse than that, she wasn't sure what she felt. Embarrassed, yes. Humiliated, too. Crushed? Well, sure, the man she loved had cheated on her, then handed her the ultimate rejection by jilting her, practically at the altar. Wouldn't any woman be crushed?

"Here, nice and chilled." Nick held out a glass of wine, then sat down beside her holding one for himself. He raised his glass and toasted, "To you. And to the future."

She gulped a lot of it down at once, almost choking. Barely taking time to catch her breath, she tilted the glass again, but Nick caught her wrist. "Hold on, this is a particularly good label. It's a wine to be savored. Let's take our time."

"Right." She stared into the pale liquid, adding bitterly, "God knows, I don't have anything else to do tonight."

Nick, too, stared into his wine. "I thought you might feel better if you talked a little about it."

"Why? It won't change anything."

"I'm not so sure about that."

Curled into the corner of the huge sofa, Rachel studied his profile. Was he speaking from experience? Nick had been married once. Although they'd never discussed it, she knew about the death of his wife and young son in an accident involving a drunk driver. It had happened before she met him, five or six years ago. She had never heard Nick mention his wife's name or speak of his little boy.

"It hurts to be jilted, Nick, but I don't think it's even in the same ballpark with the kind of loss you've lived through."

"Maybe not." He was hunched forward, elbows propped on his knees, twirling the wine glass between both hands. "But any loss is painful at the time it's happening. It doesn't hurt to reach out to people. If they're there."

She was silent for a few moments. "It's hard to talk about feelings if you're not even sure what they are."

He gave her a sidelong look from those incredible gray eyes. "Well, you know you're shocked, embarrassed, unprepared. All of that can be lived down and believe me, people forget fast. The main thing to remember is this. Don't let Jared make you feel you did anything to make this happen. Or that there was something you might have done differently and it wouldn't have happened."

"Great." She set her wine aside. "You're saying there was so little I have to offer that Jared would have walked out on me eventually anyway?"

"No, I'm not saying that!" He looked appalled.

"Then what are you saying, Nick?"

He straightened and set his glass on the coffee table in front of him. "Jared's my half brother. My folks spoiled him. He shamelessly manipulated Bethany, my stepmom, who could never bear to refuse him anything. And Dad has just sort of gone along with it all these years. Maybe it sounds disloyal to say it, but he's typical of the Me Generation. He wants what he wants when he wants it. He has zero tolerance for anything that doesn't promise instant gratification."

"Sex."

"What?"

She shook her head. "Tell me something, Nick. Did you honestly have no idea that Jared was cheating?"

"I honestly had no idea."

"He would have cheated on any woman, it's not just me?"

"I can't say that for sure, but—"

"Then it *is* me?"

"Rachel—"

She felt tears welling up again and jumped to her feet. "What is it about me that drove him to someone else, Nick? What's wrong with me?"

"There's nothing wrong with you." He sighed and stood up. "See, you're doing exactly what you shouldn't do."

"Then why her? Why Denise? What did she have that I don't have?"

His hands went into his pockets. "Maybe she was just…there."

"She worked in the office with him, of course she was there. But *I* was his fiancée! I was there, too."

"Jared needs a lot of attention."

She looked at him. "So?"

Nick shrugged. "His women have always lavished special time on him, they've been at his beck and call twenty-four hours a day, they've pumped him up, stroked his ego, they've catered to his need to be the center of attention."

"Oh, give me a break! You sound like my mother. That's the role she assumes in a relationship and you see how lasting her relationships have been." Rachel's mouth twisted bitterly. "I swore I wouldn't pander to a man like that. I have a career, a demanding one. Jared knew that when he asked me to marry him. He accepted that I have other interests that might not include him sometimes. And as his wife, I would have expected him to have interests that didn't include me." She paused, then threw out an arm. "Look at us, you and me. We work together frequently. You know there are other things in my life besides Jared. How could he not know it? I thought Jared understood this."

"Maybe he did and maybe that's why he turned to Denise."

She stopped, holding her hair away from her face with one hand. "Explain."

"Maybe Denise gave him all the time he wanted, all the attention he craved. She was right there in the office with him willing to pander, as you call it, to his ego."

All the starch went out of her suddenly. "Even so, he shouldn't have fallen for it if he really loved me."

"I don't know if Jared knows what love means, Rachel."

She sank back onto the sofa with a morose expression. "But even for me, a career wasn't enough. I wanted a family, Nick. A b-baby, maybe two."

"You'll still have them."

"No, I'm thirty-three years old. Men can put off these things indefinitely, but women can't."

"Jared proved by his behavior that he's too immature to be a father, Rachel."

She sighed. "Which brings me right back to what I said a minute ago. I guess I ought to consider myself lucky that I'm not marrying him tomorrow."

"Well, it's a thought."

She drew in a sobbing breath. "B-but it's just s-so *awful*, Nick!" Covering her face with her hands, she burst into tears.

"Ahh, Rachel…" Nick sat down and began patting her shoulder, then he was stroking her hair and murmuring while she indulged in a torrent of tears. When it didn't seem that she was comforted, he muttered an oath and hauled her fully into his arms. Rachel reacted with a fresh rush of weeping. Clutching his shirt with both hands, she buried her face in his chest. He felt so solid, so dependable. Nick was a man who could be trusted, she knew that instinctively, and it was reassuring to be comforted in his arms. He was kind and sympathetic. She probably wouldn't be able to hold her head up tomorrow, but just now, tonight, somehow it didn't seem as important as it had when he'd first told her the bad news.

Drawing in a shuddering breath, she lifted her head a bit and looked at him. "Tell me the truth, Nick. Why did he do it? Is it because Denise is…is more beautiful?"

Nick's mouth hiked up in a half smile. "She's cute, Rachel. She's perky. *You're* beautiful."

She didn't believe him, but it was nice hearing it. "Am I too serious? No sense of humor?"

"This from the lady who, with just a smile, charms my crew into working on holidays? I don't think so."

"Okay, I'm too fixated on my job. No man likes an overachiever—that's it, isn't it? It's a power thing." His hands were on her arms, above her elbows. He ran them down to her wrists, lifted her hands and kissed both palms. *Kissed them!* She stared at his dark head in shock. Nick had never, ever even hinted at anything personal.

"These hands were made for creating fabulous architecture," he murmured. "And for making some lucky man extremely happy. That could be powerful, yeah. But it sure doesn't turn me off."

With the touch of his lips still on her palms, Rachel's heart was suddenly beating fast. So vivid was the feeling, she wondered if he'd left a mark. But she couldn't look. She was too trapped by the look in his eyes. That compelling, unreadable gaze held her in thrall as surely as if they were connected by some invisible force.

Nick leaned forward and touched his lips to the corner of her eye. She blinked tearfully. "He isn't worth a single tear, Rachel," he said gently, as her eyes closed on a sigh. Then he was cupping her face in his palms. "In no time, you won't even remember what he looked like." He kissed the tip of her nose. "You'll wake up one morning and wonder what you ever saw in him." He nuzzled the hair at her temple, kissed her ear. Next, he nipped her lobe, then used his tongue to soothe it.

Rachel shivered, as a torrent of sensation erupted inside her with the speed of wildfire. Her heart was beating madly and she was hanging onto his shirt now, not in anguish, but as the only solid thing in an upside-down world. This was Nick kissing her, not Jared! And she was liking it, really liking it. And it felt so right.

He drew back just a bit and waited for her to open her eyes. For a long moment, they regarded each other as two people who sense uncharted waters ahead, undecided whether to plunge in. She could call a halt right now, she thought dizzily. One small move and he'd let her go. He would have done his duty as best man and he would leave. Afterward, neither of them would ever refer to this brief moment of insanity again.

But then Nick's gaze dropped to her mouth and she found herself wondering what it would be like to be *really* kissed by Nick. With a sigh, she closed her eyes again and his lips closed over hers while his arms went around her with almost fierce possession.

His kiss was like none Rachel had ever experienced. It was dark and deep and compelling, like Nick himself. It was wild and sensual and demanding. It reached down into a wellspring of emotion that Rachel never knew existed inside her. It swept her away on a wave of such irresistible need that she was left breathless, her body yearning, her heart hungry.

And when he stood, sweeping her up into his arms to head for her bedroom, Rachel answered the question in his eyes with an unhesitating yes.

IT WAS A couple of hours later when Nick left. He got all the way home, let himself into his house, poured himself a stiff drink and knocked it back in one gulp before letting his thoughts loose. With a groan, he braced both arms against the bar and gazed down at his feet. What the hell had happened back there? What was he *thinking,* for chrissake! Had he lost his freakin' *mind*? He'd gone to tell his brother's fiancé that she'd been jilted and, instead of comforting and reassuring her, he'd taken her to bed! She'd been so sweet and so damn sexy that he'd somehow forgotten the hard and fast rule he'd lived by for the past eight years.

Good God, he was as bad as Jared. No, he was worse! Jared had at least planned a future with

Rachel. There was no question of a future for Nick and Rachel. Or any woman. He'd been there and done that. And he had sworn never again to put himself in harm's way.

Chapter Two

RACHEL KNEW SHE was pregnant a full month before she finally broke down and bought the kit to do the test. She drove home carefully that morning with the plastic bag on the passenger seat beside her, almost as if it held something fragile and precious inside and not the instrument that was sure to spell big-time change to her entire way of life.

And Nick's.

Oh, God, Nick.

She had seen Nick many times since that night. Not Sunday, her canceled wedding day. She'd spoken only to her mother and Paige for the first thirty-six hours after being jilted. She had to get used to the feeling *and* to work up the courage to face other people, not the least of whom was Nick. At the time, she hadn't been sure which was worse.

But Nick had been discretion itself. On Monday morning, she had taken her courage in both hands, meeting him at the construction site just as if nothing was amiss. Perhaps she herself had set the tone for how the two of them wished to deal with what they'd done, which was *not* to deal with it.

At any rate, Nick must have given his men some explanation for her showing up on the job site two weeks earlier than scheduled, as no one seemed surprised to see her, nor did anyone mention her wedding-that-wasn't. Her embarrassment at Jared's contemptible behavior was completely ignored.

Now she stared with dismay at the tiny strip confirming her worst fears. An unplanned pregnancy could not be ignored.

What next? Even the prospect of being jilted again was less harrowing than telling Nick Preston that she was having a baby. What would he say? What would he do? What if he wanted her to get an abortion? But no, she couldn't see Nick choosing that option. On the other hand, she couldn't see him ignoring the presence of his child either. Which presented the intriguing prospect of having Nick in her life on a far more intimate basis than she'd ever dreamed. Of course, some might describe intimacy as the experience they'd shared making this baby. But Rachel knew better. One sexual encounter between a man and a woman didn't even come close to creating the kind of intimacy she craved.

Or did she? Crave intimacy, that is. Didn't Jared turn to Denise because Rachel came up short in the intimacy department? With a frustrated groan, she tossed the little strip in the trash and headed for the telephone. The bald truth was this: she could weigh her options, tippy-toe around the what-if's regarding Nick and rationalize behavior until doomsday, but nothing was going to change the fact that the man had to know and he had to know now.

"HI."

"Nick, hi. Thanks for coming." Standing back, Rachel waited until he stepped into her tiny foyer before closing the door. Ordinarily she would have expected to be nervous over this visit, but she was too nauseous to feel nervous. Unlike other pregnant women, her morning sickness seemed to happen in the late afternoon and evening. She wondered if she looked as green as she felt.

Nick waited as she closed the door, then followed her into the living room. As they walked, he said, "I would have been here sooner, but my secretary didn't give me your message until a few minutes ago. I came right over."

"Can I get you something? A beer? A glass of wine? Something else?"

"Beer's fine." She moved around the bar that separated the living area from her tiny kitchen and opened the fridge. She pulled out a Heineken and took an opener from the drawer to remove the cap. After sliding it across the bar to Nick, she headed back to her chair. "You aren't having one?" he asked.

"Not tonight." Her smile was fixed, mechanical. She often joined Nick for a beer after leaving the job in the evening, but those days were over for the next several months. She sat gingerly on the edge of a big club chair, fingers laced, knees tightly together. "So, how was your day?"

He regarded her intently. "Okay. And yours?"

"I spent most of it trying to work out a problem in the design of an elevator in a very spiffy house for a client in Sugarland."

"An invalid."

"Yes. The daughter. Cystic fibrosis."

He grunted. "Tough."

"Yes." She seemed to realize he was still standing. "You want to take a seat, Nick? What I'm about to say might come a little easier if I don't have to crane my neck to see you."

With another sharp look at her, Nick sat.

Rachel cleared her throat and forced herself to

look him straight in the eye. "Remember when you came to tell me that Jared had run off with Denise?"

"Yeah."

"Well, you said you felt uncomfortable being the one to tell me something like that."

"Uh-huh." He was frowning now, obviously wondering where she was heading.

She cleared her throat. "The shoe's on the other foot now, Nick. I hate to be the one to tell you this, but I have to." Her gaze shifted from him for a second as if to draw a quick breath and fortify herself for what came next. "Maybe I should have mentioned it before...then again, I wasn't exactly sure." She gave a tiny shrug. "Why alarm everybody for no reason? But all doubts are removed now, so it looks like I can't put it off any longer."

"Is this about Jared?" Nick asked, his beer forgotten.

"No. Well, yes, in a way..."

"Yes or no?"

"No, not really."

"What, then?" He was showing impatience.

She closed her eyes. Opened them. "I'm pregnant."

"Pregnant?" He looked genuinely confused, as if he didn't understand the word.

"It's true, Nick. I'm pregnant. I bought the kit a couple of days ago and the strip came up positive." Unable to meet his eyes for a moment, she studied her hands. "As you can imagine, I didn't want to believe it, but I saw my OB-GYN this afternoon and she confirmed it. I'm about six weeks along."

Even before she finished, he was up and prowling the room. "Goddamn it! I can't believe this!" he said, shoving fingers through his hair. "I thought it was bad when he dogged out the night before the wedding, but to leave you pregnant on top of everything else...is...is just too rotten even for Jared."

He regarded her with a look of genuine puzzlement in his gray eyes. "What happened? Were the two of you just careless since your wedding day was near?" He shook his head. "And even so, I would have thought you'd want to wait a while before having kids. Adjust to each other, to marriage, to the change in your lives. You know what I mean."

Eyes closed, she was shaking her head. "Nick, please..." She stood up, too. "This is not Jared's baby."

"Not Jared's baby?"

She could see that he still didn't get it. "No,

there's no way this could be Jared's baby. You're the father, Nick.''

He stared at her in utter shock, then turned and strode to the window. His next words were growled at her over his shoulder. "That's not possible. It's got to be a mistake."

"It's not a mistake. I'm pregnant. It happened the night we…when you told me the wedding was off."

"Shit."

It hurt. She couldn't help the small sound that escaped.

His shoulders slumped suddenly and he rested his forehead against the pane, still not facing her. "Sorry. I'm just—"

"Surprised? Shocked? In denial?" She gave a short, shaky laugh. "Join the club."

He turned. "How can you be sure? I mean, you're six weeks along, but doctors can be wrong. It could be eight weeks, right?"

Rachel regarded him in silence for a moment. "No, Nick," she said steadily. "I couldn't be more or less than six weeks because there is only one possible moment in the past two years that I could have become pregnant. And that was the night that you and I were together."

"You and Jared were that careful? You're certain of that?"

"Jared and I never...went that far."

"You're kidding," he said with open disbelief.

She sighed wearily. "Forget Jared and me, Nick. And forget trying to find a way to wish this whole business away. It happened. You and I were both consenting adults that night. Make that *irresponsible* consenting adults. So the damage is done. The reason I called you over tonight was to tell you—silly me, I thought you'd want to know, considering. Anyway, if you have any ideas or suggestions to make this whole thing less...less devastating, let's have them."

Nick still stood over her looking as if his whole world was crashing around his feet. Rachel wasn't sure what reaction she'd expected from Nick, but it wasn't the desperate denial she saw on his face. "I don't understand why you and Jared didn't have a sexual relationship," he said, still baffled.

"Does it matter?" she asked wearily.

"Yeah, it does. Jared has always been famous for the number of women eager to share his bed. Now you're telling me he didn't demand a sexual relationship with the one woman who was to become his wife?"

"'Was' being the operative word," Rachel muttered. "And although it may sound...odd with so many people openly sexual and living together before marriage, I simply wanted to wait. Jared wasn't exactly enthusiastic about it, but he said he understood. He said it would make our wedding night even more meaningful." She got up again, quickly. "As for 'demanding' a sexual relationship, one hint that he would try to force intimacy would have driven me away."

"And instead, he chose to walk away."

"I suppose so, if you believe that I have so little appeal that I had to hand out sexual favors to hold a man," she said, stung at the implication.

"I'm sorry," he said, shaking his head with regret. "I didn't mean it that way, Rachel. I just meant that, knowing Jared and how he might interpret the fact that his fiancée wasn't sufficiently turned on to go to bed with him, I'm not nearly as surprised that he turned to Denise."

"Who apparently couldn't say no."

"Or chose to say yes."

Rachel flung out an arm with impatience. "Which doesn't have any relevance to what we're talking about here and now. I need to know what you're thinking about all this, Nick. I need to make some plans. I think I'll take a trip to the beach—I have a friend who owns a condo at Perdido in Florida. I'll spend a few days there to consider all the options and then—"

"For example?"

"What?"

"What options are you considering?" His gaze sharpened on her. "You aren't thinking about getting rid of it, are you?"

She looked at him. "If I were, how would you feel about that?"

"No! There are all kinds of things you can do. There's adoption or if you choose to keep it, there are full-time nannies, or if you wanted to stay home with it, I could subsidize you for as long as you were happy doing that."

"It? *It?*" She shook her head in disgust. "Stop calling my baby 'it,' Nick." She put a hand to her tummy. "This is a living, breathing baby. He may be only as big as a peanut today, but he's still a person, an individual. Not an 'it!'"

"He could be a girl," Nick said.

Rachel rounded the bar, heading for the kitchen. She got another beer, opened it and passed it over to him. "Look Nick, as I said, this was something I felt morally obligated to tell you. For some reason, you've chosen to treat the prospect of a baby as something that can be handled the same as any other sticky problem you might encounter on the job. But to me, it's nothing like that. I'm shocked, yes. Stunned, to tell the truth. But I could never consider any option except having the baby and loving him from the moment I set eyes on him for the first time.'' She hesitated, putting both hands over her still-flat tummy, and said softly. "Actually, I'm already in love with this baby."

Nick stared at his beer, knowing that if he looked at her, his expression would give her the wrong idea. Jesus, he couldn't believe he had been stupid enough to box himself into a situation like this. He didn't want another child. When you were a parent, life was just one long, never-ending series of ups and downs. And if tragedy struck again, your heart was ripped out by the roots. He knew the drill and he wasn't made of the right stuff to take all that on again, not even with Rachel. No way.

He looked at her. "Did you do it on purpose?"

"Pardon me?"

If her quiet tone wasn't enough to alert him, he recognized that particular glint in Rachel's eyes and he knew it meant she was ready to blow. But he'd never been the target of her ire. He plowed on recklessly. "I want to know if you knew what you were doing. One reason you were marrying Jared was that you wanted children and you weren't getting any younger. You said that. So when he walked off, did you decide that one

of us was as good as the other as a sperm do-
nor?''

"Oh. *Oh!*'' Eyes flashing, Rachel sucked in a
deep breath and blew it out furiously. He thought
she might literally bite his head off. Instead, she
whispered in a voice shaking with fury, "I'm
only going to say this once, Nick Preston. After
what you just said, don't even finish that beer.
You aren't welcome to drink my beer.''

She thew out an arm, pointing to the door.
"Just leave right now while I still have myself
under control. Otherwise, I don't know if I can
keep from attacking you with my bare hands.''

"Dammit, Rachel...''

"I'm warning you, Nick...''

He opened his mouth to apologize, but what
came out instead was, "I think I'm entitled to an
answer, dammit. Did you set me up?''

"Get out of here!'' she screamed, losing it.

He slammed his beer on the bar and stalked to
the door. But before walking out, he turned and
looked at her. "When you cool off, we'll talk
again.''

Chapter Three

"WAS THAT NICK'S car I saw pulling out of your driveway, Rachel?"

"Yes, Mother."

Miranda went to the window and peered through the blinds as if there was a chance Nick might still be in sight. "He certainly seemed in a hurry." She turned to look with faint accusation at Rachel. "Did you two have an argument?"

"Why would you think that, Mother?"

Paige piped up. "Because he revved up his car so much that it made black marks when he shot down the street."

"That was very irresponsible," Rachel said stiffly.

"I wonder why?" Miranda said, looking thoughtful.

"Rachel, can I have a popsicle, please?" Paige asked.

"May I." Miranda absently corrected the young girl while still regarding Rachel.

"Yes, you may," Rachel replied, glad for an excuse to avoid her mother's scrutiny. Of all people to pop in unexpectedly after the scene with Nick, Miranda was the worst. She simply wasn't ready yet to confide in anyone about her pregnancy. Besides, she was still shaken that Nick could suspect her of doing something so devious as deliberately scheming to get pregnant. What had she done to make him think she would do something so underhanded?

"My favorite's orange, Rachel," Paige told her.

"Orange, it is." Rachel handed it over.

"What's wrong, Rachel?" her mother asked.

"Nothing. I'm just tired. This has been one stressful day."

"Trouble on the job with Nick?"

"Actually, I didn't go to the job site today. I worked on the design of a house in Sugarland." Picking up a sponge, she swiped at the bar a time or two. Hoping to distract Miranda, she said, "It's going to be fabulous. It's located near the house you lived in when you were married to George. You should drive by and take a look, Mother."

Miranda studied the diamond tennis bracelet on her right wrist. "It was George who bought this for me," she said, turning it to catch the light overhead. "He had such fabulous taste."

"How come you divorced George, Mama Miranda?" Paige asked, licking the popsicle.

"He was an old fuddy-duddy, darling."

"What's that mean? He's like Elmer Fudd on the cartoon channel?"

With a humming sound, Miranda seemed to consider it. "That's right, punkin."

"Mother…" Rachel said with exasperation.

"Well, it's true. You know as well as I that George was stuffy. But he did have incredible taste. And incredible money."

"My daddy has a lot of money and he's got incredible taste, too. Is he a fuddy-duddy? Is that why you divorced him?" The popsicle, forgotten for the moment, dripped orange streaks on her fingers.

"No, darling!" Remorseful, Miranda caught her small face between her hands and kissed her nose. "After we married, your daddy and I just didn't get along as well as we anticipated. So when he met your new stepmother, I knew right away they were more suited to each other, so I gave him a divorce and no hard feelings. But…I did tell him, 'Donald,' I said, 'there is one condition.'" She tweaked the little girl's nose. "'Let Paige come and live with me if she wants to.'

And because your daddy and I parted such good friends, he was happy to do that. And with JoAnn's blessing, I might add.''

Standing behind Paige, Rachel rolled her eyes over Miranda's sunny, entirely false account of the facts of her divorce from her fourth husband.

Cocking her head, the little girl wrinkled her nose in thought. "If you're such good friends, Mama Miranda, why did I hear you telling Rachel that Daddy had lost his freakin' mind when he met that bimbo JoAnn?''

Miranda held up a finger. "Now you know that's not a nice word, honey.''

"Okay, but what's the answer anyway?''

"I suppose you're old enough for the truth.'' Miranda sighed. "JoAnn is qu-i-ite a few years younger than your daddy, sweetheart.''

"She sure is.'' Paige noticed her dripping popsicle and hastily began licking again. "She's twenty-four and he's fifty-six.''

"Well, it happens, darling. Men have such funny urges sometimes.'' Miranda took a seat on a bar stool and accepted a cup of coffee from Rachel. "Paige, Rachel mentioned a new game she's just installed on her computer. I'll bet you'll love it, right, Rachel?''

Apparently her mother was determined to poke and pry tonight. Resigned to the inevitable, Rachel handed Paige a paper napkin. "If you want to try it out, click on the icon the way I showed you last week, Paige."

Paige studied both women. "You want to talk private stuff, right?"

"Yes," Miranda said.

Rachel sighed.

"You may as well tell all, Rachel," the little girl said knowingly, heading down the hall. "Mama Miranda won't give up 'til you do."

"So, what's the problem with you and Nick?" Miranda asked as soon as Paige was out of sight.

"I didn't say there was a problem, Mother. Nobody could have been a more loyal friend than Nick has been to me lately."

"Well, I'm hardly surprised to hear that." Miranda sipped the coffee Rachel had poured for her. "He's a lovely man. But you've been so hurt and angry with Jared that I was afraid you might shift those feelings to Nick. Transference, Dr. Sims would call it."

Dr. Sims was Miranda's therapist. "Please, Mother, no pop psychology tonight."

"Don't try to distract me, honey. It would be terribly unfair to punish Nick for Jared's deeds, Rachel."

"What I feel for Nick has nothing to do with Jared, Mother."

"Then you do have feelings for him?"

"Not *that* kind of feeling, Mother."

"Too bad." Miranda's expression filled with regret. "I was hoping the two of you would eventually get together."

Oh, Lord, if she only knew. But as unconventional as Miranda was in her outlook, Rachel didn't think her mother's idea of her and Nick "getting together" would include a surprise pregnancy. "We've seen each other almost daily since I was jilted. Isn't that enough?"

Wrinkling her eyes, Miranda made a little sound with her tongue and teeth. "It's not exactly what I had in mind, darling. I just know if you set your mind to it, Nick would notice you as a woman." She held up a hand as Rachel's expression darkened ominously. "Now let me finish, Rachel. You work with Nick every single day, the two of you have tons in common, you're good friends and you even share the same political philosophy, to my everlasting mystification. Now, in anybody's book, that is a recipe for a lovely marriage."

"Mother..."

"Okay, okay. But you could at least start dating."

Rachel leaned forward, both hands on the bar, and looked Miranda straight in the eye. "I'll say this once and only once. And I hope you won't consider it disrespectful. Stay out of my love life." She pointed to her lips. "I'll say it again— so read my lips, Mother. Stay...out...of... my...*love life!*"

Miranda shrugged. "It was only a thought, dear." She made a face, pained and regretful. "He's just such great marriage material, Rachel."

"Moth-the-er-rrr!"

"WE'LL HAVE TO get married."

"Excuse me?"

"It's the only answer, Rachel." Nick tossed his briefcase on her couch and stood before her with his hands on his hips. "I apologize for saying a bunch of stupid stuff last night. I was caught off-guard. Hell, you could have knocked me over with a feather when you told me it was my—" A quick look at her face and he back-pedaled quickly. "Not 'it,' not 'it.' I meant to say baby. My baby."

He glanced toward her kitchen. "How about a beer? You have one, too. No, I guess you can't, can you? Hell, I don't need it myself. What else have you got?"

"Ginger ale?"

"Great. Fine." He drove his fingers through

his hair. "I didn't sleep much last night, Rachel. After I left you, I drove around for hours. In fact, I closed the bar at the club. I know, bad choice. That's no way to solve a problem, but I was so bowled over that I needed to try and put all this in perspective. I mean, I didn't think I'd ever have—"

He cleared his throat, accepted the drink she passed over to him from behind the bar, and took a long swallow, grateful for any delay. He hadn't spoken about the loss of his wife and son since the day it happened and he didn't want to go there today either. He stared hard at the glass in his hands, forcing himself past the quick mental image of the mangled car that had been totaled by a drunk, wiping out Michelle and Joey as if they'd been so much dust in the road. Last night, as he'd faced the prospect of having another child, he wasn't sure what he felt. But he was sure where his duty lay.

Five years ago, he'd often wondered if he would make it through that time. But he had. And he'd come out of that whole horrible nightmare with new guidelines for survival. Top of the list was that he wouldn't marry again, wouldn't be a father again, wouldn't put his heart on the line like that ever again.

Well. Never say never.

He forced himself to meet Rachel's eyes. Beautiful eyes, he thought, not for the first time. A startling clear amber. The perfect shade to go with her streaky blond hair. "You said yourself you wouldn't consider abortion."

"No."

"And since you admitted one of the reasons you were getting married was to have a child, I know adoption isn't an option."

"I was getting married because I thought I'd met a man I wanted to share my life with, not because I wanted to get pregnant, Nick."

"Okay, that's how you felt then," Nick said, studying her intently. "How do you feel now?"

"Like a complete idiot for placing any trust in a man."

"Jared's the idiot here, Rachel," he said quietly. "Not you. And you shouldn't judge the whole male population by what he did."

She drew a deep breath. "I really don't want to talk about Jared anymore, Nick."

"Good." He drained the last of his ginger ale and set the glass down with a solid thunk. "Because we've got more important issues to settle tonight. So what do you think about us getting married?"

She simply stared at him.

Nick cursed himself for a lack of finesse. He

should have practiced a more subtle way of telling her, built up to it. By just blurting it out, she was probably thinking that he wasn't much different from Jared.

"I've spent twenty-four hours thinking it over, Rachel. I won't lie, I never thought I'd get married again, but I can't let a child of mine come into this world without a name."

"He'd have a name, Nick. Mine."

He was shaking his head. "You know that's not enough today, Rachel. That kind of thinking has screwed up the lives of too many kids. I can't let it happen to mine." He paused, regarding her thoughtfully. "You don't really believe it's okay for kids to have just one parent, do you?"

"No, not really. But think about what you just said. You spent twenty-four hours thinking about this. Twenty-four hours, Nick." She looked at him, waiting for him to get it. "That's ludicrous. I spend longer than twenty-four hours to decide how much closet space is needed in the houses I design. You took three weeks to choose the foreman for the job we're working."

"That's different."

"You bet it is. A marriage will affect both our lives—and the baby's—forever. I need more time—weeks, months, maybe—to think about it."

"And time is what we don't have, Rachel. That's just the point. I have the baby's welfare at heart, but I was also thinking to save you more embarrassment. You know what people are going to think."

"That Jared's the father." Rachel sighed, leaning one hip against the kitchen counter. "So let them think what they will, Nick. I still refuse to be stampeded into a marriage of convenience."

"It'll work, Rachel!"

She gave him an exasperated look. "And you're sure of that, are you?" Before he could reply, she added, "Based on exactly what, Nick?"

He left the stool to begin pacing. "We have a lot in common. Our careers put us in close contact daily so I'll bet we've had a chance to get to know each other better than most folks who actually get married after a conventional courtship. We're friends, too, which seems to me a good solid basis to build a lasting relationship. We come from similar economic backgrounds and we even share the same politics."

"Now you sound like my mother," Rachel muttered.

Momentarily distracted, he stopped to look at her. "You talked about marrying me with Miranda?'' Another thought struck. ''She knows you're pregnant?''

''No! We were just...talking.''

''About me?''

''Only in a general sense.''

''Uh-huh.'' He knew that expression. She wasn't going to say anymore. ''Look at me, Rachel.''

She did, but warily.

''When we were together six weeks ago, it felt pretty awesome to me. How about you?''

''I don't see how that's relevant.''

''If ever there was a time for blunt honesty, Rachel, it's now,'' Nick said. ''Don't be afraid to hurt my feelings because, as you say, whatever we eventually decide is going to affect three lives from here on out. We're linked together for all time—you, me and the baby.''

''True.''

''So, answer my question, please. What about that night?''

She left the kitchen to begin pacing nearby in agitation. ''I couldn't believe it happened, to tell you the truth! I can only think that it was the shock of being jilted. Maybe I needed some reassurance that I wasn't totally unattractive to a man. Or maybe I just wanted to forget everything for a while...'' She glanced uneasily at him.

"This is a terrible thought, but I wouldn't be the first person to use sex as an escape, would I?"

Nick was stunned at the feelings rushing through him. He found he didn't like the idea that just any man could have been in his place that night with Rachel. That just any man could have felt the response that had rocked him to his core. Rachel had breached defenses he'd set up years ago, leaving him shaken to find he was still alive emotionally. And she was calling it an "escape."

His gray eyes narrowed. "You're saying any man would have served the purpose that night, Rachel?"

She spread her hands. "I'm saying I don't know."

"You don't know." His fists went deep in his pockets. "Well, if you really mean that then I suppose any plans to marry are premature."

"I'm just saying we shouldn't rush into anything."

"Have it your way." His words came out clipped and just short of anger.

With a look of distress, she made an apologetic gesture, lifting one shoulder. "I appreciate that you believe you're doing the right thing."

"Yeah."

"I mean...I just think it's best to step back

and consider the…situation before jumping into
marriage.''

"The 'situation' is pregnancy," Nick growled.
"And even though you might like to put everything on hold, that's not Mother Nature's way.
So do your 'considering' pretty fast, Rachel. He
was big as a peanut yesterday. Next week, he'll
be double that. As for me, I won't change my
mind about what I think is best, and I'll try to be
patient while you decide what you think is best."
He turned abruptly and headed for the door.
"Hopefully, we'll agree on what that is before
he's seven and a half pounds."

"And if we don't?" Rachel asked coolly.

"We will." He had the door open, but he
turned back. "There was something I meant to
say when I first got here tonight." He took a deep
breath, then spoke gruffly. "It was wrong to react
the way I did when you first told me about the
pregnancy. I know you're not the kind of person
who would ever do something like this deliberately. I was shocked and I spoke without thinking."

"It's okay." She managed a small shrug. "I
was pretty shocked myself, but I'd had several
weeks to come to grips with it."

"I should have had more control. I'm sorry."

"I said it's okay, Nick."

After a keen look, he said, "One more thing. I could never feel good about myself again if we didn't do the right thing about this baby. He didn't ask to be brought into this world and he deserves a mom and a dad."

Rachel waited until the door closed behind him before she sat down and burst into tears.

Chapter Four

RACHEL WAS AT the job site the next morning hoping that her face bore no evidence of the teary episode the night before, but just in case, she wore her darkest sunglasses. She wasn't even sure why she'd broken down that way, unless it was just another crazy symptom of her condition. According to the books, pregnancy worked havoc with a woman's emotions and it seemed nobody pushed her buttons the way Nick did.

She'd been so angry over the way he'd reacted when she told him about the baby that she'd spent half the night conjuring up ways of punishing him. Then when he'd apologized and offered to marry her, she'd spent another miserable evening bawling her eyes out. If she kept this up, she'd be such an emotional basket case that she wouldn't have to worry about making the decision whether to get married or not, because Nick would no doubt withdraw the offer.

And that was another troubling thing. She didn't like the idea of Nick offering to marry her out of some duty-bound urge to do the right thing by her and the baby. But for some reason, she didn't feel like examining that odd reaction too closely. Why else would he want to marry her? Why else would she want him to marry her? It wasn't as if she loved him.

Donning a hard hat, she started across the work site. Jim McMurray, the job foreman, waved at her from a scaffold on the second level. She felt both relief and a little pang of disappointment that Nick was obviously not around today. She would give Jim the change orders, answer any questions he might have, and then escape before Nick returned.

She'd have to walk the single plank which bridged a wide ditch being excavated for the plumbing since there was no other way to get across and inside the building. Starting off, she wobbled a bit and her hard hat slipped, obscuring her vision. Off-balance, she grabbed at it, but too late. It toppled to the mud below. Now, halfway across and struggling to keep her footing, she missed something Jim was yelling at her as the scaffolding was lowered.

She wasn't sure when she realized she was in danger. Two levels above her head, a load of two-by-six framing studs was suspended by a steel hook on a huge crane. Jim's frantic gestures

made her look up in time to see the cables holding the studs shift. She knew in a heartbeat that
the load was going to fall. Stranded as she was
midway across the plank, it was not possible to
reach the other side fast enough.

Her first thought was for her baby. She had to
make the huge leap to safety or be crushed by
the falling lumber. Moving on instinct alone, she
got ready to make the effort and then somehow,
someone grasped her arm, pulling her with such
desperate force that she was lifted off her feet
and jerked the whole length of the plank as the
lumber crashed down.

Coming up hard against a broad chest, the
breath was knocked out of her. And then both
she and her rescuer were falling to the ground,
but in a way that shielded Rachel from a hard
landing. For a moment or two she lay stunned
and breathless, cradled securely in Nick's embrace. She wasn't certain when she realized that
Nick was her rescuer, possibly as they'd tumbled
to the ground in a tangle of arms and legs and
other body parts. Or possibly as she heard his
voice in her ear hoarse with panic before he
jerked her to safety. Or maybe when it was over
and his panic became profanity. Whatever the
clues, as she looked up into his eyes through

cocked sunglasses, her body pressed to his, the whole scene seemed oddly familiar.

With a look on his face that defied any word she could come up with, he snatched off her sunglasses. "Are you hurt?"

Impossible to know. Sprawled in the V of his legs, touching him in places she felt only once before, Rachel wasn't sure whether she was hurt or not. Nothing seemed broken. Nothing seemed sprained. Or strained. Except possibly her dignity. But it had been a close call.

"I'm okay. I think."

He sat up, bringing her with him. But even though his features were grim and his gray eyes storm-dark, he handled her gently. Still supporting her, he got to his feet, and when she stood before him, she realized he was furious. Silently, he ran unsteady hands over both her arms, grunting with disapproval when he found a nasty scrape on her elbow.

Nearby, Jim McMurray picked up her fallen papers and knocked them against his leg to clear away the mud. "Gosh, that was a close call, Ms. Winthrop. Good thing Nick spotted you crossing that plank when he did. Jeez, I never saw a man move that fast."

"Yes," she said flatly. But when she reached for the change orders, Nick intercepted them.

Holding the papers in one hand, he claimed her uninjured elbow in the other and began hustling her out of the building, his face a dark cloud.

"There's a first-aid kit in the trailer," he told her gruffly.

"Really, it's nothing, Nick. I'm okay."

"Humor me." He was already halfway across the grounds, heading for the double-wide he used as an on-site office. After a few steps, he stopped and looked back at McMurray. "I want to know what happened to that cable, Jim. Somebody could've been killed."

"Yes, sir."

The trailer was well insulated and blessedly empty. When Nick closed the door, the noise of the backhoe and street traffic ceased abruptly, leaving them in a cocoon of charged silence.

One look at Nick was enough to tell her that he was still battling the urge to rake her over the coals. He tossed her sunglasses on a work table before speaking. "Do you realize what a close call you just had, Rachel?"

She was not a nitwit. "Of course, but—"

"No buts. What were you thinking?"

"I wasn't thinking a load of two by sixes would fall on my head," she replied testily. Usually she held her own when she and Nick disagreed, but right now her knees were still shaking and she wanted to sit down.

"Where the hell was your hard hat?"

"I... It fell off when I lost my balance on that plank." She glanced around in distraction, needing to sit. The work table was cluttered with plans and drafting materials. Used coffee cups, stinky cigar butts and yellow sticky notes were everywhere. Definitely a male retreat. Rachel spied a chair and sank gratefully into it.

"And what was the idea of those dark glasses?" Nick demanded. "The day's overcast. It's no wonder you couldn't see where you were going."

"I...uh, give me a minute, Nick." Now that the incident was over, reaction was setting in. Her limbs were trembling and she felt a little dizzy. And nauseous.

She put a hand to her forehead, hoping to clear her vision and banish the roaring in her head. She knew Nick was saying something else, but his voice was receding into a hollow hole. When stars began popping, she knew she was going to faint.

One minute Nick was telling Rachel in no uncertain terms that, architect or not, she was subject to the same safety rules and regs as the lowest ranking laborer and, in the next, he was leaping to catch her as she slid without a whimper off the chair to the floor.

He stood holding her with his heart pounding, looking around frantically for help, but nobody on the site knew what to do for an unconscious woman any more than he did. Striding to a couch, he cleared away building specs and newspapers with a single swipe and gently laid her down.

"Blood to the brain," he muttered. "Feet elevated." Reacting to scraps of first-aid facts that came to him, he was gripped by an all-encompassing fear. He cursed himself for jumping down her throat before she had a chance to pull herself together. She'd just avoided an accident that could have been fatal only to get chewed out by him, not because he was mad at her, but because it had scared the hell out of him to see her in danger. When had Rachel become so important to him?

Whoa. He didn't want to go there.

Dashing to the small bathroom, he wet a few paper towels and ran back. Dropping beside her on the couch, he gently sponged her cheeks, her forehead, her throat, but she remained unresponsive. Truly alarmed now, he scanned her pale face anxiously, searching for a hint of movement. Her hair had worked loose from a French braid and he pushed a few strands from her cheek, finding it soft and clingy. Stroking her temples with his thumbs, he tried to draw a sign of life from her. But her eyelids remained closed and still.

"Rachel, Rachel, please wake up." Fumbling for her wrist, he tried to find a pulse, but he was so shaken, he couldn't feel anything, so he began unbuttoning her blouse to get at the pulse point in her throat. He found it beating steadily and strong. She gave a small moan. Weak with relief, he levered her up and just held her fast against his chest.

Quick images of another time and another limp and lifeless woman flashed before him, but with an angry sound, he closed his mind to shut them out.

Rachel moaned again.

"Rachel! Are you okay?"

Rachel fought through a blanket of fog toward consciousness. She heard Nick's voice, knew that she was close and safe in his embrace. He didn't sound angry anymore, just concerned, but she couldn't quite find the will to answer him.

He cupped her face in one hand, frantically urging her to wake up. She should wake up, she thought, but it felt good—safe—being held this way. For a few seconds more, she let herself simply bask in the luxury of being cared for.

And then Nick began fumbling for the buckle of her belt. Working it loose, he unbuttoned the waistband of her jeans and pulled the tail of her blouse free. Undressing her. He'd done this once before, she thought dreamily, but she'd been wearing silk and lace then, not a man's shirt and jeans.

"Rachel, please say something,' he pleaded.

"I'm going to be sick."

"Oh, jeez, oh, no." Lifting her up, he hustled her to the tiny bathroom and turned on the water at the sink. Holding her upright with an arm around her waist, he snatched a handful of paper towels, thrust them beneath the water and began wiping her face for the second time. "Take deep breaths," he told her, patting her cheeks and her throat, inadvertently dribbling water into her bra. "Slow and easy does it," he said in a voice totally unlike the wild man who'd hustled into the trailer, scolding her for her carelessness.

"I think it's passed," she said shakily, pushing the soggy paper towels away. "I just need to sit down until I get my bearings."

"You need to lie down."

"Only for a minute."

Scowling, he urged her back toward the couch with an arm still firmly about her waist. Sitting, not lying, she rested her head against the back of the couch and watched him pull a light blanket from a built-in cupboard. Because the thermostat in the trailer was set cold enough to preserve fresh meat, she said nothing when he draped it over her. Or when he sat down on a small space beside her. Or when he subjected her to a keen inspection.

"Better now?"

"I think so."

He glanced once at her abdomen. "Baby's okay?"

"Baby's okay. Nausea's gone." She placed a hand over her tummy. "I guess I was a little shaken by such a close call."

He let out a breath. "And I shouldn't have jumped on you before you'd had a chance to pull yourself together."

She met his eyes, managing a smile. "But it would've been okay to jump on me afterward?"

"Well..." He had the grace to look chagrined.

"I'll think twice before I walk over another plank like that."

"Good. For two reasons. One, there have been a couple of accidents on this job. Maybe it's hexed, I don't know. Second, a close call like that can unravel even experienced construction types."

She was beginning to feel more like herself. "But did they faint?"

"No, but they weren't pregnant, either."

"I guess I can chalk up another lesson learned about being pregnant," she said dryly. "Nausea can strike anytime, any place."

"Has it happened before?"

"Oh, yes."

"I'm sorry."

She gave him a wry look. "Comes with the territory, I think." Then she wrinkled her nose. "Along with a few other surprises."

"Such as..."

"Well, pregnancy is an emotional roller coaster, which isn't all that surprising, I suppose. But I learned something else when I looked up and saw that stuff come tumbling down and I knew I couldn't move fast enough to get out of the way." Her gaze drifted beyond him as she tried to put her feelings into words. "My first thought was for the baby. There was fear like none I've ever felt, a deep, almost primal emotion that nearly stopped my heart cold, Nick. I knew then that even though the baby was unplanned and I'd reacted with shock and a mixture of emotions when I first realized I was pregnant...even with all that, I didn't want anything to happen to this child."

"It scared the hell out of me, too," Nick said, on his feet again. He'd stood up abruptly while she was talking. Now it seemed he wouldn't quite meet her eyes. "So you're sure you're okay? You don't need one of my men to drive you back to your office?"

"No, thanks," she replied after a curious look at him. She knew a dismissal when she heard it. Tossing the blanket aside, she stood up. "I need to swing back by my house and change. I'm soaked."

"Yeah, sorry about that." He watched her button up her shirt, leaving it loose over her jeans.

"No problem. Did I remember to thank you?"

"No thanks necessary."

She'd give a lot to know what Nick was thinking right now, but his face was an unreadable mask. Even though they'd been as intimate as it was possible to be with each other, at the moment she felt as if they were two strangers talking.

"If you don't mind, I think I'll put off discussing the change orders just now," she said, glancing around for the plans she'd brought with her. "Look them over, will you? If you recall, there have been a substantial number of changes already on this job. I've explained about expense and downtime to the clients, but nothing I say seems to penetrate. Hardly a day goes by that the nephew, who is a part-owner in this particular venture, doesn't pop in to float yet another idea. I can seldom talk him out of it. Seems they're only happy for as long as it takes to think of something different.''

''Speaking of the nephew, I had to ask him to cut back on impromptu visits to the site. His questions were disruptive to the crew,'' Nick said, following her to the door of the trailer.

''Lucky you. I'd declare my office off-limits if I could,'' Rachel said dryly.

He opened the door for her. ''Have you thought about cutting back on your schedule?''

''Not really.'' Rachel stepped down out of the trailer with the distinct feeling that she was being hustled on her way.

''I'll give you a call,'' he said.

''Sure.''

She was climbing in her car when she suddenly realized what seemed odd about Nick today. He'd been concerned about the baby and her close call and she was sure that his agitation when she fainted was genuine. But his reaction seemed disconnected in a personal sense, almost as if he'd distanced himself from her. And he had not mentioned marriage again.

Chapter Five

"GUESS WHO I saw at La Madeleine having lunch today?" Miranda reached for the cheese mill and ground fresh parmesan over a huge salad.

"I have no idea." Sitting on the floor surrounded by boxes and packing material, Rachel checked off another name from her gifts-to-be-returned list. Although Nick and his sister had done most of the work, there were several gifts Rachel felt she should return personally.

"Let me guess!" Paige said. "Give some clues, like male or female, old or young, we like 'em or we don't. Then we'll guess, right, Rachel?"

"I guess so, sweetie."

"We're extremely disappointed in him," Miranda said, mixing oil and vinegar with a French whisk.

Paige closed a kitchen cabinet with a bang. "Good clue! It's a boy! So is he old or young?"

"Woefully immature," Miranda said.

Sensing where this was going, Rachel frowned. "Mother..." she said in a warning tone.

"Jared!" Paige said, wrinkling her nose. "Am I right?"

"You guessed it, baby." Miranda came out of the kitchen with the salad and set it on the table.

"Yuck," said Paige. "He's my most unfavorite person."

Rachel made another notation on a tablet after opening a box containing a beautiful crystal vase, then said dryly, "I thought we were never going to mention his name again as long as we all lived."

"I just wanted to let you know that he was with That Woman," Miranda said, putting napkins around the table. "And she's hardly five feet tall, Rachel, and *plump*. There's no other word. And I hope you weren't thinking that red hair is natural."

"No more than mine is naturally blond," Rachel muttered.

"You most certainly are a natural blonde," Miranda huffed. "Your hair was absolutely golden in your childhood."

"That was then, this is now."

"Will I still be a blonde when I grow up?"

Paige asked, crossing her eyes to look up at her long white-blond bangs.

"Yes," Miranda said.

"It won't matter if you aren't," Rachel said.

"I don't know what he was thinking to choose That Woman over you," Miranda grumbled.

"Let it go, Mother," Rachel said, stuffing white paper around the crystal vase. "I have. To be honest, I should never have let our relationship get beyond simple friendship. Jared needed more than I could offer him. Denise was there to fulfill those needs."

She looked up to find Miranda studying her intently. "Exactly what needs, Rachel?"

But Rachel was regarding the table, now set with four places, not three. "Mother, who's coming to dinner?"

Miranda was saved by the chiming of the doorbell.

"I'll get it!" Paige shouted, racing to the front of the house.

"That must be Nick," Miranda said. Untying her apron, she gave Rachel a critical once-over. "You might want to slip into the bathroom and freshen up a bit, Rachel."

Rachel scrambled to her feet. "Why is Nick here? What are you up to, Mother?"

With a warning look, Miranda shushed Rachel

with a finger to her lips and whispered, "Nick very thoughtfully agreed to pick up the rest of the gifts when you've boxed them up and take them to the UPS place. And since dinner's ready and there's more than enough food...well, why wouldn't he want to join us?"

"And you didn't think to consult me before arranging this?" Rachel's tone was low, but charged with outrage.

"I can't imagine that you'd object, dear. It's such a hassle loading up those boxes and waiting in that line."

"It's just as much a hassle for Nick!"

"He'll probably ask one of his men to do it."

"At a cost of sixteen dollars an hour? I don't think so." Exasperated, she gave her mother a piercing look. "Does he know I'm here?"

"I may not have mentioned that."

"Mother!"

"It's Nick!" Paige announced, skipping along beside him. "He's all ready to pick up the gifts and stuff but I told him Rachel hadn't finished yet."

"Hello, Nick," Rachel said.

"Rachel." He nodded, then gave Miranda a smile after glancing at his watch. "Am I interrupting dinner?"

"No, no, you can join us. You're just in

time." Miranda bustled around the table carrying a bottle of wine. "Here, open this, if you will, Nick. Rachel, you're about done there, aren't you?"

"Not quite," she said, her teeth on edge.

"Well, it can wait and dinner shouldn't. Now, let's see...I have the salad on the table, the pasta's just about ready." She gave Nick a bright look. "You like fettucine alfredo, I hope?"

Nick avoided looking at Rachel. "Um, yes."

"We have shrimp cocktails, too!" Paige chirped. "I helped Mama Miranda make 'em."

"Sorry, I'll have to pass. I've already eaten," Rachel said with a devilish wish to throw a monkey wrench in her mother's shameless manipulations. But when she saw the chagrin on their faces—Nick's included—she relented. "Just kidding," she added weakly.

"Nick, you pour the wine," Miranda directed when they were all seated.

Rachel put a hand over her glass. "Nothing for me. I'm trying to cut calories," she explained to her puzzled mother.

"Dieting, dear? Whatever for? You're a perfect size eight, isn't she, Nick? With her height, she doesn't have to worry, lucky girl."

"She's perfect," Nick said.

"We were just talking about Jared," Paige

said, offering her helpful contribution to the table conversation.

"Is that so?" Nick glanced once at Rachel.

"Yeah, Mama Miranda saw him and his new wife at La Madeleine today. But Rachel doesn't care anymore. She's ready to let it go."

"She is, is she?" Nick said.

"Uh-huh."

Rachel closed her eyes and wished herself at home. At a movie. On the moon.

"That sounds like a very intelligent thing to do," Nick told Paige.

"We all like you better than Jared anyway," Paige said, dimpling at him, like a budding coquette.

"I'll get the shrimp cocktails," Rachel said, rising abruptly. In the kitchen, she placed the four appetizers on a tray and stood for a moment trying to collect herself. She liked order and control in her life, but ever since her wedding-that-wasn't, it seemed everything had spiraled out of control. Just a few weeks ago, she'd planned to be a married woman now with all the changes that entailed—a different home, a different lifestyle, a sharing of decisions and personal space with a husband. Instead, here she was pregnant and unmarried, her immediate future uncertain, her mother unsubtly pushing her at Nick and Nick himself giving off mixed signals.

"Need some help?" Nick asked.

She gave a start, almost up-ending the tray. "No, it's...I've got it. I was on my way."

"You're upset. What's wrong?"

"Nothing that concerns you, Nick. Look, you've done enough by returning all those other gifts. I can handle everything that's left. My mother shouldn't have called you over here tonight. I would have saved you a trip, but she conveniently failed to let me know you were coming."

Ignoring her protests, he took the tray from her. "It's no trouble to take the packages to the UPS office. You know how I feel about the responsibility for returning them. Besides, I'd planned to give you a call tonight. I found out what happened with that crane accident today."

"You did?"

"Yeah. The crane had been rigged out with a substandard hook. With that kind of weight, all it took was a slight shift in momentum and the additional stress snapped it."

"How does it happen that we're working with a crane outfitted with substandard material? That's asking for trouble."

"I don't know, but I'm damn sure going to

find out.'' He stepped back to let her go in front of him. ''It was a deliberate act of sabotage, so I've beefed up security. Extra guards are on duty at night now.''

''Good move,'' Rachel said, thinking. ''You mentioned something once before about a couple of suspicious incidents on this project. What's going on, Nick?''

''Somebody's bent on causing mischief,'' he replied, ''which makes it next to impossible to keep the area safe until I figure out who it is and why it's happening.''

''I don't know what else you can do after putting in extra security guards,'' Rachel said thoughtfully. A construction project was a high-risk work environment under the best conditions, but deliberate sabotage was criminal. Someone could get hurt. ''I assume you'll caution the men to be extra careful,'' she said, heading for the door. ''In the meantime, I'll speak to the client. Not that I expect her to be much help. She and her nephew treat the project like it's a vacation cottage and not a multimillion-dollar investment. But who knows, she may give us a clue.''

''It's worth a try. I'd planned to drop by your place this evening to discuss it. But no matter what, until I get to the bottom of this, I want you to stay away from the site.''

She stopped short, almost causing him to spill the shrimp cocktails. "Don't be ridiculous! How can I monitor the project if I don't have access to the site?"

"Someone else from the firm will just have to take over, Rachel."

She stared at him. "You aren't serious? I worked hard to get this assignment, Nick. How will it look if I tell Simon that I can't do the job after all?" Simon Laird, the head of the firm, had very reluctantly bowed to pressure from his staff to hire two women architects. It had taken two years to reach the point where she was senior project officer on the job. She'd suspected at the outset that she'd gotten this particular project because the client, Agnes Armstrong, was a woman and known to be demanding, but the opportunity to prove herself had been too good to pass up.

"You don't have to tell Simon," Nick said, scowling. "I'll do it for you."

She rolled her eyes. "Oh, great. And that's sure to make me seem like such a professional."

"You're pregnant," he said in a low, but fierce tone. "I think that should be your main focus right now, not some hell-bent desire to be viewed on a par with the man you work with."

"And while we're at it, why don't I just toss all the respect I've worked so hard to earn? Get real, Nick. If I back away from this now, I'll never be taken seriously again, pregnant or not. Simon Laird's from the old school. It's no secret he resents the two female architects. I can just hear him now telling everybody he was right. The going gets tough, women can't take it. Worse yet, once my pregnancy is visible, he'll say I'm trying to avoid carrying the same workload expected from a man.''

''We're not talking about equality in the workforce, Rachel. This is about your safety. And the baby's. I'm not prepared to put our child in jeopardy because you don't want to seem too feminine to Simon Laird. To hell with Simon Laird!''

''Be quiet!'' She gave him a fierce look while gesturing with her eyes toward the dining room. ''Unless you want to make the big announcement tonight.''

Still scowling, Nick lowered his tone. ''And speaking of that, when are you planning to tell your mother?''

''When the time is right,'' she hissed.

''And when is that?''

He should have looked ludicrous balancing four fancy shrimp cocktails on a silver tray, but with his gray gaze hard as nails and his strong jaw clenched, he simply looked forceful and determined. And uncompromisingly male.

Giving in, Rachel put a hand to one temple. Her answer came wearily. "I don't know, Nick."

"Your mother's got to know sooner or later, Rachel."

"And I'll tell her. Soon."

He hesitated, then drew in a deep breath. "We could tell her tonight, the two of us."

She regarded him steadily for a moment. "You look as if you'd rather face a firing squad."

"I'm not proud of what's happened," he said, looking away. "First my brother shirks his commitment to you, then instead of helping to ease the scandal, I seduce you."

"Oh, come on, Nick!" she said irritably. "It takes two. I was just as much to blame for what happened that night as you."

He shrugged. "Believe what you want, but I still feel responsible."

Miranda appeared at the door, studying both of them shrewdly. "You feel responsible for what, Nick?"

"There was an incident at the work site today," Rachel said quickly. She wasn't going to be stampeded into telling her mother about her pregnancy until she was good and ready. And especially not in front of Paige.

"Rachel had a close call," Nick explained. "A

crane hook gave way just as she walked under it.''

''Rachel! You never said a word. Were you hurt?''

''No, Mother.''

''I discovered later that the accident was rigged,'' Nick said. ''It looks as if somebody's trying to sabotage the job.''

''Sabotage?'' Miranda frowned.

''It's nothing I can prove yet, but a waterline was struck when digging the foundation, causing expensive delay while it dried out. Then there was a bomb threat.''

''A bomb threat?'' Miranda looked horrified.

''In the building next door,'' Nick explained. ''It was a hoax, but it shut us down a whole day. The most recent was when kids—''

''We thought they were kids,'' Rachel put in.

''Somebody,'' Nick said, ''jump-started a bulldozer and rolled it right over a whole shipment of new plumbing supplies, destroying everything.''

''My goodness!'' Miranda murmured.

''So, to be on the safe side,'' Nick said, ''I was trying to persuade Rachel to stay away until we find out who's behind it.''

''That certainly sounds like the smart thing to do,'' Miranda said, looking at Rachel.

"It's not smart at all, Mother. I'm the project architect. As I've told Nick, it's professional suicide if I react differently than any other man. You know Simon Laird. You know what he'd think."

Miranda took the tray from Nick and headed for the table. "Leave Simon to me, dear. I'll just drop by and have a talk with him tomorrow."

"Over my dead body, Mother! Don't even think it!" Rachel threw up her hands. "First Nick, now you trying to protect me." She looked at Paige. "I guess Paige will be next. Perhaps she has an idea how to cushion me from the big, bad world," she grumbled.

"I could have everybody in my class at school write letters," Paige suggested helpfully. "We all had to write the governor once about giving money to education and stuff. The teacher said it worked, so we could write this Simon person, I guess."

Rachel laughed and ruffled the little girl's hair. "I was just kidding, sweetheart. So was Nick. And so was my mother. Nobody needs to help me out at my job. And when you choose a career, you won't need anybody to help you out either."

"I sure hope not," Paige said, popping a shrimp in her mouth. "Because who would it be? My daddy's just interested in his new wife and my mother's always going somewhere and can't be bothered with me. And Mama Miranda might get tired of me, too, one of these days." She looked thoughtful as she munched, then added artlessly, "When you aren't part of a real family, it's hard to know who you can depend on."

"Oh, baby!" Miranda rushed to the child's chair and swept her up in a warm hug. "You can always depend on me, Paige. And Rachel. Isn't that right, Rachel?"

"Yes, it is," Rachel said quietly. She met Nick's gaze over the little girl's head. Their own baby deserved a secure home with a carefree childhood. Nick had said so himself. Too many kids' lives had been screwed up when their parents made bad choices, yet he seemed to be backing away from his earlier suggestion that they get married. On the other hand, he seemed more than ordinarily concerned about her safety, about protecting her. It was very confusing.

With a sigh, she took a seat and shook out her napkin. Only one thing stood out clearly in all this. She had to know exactly where Nick stood before she made any lasting decisions.

"ARE YOU READY to tell me what's going on, Rachel?" Hands propped on her hips, Miranda watched Rachel loading dishes into the dishwasher.

"I'm doing the dishes, Mother." Closing the appliance with a thump, Rachel rinsed her hands and ripped off a paper towel to dry them. "And now, I've got to go. I've got an early meeting tomorrow."

Arms akimbo, Miranda regarded Rachel steadily. "I know it's something. And I'm almost positive it has to do with Nick Preston. Are you seeing him? Are you finally turned on to a real man?"

"I've never had a date with Nick, Mother."

"Then you ought to. He's interested, I can tell. The way he always finds time for you tells me volumes! Did you see his face when he walked in?"

"That was shock!" Rachel tossed the wadded-up paper towel. "He didn't even know I was here, Mother. He came because of the gifts. He's still assuming Jared's responsibilities."

Miranda thoughtfully tapped a forefinger against her lips. "Yes, but once he saw you, I could feel the vibrations from across the room."

Rachel swept up her purse and keys. "I can't wait for Paige to get out of the bathtub, Mother. Tell her I had to run, will you?"

"You don't feel anything for Jared, do you, Rachel? That's over, isn't it?" Miranda's gaze was sharp with concern.

"Rest easy, Mother. It's hard for me to remember what that man's face looked like."

"Good," Miranda said, following her to the door. "Because it's not half as attractive as Nick's."

Rachel laughed and hugged Miranda. "You're impossible, Mother."

Instead of letting go, Miranda held on to Rachel's arms and looked right into her eyes. "You can tell me anything, darling, you know that, don't you?"

"I know," Rachel said, touched.

"Are you pregnant?"

Rachel's mouth fell open. "Why…what… what a question, Mother!"

Miranda sighed and pulled away, opening the door. "Too personal, hmm? But you just haven't been yourself and I refuse to think Jared broke your heart, Rachel. You just didn't seem… crushed enough when he bolted. But since then, I've wondered if perhaps…maybe you and Jared might have been just a teeny bit careless." She held up a hand as Rachel made a choked noise. "Not that I'm passing judgment, dear. But I know how things can just escalate in the heat of the moment. A man's passion can be contagious. I remember once when Donald and I—"

As Rachel waited in speechless anticipation,

Miranda suddenly shook her head as though re-thinking the impulse to confide that particular moment in her relationship with Paige's father. "Oh, goodness," Miranda said, putting a hand to her cheek. "Maybe I shouldn't go there. But you get the point anyway, don't you, dear?"

"Relax, Mother," Rachel said dryly. "Jared Preston won't be the father of your first grand-child."

Close, but not quite.

Miranda sighed dramatically. "Well, that's a relief." Then she was frowning again. "So if it's not Jared, is it your job? You aren't worried about your ability to do the Armstrong Building, are you? I know Agnes. She's very demanding and Charles, her second husband, spoiled her shamelessly. But she's pleased to have you as project architect. She told me so."

"I'm not worried about the job, Mother, but you heard Nick tonight. Whether Agnes is happy or not, he can make it difficult for me if he insists on 'protecting' me!"

Miranda leaned against the door facing. "Now you see? That's what I mean. There's more to it then just simply looking out for you, Rachel. I think Nick's feelings go far beyond the relation-ship you've had as co-workers."

Cringing at how accurate Miranda was, Rachel said a quick, "Good night, Mother," then scooted past her and escaped.

Chapter Six

RACHEL DIDN'T BELIEVE for a minute that she'd persuaded Nick that it was necessary for her to continue personally supervising the project on-site no matter what it implied about her professionalism to Simon Laird. So she was waiting on the steps of the trailer at the construction site when he arrived the next morning.

He got out of his truck scowling. "What do you think you're doing, Rachel?"

She stood up, dusting off the seat of her pants. "Good morning to you, too."

"Where are the security guards?"

"One's on patrol around back. The other went to get some coffee."

Nick swore. "He can get coffee after he clocks out!"

"I told him it was okay. I'd keep a lookout until he got back."

In the act of unlocking the door, he turned with a frown. "And what if the thugs had shown up while you were on guard? Are you armed? Or is your tae kwon do so keen that no weapon is necessary?''

She looked at him. "Come on, Nick, don't start. It's broad daylight. Even stupid thugs wouldn't be so brazen." She regarded the paper sack in his hands with interest. "Please tell me you have doughnuts in there."

Handing the sack over, he pushed the door open and waited for her to go inside. "Did you skip breakfast?"

"Not exactly." She bit greedily into a doughnut and closed her eyes to savor it. "Umm, delicious. It's still warm."

"What do you mean, not exactly?"

"The thought of food is nauseating when I first get up, but an hour or so later, I'm famished!"

"Then from now on, don't leave home until you're able to eat something!" He took the sack from her before she could grab another doughnut. "Something nourishing. There's o.j. in the refrigerator and some fruit over there by the microwave. Think of the baby."

"Yes, Daddy." Rolling her eyes, Rachel did as she was told. Proper nutrition during her pregnancy was important to her. But she wasn't thinking about nutrition this morning. She watched Nick measure out coffee from a vacuum can and put water in the coffeemaker. In a matter of minutes, he had the coffee dripping, the cups ready, and was taking cream and sugar from the cabinet.

"We need to talk, Nick," she said, placing her empty juice glass in the sink.

"Shoot." Leaning against the counter, he crossed his feet at the ankles. He had the longest legs, she noticed. And the way he filled out his jeans...well, her mother would definitely call such assets to Rachel's attention.

"Two things," she said, sounding breathless. Damn! She was already nervous about this, and getting distracted wouldn't help.

"Two things..." he prompted, waiting.

"We need to come to some agreement about access to the site, Nick. You can't tell Simon Laird that it's too risky for me to be here. Believe me, it would deal a death blow to my career. You do see that, don't you?"

He crossed his arms over his chest. "I know where you're coming from, Rachel, but under the circumstances, I think safety ought to come before your career concerns."

"Those circumstances being that I'm pregnant."

"Yeah."

She put her hand over her eyes for a moment, then looked up. "What if I promise to let you know in advance when I need to be here and I agree to have you or Jim McMurray accompany me at all times? That is, until you flush out whoever's doing this,'' she added.

He pushed away from the counter without replying. After pouring coffee into a mug, he offered it to Rachel, who refused.

She watched him move to the tiny window above the sink and stand looking out for a minute or two as the crane operator climbed into the cab and started the motor. The lumber that had slipped the hook yesterday was now neatly restacked and ready to be lifted again.

"I know I sound stubborn and unreasonable," he said, his eyes on the heavy load slowly rising. "But an odd thing happened yesterday when that lumber slipped the hook. I thought you were going to be hurt, maybe killed, right before my eyes and it scared the hell out of me."

"It scared me, too, Nick," she said, wishing he would face her. It was hard to tell what he thought when all she could see was the back of him. "But I don't think that's odd. Anybody would get a fright seeing something like that. It's human nature."

He dumped his coffee, then put his mug in the sink before facing her. "You don't understand. It was after I knew you were safe. That was bad enough, seeing you almost crushed beneath a ton of lumber, but it was afterwards, when we were in the trailer and you fainted.''

''Was that so surprising? Pregnancy can trigger—''

''I know all that,'' he said, suddenly impatient. ''Pregnancy is tricky. I've been through it once, remember?''

Rachel realized that she didn't want to hear about his first wife's pregnancy. ''Then I'll try not to faint again,'' she said stiffly.

''But you might,'' he insisted. ''Or you might have other complications. You might have a reaction to medication. You might step in front of a bus. There are dozens of hazards that might happen. And when the baby comes, there's even more at stake.''

She regarded him in total confusion. ''What are you talking about, Nick?''

''I'm saying that I panicked when I thought you were going to be hurt and I panicked again when you fainted. From the start, I tried to keep from getting involved. I mean...after we did what we did. And then you were pregnant. And it happened anyway.'' He turned from her, looking out the window again. Something about his tense stance and the way he braced his shoulders told her he was fighting some strong inner emotion. "I just don't think I'm up to this again, Rachel," he said quietly.

Rachel struggled to sort out what he wasn't saying. Did he care enough that his comfort zone was threatened? If so, it had to be the baby, because he had no profound feelings for her, did he? "I need to understand this, Nick. Are you talking about emotional involvement?"

"Yeah, I guess." It was a reluctant admission.

Feeling a compelling need to touch him, she managed a shaky laugh. "Funny you should bring that up," she murmured. "You make it a little easier to mention the other matter I wanted to talk about."

"What is it?"

"I have the feeling you've been backing away from the idea of marriage. I wanted to ask you if that was still an option."

Rachel had been sleepless half the night worrying over how to put that thought to Nick. It was awful asking a man if he still wanted to marry her. But it was for the baby, she now reminded herself for the tenth time. Which had been Nick's original argument when he'd suggested it. But now what? Had he, in essence, just withdrawn the offer? She was confused by the tangle of emotions going on inside her. Not just humiliation, but bewilderment and hurt and yes, disappointment. Lord, first Jared, now Nick. Was she being jilted again?

"I didn't expect to ever marry again," Nick muttered, fiddling with a pair of pliers left on the counter.

"I know you suggested it strictly because of the baby," she replied, managing to keep her voice steady.

"I'd give you anything you needed in the way of child support," he told her. "Financially, I've done pretty well the past few years."

"I never thought otherwise."

"My house..." The pliers made a clatter as he dropped them in a drawer. "It's in a good neighborhood. You and the...the two of you could live there. I'd get a condo. Your place may be okay for a baby, but when he's older..."

"I didn't plan to stay in my place," she told him coolly. "And I can afford to buy a house on my own."

"Not if you don't work for the first year." He turned to look at her. "You do plan to stay at home with him for a while, don't you? While he's little?"

"Frankly, my plans are still somewhat hazy, Nick. But you needn't be concerned. Rest assured I'd do what's best for our child. With or without you."

She went over to the table where she'd dropped off the plans yesterday after the accident. Heartsore, she acted on an impulse to hurt him back. "Naturally, I'll keep you informed, but at a safe distance, since you're a little squeamish up close. Now, before I get back to the office, we need to go over these change orders. When I dropped by yesterday, I didn't—"

"Screw the changes!" he snapped, his tone vibrating with emotion. "I was about as 'up close' as it's possible to be when my wife and son were suddenly wiped out of my life by a drunk driver five years ago," Nick said, locking his gaze with hers. "Can you believe that I don't even remember the next six months? It was hell, worse than hell. And for the next two years I was only half-alive. I worked seven days a week, fourteen, eighteen hours a day trying to forget. What I'm trying to get through to you now is that I can't take a chance like that again."

Her heart was beating so hard, he must surely have heard it. "I'm sorry. I...I do understand, Nick."

He turned away, holding onto the counter with both hands. "No, I'm the one who's sorry. Believe that. After what Jared did to you, now this—"

She took a step, touched his arm. "It's okay."

"I know the baby needs a father," Nick said, his voice low and rough. "I'm not stepping out of the picture entirely, I swear I'm not. I just don't think—"

Her eyes were suddenly stinging. "You just don't think you can be the kind of father you were to your...your first little boy," she said, her throat threatening to close up tight. "Is that it?"

He shrugged, but she knew it was true. In spite of that, she longed to slip her arms around his waist, to rest her cheek against his shoulder and promise that he'd never have to survive another personal tragedy. It came to her then that as long as Nick was afraid to open his heart, he would always be half-alive. An accidental pregnancy coupled with a marriage of convenience would not fix what had been broken five years ago. Only if he cared enough would he be able to risk everything again.

"Nick, look at me."

He turned with eyes so tortured that she almost lost the courage to say anything. "Maybe I have no right to talk of loss, certainly not the kind of loss you've suffered, but it seems to me that nobody's life comes with any kind of guarantees. Oh, I know this sounds so trite, but bad things do happen to good people, Nick."

Nick drew in a deep breath. "Don't say any

more, Rachel. Take it from me, you're in over your head.''

Rachel watched him turn from her again, but she plowed on. "Some of us seem more fortunate than others. I know it appears unfair, Nick, but that's the way it is. It's a mystery why some people luckily draw intact families, enjoy advantages, education, get decent jobs. They marry, have healthy children and live to see them grow up.''

He made a sound and Rachel's heart twisted. Slipping her arms around his waist from behind, she rested her cheek against his back. The sound of his heartbeat was strong, heavy, but somehow forlorn. Oh, something about this man touched her so!

"For most people," she said softly, "the ups and downs don't seem so extreme, but once in a while, a good person is dealt a really killing blow. And there aren't any words to make it seem anything but what it is. Killing.'' Eyes closed, she gave him a compassionate squeeze. "But is closing yourself off any better than being half-alive?''

Nick's hands covered hers at his waist. "I almost died," he said hoarsely. "I woke up every day hating to find myself still living. I *wanted* to die.''

She couldn't speak for a moment, imagining Nick wounded and isolated, imprisoned by grief. Surely no one would have to live through anguish like that twice in a lifetime. But that assurance was given to no one. "Do you ever think there might have been a reason that you didn't die?" she asked, desperately seeking something—anything—to reach him.

"Sheer bad luck."

She managed a shaky laugh. "Oh, Nick, I don't think so." With a sigh, she started to pull away, but Nick turned and framed her face between his palms, studying her without a word for a long moment. "I know what you're thinking, Rachel. That this baby is my reason for having survived."

She searched his face with the same intensity. "Why couldn't that be true?"

"Maybe it could...in a world where there's some rhyme or reason to the way things are."

Outside, the powerful roar of the heavy equipment starting up shook the walls of Nick's office. Was that the reason for the odd quaking inside her? Rachel wondered. Or was it that she was once again as close to Nick as she'd been the night they both wanted to forget?

"Nick..."

"I don't want to talk anymore," he said

roughly. Then as her eyes went wide, he lowered his mouth to hers. In a heartbeat, she opened to him and the kiss deepened. Her arms went around his neck as he pulled her close, then both were caught in the same explosion of passion and need that had gotten them in trouble before. She moaned when his hands, gently framing her face, slid back to fist in her hair. And then his kiss became much more than a blending of their lips. Now it was wild and hungry, as if the need in him, rigidly contained, threatened to break its bonds. He shifted then and pressed his thigh hard against her softness.

"It drives me crazy, thinking of this," he told her, breaking the kiss to run his mouth over her face, her throat. "Do you feel it, too, Rachel?"

"Hmm..."

Now her blouse was open. With a soft moan, he filled his palms with her breasts, his thumbs grazing her nipples. She felt the warmth of his breath on her, and then somehow his mouth was there, open and hot.

"Oh!" Keen sensation washed through her, flooding her mind with pleasure. She thrust both hands into his hair and held on, panting and pleading. Nick, incited by the power of her response, urged her backwards until she was against the counter. Burying his face in the soft fullness of her breasts, he reveled in the taste of her while his hands, hotly possessive, sought out other secret places. He ran a palm past her belly, seeking the hot, damp heat between her legs. Then his touch became even more intimate.

Clinging weakly, Rachel couldn't think and didn't even try. Nick was merciless, steering a course of excruciating pleasure with relentless skill, murmuring in her ear, kissing her, tormenting her. Impossible not to move with him, not to fall into that mindless, compelling rhythm. And then she was in a frenzied free fall.

"Ahh, Rachel...yes, yes..." When her climax came, a shuddering, shattering convulsion of bliss, Nick groaned like a dying man and then fastened his mouth on hers again as if to feast on her pleasure.

Stunned and disoriented by the sheer power of what happened, Rachel clung to him to keep from falling to the floor in a boneless heap. Nick held her fast, breathing hard.

"I can't believe I did that!" she murmured when she was finally able to talk.

"Was it good?" Nick's tone was almost guttural.

She turned her face into his neck. "You know it was."

"Yeah." His low, rough laugh held traces of her own bewilderment.

Still not looking at him, she said, "But you didn't...you haven't—"

"Wrong time, wrong place." He stroked her hair. "It'll keep."

Did that mean there would be another time? Or another woman? Shaken by the thought and now totally confused, she withdrew to try to fix herself up. She must look as if she...as if she'd been doing exactly what she was doing. Avoiding his gaze, she smoothed her hair and began tucking her top back into her skirt.

"I know I look a fright," she said, embarrassed. What on earth had happened? What was it about Nick that once he touched her in that way, she forgot all restraint, all sense of propriety? And if his reaction was anything to judge by, he was as quick to lose control as she was. "Anybody could have walked in here, Nick."

"Yeah." He watched her trying to smooth the tangles from her hair. "Maybe it's the pregnancy."

She was suddenly irritated. Pregnancy definitely had her hormones in an uproar, but she hadn't been pregnant the first time this had happened. "Still in denial?" she demanded.

"I've never denied that I like making love to you."

She regarded him steadily. "I don't remember ever having a discussion about it."

"Rachel—"

Suddenly, with a quick knock, the door was flung open. "Nick! Hey, man, you in here?"

Jared!

"You're out early this morning, Jared," Nick said, sounding remarkably calm to Rachel considering what his brother had almost interrupted.

"Not only me, it seems." Upon seeing Rachel, Jared's grin faded into almost comic dismay. "Rachel. Whoa, this is a surprise."

"Why?" Rachel replied coolly, but her heart was racing. Lord! What if he'd come in two minutes sooner? "You know I'm the project architect on this job."

Jared moved slowly toward them as if sensing the charged atmosphere. "Sure, but as Nick says, it's pretty early."

"Rachel and I both like an early start," Nick said. "So, what's on your mind, Jared?"

But Jared's gaze was on Rachel, who resisted the urge to touch her face. What if he saw whisker burns! "You're looking great, Rach. So, how've you been? Believe it or not, I've picked up the phone a dozen times to try and explain what happened.''

"Really?''

"Yeah, really.'' Ruefully grateful, he sighed. "To tell the truth, Nick here was doing a much better job of damage control than I ever could. So it just seemed best to let it ride. I mean, for the time being.'' He glanced at his feet, then favored her with his famous lopsided grin. "Plus, you'd probably hang up on me.''

"There's definitely that possibility,'' Rachel said dryly. She'd been curious to know what, if anything, she'd feel when she saw Jared again and, with a sense of relief, she realized she felt nothing. His handsome face left her unmoved, as well as his charm and his words. But how could it be otherwise when her whole body was still tingling from Nick's magic?

"It's never too late to right a wrong, Jared,'' Nick spoke up, unsmiling. "So now's your chance to give Rachel the apology you owe her.''

"Hey, that's right.'' Jared spread both hands and said, "Rachel, I apologize.''

Rachel was almost amused. He'd turned her life upside down, but now he'd apologized, so clearly to him it was over and done with. And suddenly she realized she was perfectly willing to let bygones be bygones, too. Jared was now only a pale and insignificant part of her past. She could barely recall her plans to spend her life with him. What she could not imagine was a future without Nick.

Oh Lord, had she fallen in love with Nick?

"Is that it?" Nick demanded with a fierce frown.

"Well..." Jared gave a shrug as if to say, what else?

Nick put a possessive arm around Rachel's waist. "Try this—I'm sorry, Rachel. I behaved like a polecat. I embarrassed both our families. I beg your forgiveness, Rachel. And while you're at it, how about putting a little sincerity into it, Jared?"

"Well, sure. Consider it said, Rachel. All that." This time, he included both in his famous grin, as if relieved to have a sticky duty behind him. "And I hope we're still friends."

"Friends!" Nick said before Rachel had a chance. "Hell, no! You expect Rachel to just shrug and forget what you put her through? There's not a woman alive ready to forgive you, man. In fact, I can name a few who'd string you up by your toes for a lot less!"

Jared was the picture of genuine remorse. "And you'd be well within your rights, Rachel."

"I haven't got time to imagine ways of punishing you, Jared," she said.

"I damn sure can!" Nick barked, his arm tightening.

Warmed by Nick's defense, Rachel covered his hand, still firm about her waist. "Let it go, Nick," she said quietly. "It's over. And he's still your brother."

"It may be over, but it's not forgotten. And don't remind me he's my brother."

Unabashed, Jared was still regarding Rachel thoughtfully. "The truth is, Rachel seems to have recovered just fine, Nick...for a lady who narrowly escaped marriage to a polecat." His gaze moved to Nick. "You have anything to do with that?"

With a grunt of disgust, Nick moved to the coffeepot. "You haven't said yet what brought you out here."

"Business," Jared said, resting one hip on the edge of the worktable. "On behalf of my client, Agnes Armstrong."

"What about her?" Rachel asked, frowning.

Nick set his coffee down. "Yeah, what about her?"

"Actually, it's not Agnes so much as it is Melvin, her smarmy nephew." He looked at Rachel. "You know my firm represents Agnes, including her estate planning. Melvin's her heir. In the past when she's been involved in a building project, he was usually just a glorified gofer, but on this one, she allowed him in as an active partner.''

"I know all that," Rachel said.

"Actually, it's a limited partnership, which is no surprise to any of us who knows Agnes.'' Jared glanced out at the construction site. "He might be her heir, but she's no pushover. She's in control—or else.''

"So what's up?" Nick asked, crossing one leg over the other as he leaned against the cabinet.

"She's concerned about cost overruns.''

Rachel made a choked sound. "Well, it's about time! I warned Melvin that changes pushed up the costs. And why did she go to you instead of coming to me? What can you do to keep the costs down?''

"She had another concern. It seems she's learned of some suspicious incidents. Bad equipment, inept crews—her words, not mine—a near-disaster yesterday with a crane. She was pretty ticked. She had immediate visions of lawsuits, which is why I'm here. I wanted to hear it straight from Nick.'' He smiled at Rachel confidently. "I persuaded her not to call Simon Laird and express her concerns until I get back with her.''

Rachel gave a disgusted huff. Jared's charm worked even on Agnes Armstrong. "You could have heard it straight from me, Jared. As for the crane accident yesterday, you must know that as the near-victim, I definitely have the details. Besides, isn't it logical to talk to the architect as well as the contractor?"

"And I would have been around to see you, Rachel," Jared said in a reassuring tone, "just as soon as I talked to Nick."

"Well, you can kill two birds with the same stone right now," she snapped. Snatching up her briefcase, she plopped it on the worktable and clicked the latch. "I have a summary of the work orders, delays, all the incidents you allude to, right here. As well as an estimate of the time lag for the job. And notice, if you will, that all the changes are initialed by Agnes herself. I think you'll find the numbers agree with Nick's assessment of the situation. We worked up the numbers together. Right, Nick?"

"Right." Nick quickly scanned a page or two of the memo handed to him by Rachel. "And we haven't been just sitting around doing nothing about the problems on this job. Extra security has been hired and I'm personally reviewing the work histories of everybody on the payroll. Rachel and I are working on the problem together. In fact, we talked about it just last night.''

''Last night, huh?'' Jared transferred his gaze from Rachel's report to Rachel herself.

''Yeah, at her mother's house.'' Looking straight at Jared, Nick added, ''Where I was graciously offered dinner after a boatload of wedding gifts had been packed for shipping back to various friends and family.''

''Aw, hell, Nick. I'm really sorry about the way I handled everything.'' He had the grace at last to look ashamed. ''At the time, I was so messed up and confused that I honestly wasn't thinking straight.'' He brightened. ''But hey, seems like it's all working out better than anybody ever expected.''

''What's that supposed to mean?'' Nick demanded with suspicion.

''Nick. Nick...'' Jared rolled his eyes. ''You're not gonna stand there and tell me that I interrupted a business discussion when I busted in here a minute ago, are you?''

''I'm not telling you a damn thing!''

''No, indeed, bro. And you shouldn't.'' Jared's eyes gleamed wickedly as he looked from one to the other.

''If you're done,'' Nick said evenly, ''Rachel and I have work to do.''

"And a great working relationship you've got going here, buddy." Ignoring Nick's irritation, Jared settled back against the worktable. "Hey, nobody knows better than me that some pretty incredible stuff can happen when two people are thrown together on the job."

"Back off, Jared!" Nick was now almost snarling. "Rachel is fresh out of a rotten relationship. She doesn't need you, of all people, making snide suggestions about her personal life."

Jared managed to look hurt. "And I, of all people, would never make a snide suggestion to or about Rachel and you know it, Nick. What I'm thinking isn't snide, it's great. Almost too good to be true."

"Are you finished?" Nick snapped.

Hardly. Jared held up a finger. "Actually, I wish you and Rachel would get it on. Denise said from the beginning that it should have been you, not me, marrying Rachel. You're two peas in a pod, she said. But I kept telling her she was nuts. That you wouldn't let yourself fall in love again, Nick. Actually, we've got a bet on it and I'll be damned if she isn't gonna collect!"

With Rachel and Nick effectively silenced, Jared picked up the papers that Rachel had pulled from her briefcase. "I'll just make a little visit

to Agnes Armstrong with this report now and see
what I can do to smooth the old lady's feathers.''
He winked at Rachel. ''Meantime, I might make
a quick stop at home and beg Denise's pardon
for doubting her.

''Hey...'' At the door, he pointed Rachel's
rolled-up report playfully at the two of them to
fire his final salvo. ''There's nothing more delicious than gettin' it on at the workplace. Am I
right or what?''

Chapter Seven

RACHEL CHOSE TO believe that she wasn't a person who put off an unpleasant task just because it was...well, unpleasant. The very next day she called her mother and made a date for lunch at a restaurant near the village. Nick was right. It was past time to tell Miranda that she was pregnant.

Her mother was certain to have a lot of suggestions. She wouldn't easily accept the fact that marrying Nick was not an option, but it was bound to be her first thought. Rachel knew from experience that on her home turf Miranda was a formidable opponent. Better to hash it out in a restaurant—no pun intended—and get it behind her.

She arrived with ten minutes to spare. Twenty minutes ago. Glancing again at her watch, she decided to give Miranda a few more minutes. Was the woman *ever* on time?

As she waited, Rachel recognized Agnes Armstrong and her nephew entering the restaurant. A moment later, they were guided to a table across the room. Rachel debated whether to go over and greet her client, but decided against it after a moment. The upcoming hour with her mother was going to be bad enough. No sense compounding an already stressful situation. Besides, she had an appointment with Agnes tomorrow. Whether Jared had or had not "smoothed the old lady's feathers," it was Rachel's job as architect to give her client facts and figures.

Oddly, while she'd worked up the data to allay Agnes's concerns, her own had increased. She'd been unable to dismiss a feeling that she was overlooking some significant detail. Ordinarily she would have called Nick to discuss it, but she was still unsettled over their encounter yesterday. So a discussion with Nick was out.

She brought her thoughts back to the Armstrong project. She had to concede that her client was not overreacting. Costs were indeed up. Changes were expensive, so it puzzled Rachel why Agnes had allowed them. The woman was no novice developer. She knew changes meant delay. Rachel wondered what occupancy date had been promised to the tenants lined up for the new building.

Glancing at her watch again, Rachel had to admit she felt somewhat responsible for not having acted more forcefully when trying to curb Melvin's appetite for changes in the plans. But she'd been so caught up in wedding plans and then further distracted by the jilting fiasco. And finally, her pregnancy. In spite of all that, she sensed some other factor hovering just beyond reach. Those accidents at the site, the frivolous changes, Melvin underfoot so often...

Sipping lemon water, she watched her two clients as they chatted. Actually, Melvin talked while Agnes Armstrong merely nodded or frowned, playing with her wine glass. Rachel recalled how Jared had defined their relationship. Agnes had the power. But at least Melvin was in on the money this time and not just his aunt's gofer.

It hit her suddenly. The money. Pushing back her chair, she rose, dropping her napkin on the table. Melvin and his aunt, along with other patrons in the restaurant, stared curiously as she grabbed her briefcase and headed for the door. The explanation had been obvious all along. If she were right—and she would need Nick to help her prove it—then somebody was going to have a lot of explaining to do.

At the entrance, she left a message for her mother with the startled hostess along with her apologies for skipping out. Lunch—and her personal life—could wait. She had to get to Nick. Another accident could happen any minute.

IT WASN'T EXACTLY an accident, but another problem cropped up via cell phone as she tooled down Westheimer on her way to the building site.

"Stop crying, Paige. I can't understand what you're saying unless you calm down." Cradling the phone between chin and shoulder, Rachel signalled and turned, heading for the interstate hoping to avoid some of the noontime traffic. "Where are you?"

Paige sniffed and paused as if getting her bearings. "I'm not sure, but stuff looks familiar. I just walked from that bunch of stores in the Village."

"You walked! Why? I thought you were spending the day with your mother."

"I was! I mean, I was supposed to, but she and her boyfriend got into an argument and it was *awful*, Rachel! Mom screamed at him and he yelled back and I just had it with them. I walked off 'cause I'd rather be by myself than with two people who can't get along even for one stupid day." Her voice wobbled as she added, "Besides, they didn't want to be with me, Rachel.

They just took me along because…because…well, just because.''

"I'm sorry, honey. Did you try to call Mama Miranda?"

"I knew she was having lunch with you," Paige said. "When she didn't answer her cell phone, I decided to try your number."

"You did the right thing, Paige. I'll pick you up." Rachel set the phone on speaker mode and rummaged in her bag for her pen. "Tell me what stores you can see so I can get a fix for where you are."

"Oh!" Paige's voice brightened. "There's La Madeleine on the corner. Where we had brunch a few days ago."

"Great." Tossing the pen, Rachel turned to head down Kirby. "I'm about two minutes away. I have to stop by and see Nick before I take you home. You can wait in Nick's office while I take care of business, okay?"

"Okay."

"I'll call your mom and leave a message for her."

"Whatever." Paige made a disgusted sound. "But if you think she's gonna be worried because I ran away, think again. She probably hasn't even noticed."

Rachel had to believe the woman had noticed

and that she was probably worried as well, but not for the right reasons. It was sad to think that Paige considered herself unimportant to her parents. How many incidents like this would it take before she was irreparably damaged? And then who knew how she might act out her unhappiness?

"Give me two minutes, Paige. Be cool, okay?"

"Okay." A little pause, then a quiet, "Thank you, Rachel."

TWENTY MINUTES LATER, Rachel pulled into the construction site with Paige in the car with her. She saw at a glance that an electrical crew was installing power on the upper levels. If she was on the right track, Nick needed to be told her suspicions right away. He might decide to shut down the job until they got to the bottom of this bizarre situation.

She hustled Paige to the trailer office. "I need to talk to Nick," she told the girl. "There's fruit and some juice in the fridge. I'll be back in a jiffy."

"Okay."

Outside, she spent a minute squinting in the sunshine looking for Nick, to no avail, before remembering to go back and get a hard hat. After

Jared left, they'd reached a compromise on her
need to visit the site. She would have full access
provided Nick had no concern about the safety
of the particular area she wanted to see. She also
promised to call first so that Nick could accompany her personally. At the moment, he was nowhere in sight.

Now what?

She waved at an electrician catwalking an I
beam extending out four levels up. He yelled
something and, in a few moments, Jim McMurray was on his way down in the construction elevator.

"Where's Nick?" she asked as soon as Mc-
Murray reached the ground.

"On the fourth floor making certain everything
is done by the book. Talk about micromanaging!
Today he's stuck as close as I've ever seen him
on a job. He's personally inspecting every staple
and splice and conduit."

Shading her eyes, Rachel tried to find Nick
among the other men in the crew, but it was impossible to pick him out with the sun blinding
her.

McMurray reached for his ball cap and reposi-
tioned it on his head. "Nick said for you to wait
in the trailer office, Rachel. He'd be down in a
few minutes."

"I need to see him now, Jim." She regarded the half-completed building with a worried look. "Go up and tell him I'll wait for him on the first floor. Don't worry, I won't wander around. I want to see how that fountain looks now that all the stone work has been completed. I'll be okay."

McMurray shifted, looking uncomfortable. "It'll mean my job if I don't escort you to that trailer, ma'am."

A flat refusal sprang to Rachel's lips, but at McMurray's distressed look, she relented. The man was following orders—expecting *her* to follow orders, too! And she had promised. With a sigh, she turned to do as Nick wished. This time. "Just tell him it's urgent, will you, Jim?"

"Yes, ma'am."

Shaking her head, she headed back to the trailer. For a man who refused to get emotionally involved, Nick certainly went to odd extremes to see to her safety. Make that the baby's safety, Rachel thought with a pang. The reason he was so solicitous was because she carried his child.

As she stepped inside the trailer, she was unable to see for a moment while her eyes adjusted to the dim interior. "Paige?"

No answer.

"Paige, where are you?"

Nothing. The office was empty. Paige was gone.

FOR HALF A minute, Rachel considered her promise to Nick to stay put. He would be furious but her concern for Paige outweighed her fear of Nick's wrath. She rushed out of the office and headed across the site in a mad dash. Squinting in the sun she spotted Nick in the construction elevator descending along the side of the building. He was a good six feet from the ground when he saw her. Shoving the cage open, he leaped the distance with a dark frown, but one look at Rachel's face as she ran straight into his arms and his fury turned instantly to concern.

"What's the matter? What's wrong?" he demanded.

"Paige is gone, Nick! We have to find her."

"Paige?" Holding her arms, he bent a little to see her face beneath the hard hat. "Your little sister?"

"I sent her to the office to wait," she said, clinging to his shirt with both hands. "But then after I saw Jim, I went back and she wasn't there! Nick, she was already upset over her mom, who'd had a stupid fight with her boyfriend right in front of her. Paige just walked off. In the traf-

fic at University Village, if you can believe that!
I picked her up at La Madeleine.''

Nick stared at her in disbelief. ''Paige is here?
On the site?''

''I didn't take time to drop her at my mother's
place because I needed to see you about the accidents.'' She pushed her hair from her face,
looking around frantically. ''She left the trailer
for some reason and now I don't know where she
is!''

''She can't be far, Rachel. A ten-foot chain-
link fence encloses the whole site.''

''You don't understand! The site is unsafe,
Nick.''

''Wait a minute, sweetheart. Just calm down,
all right?'' He slipped an arm around her waist
and with his other hand began stroking her back
reassuringly. ''She's probably exploring, but the
men will spot her in no time.'' Over Rachel's
head, he sent Jim McMurray a signal with a lift
of his eyebrows. ''We'll alert the crew right
now.''

''She's already upset,'' Rachel told him in a
shaky tone.

''We'll find her, Rachel.'' His hand was warm
on her neck, making it so tempting to just linger
in his embrace. A shoulder to lean on, she
thought suddenly, with longing. There was a lot

to be said for that. Realizing she couldn't take time to indulge herself, she let him go and took a step back.

"I'm sorry. It's just that I think I figured out why all the problems are happening on this job and, if I'm right, they're going to keep happening. For an unsuspecting child, it could be downright dangerous."

Nick's eyes narrowed. "What've you figured out?"

She had turned now and was studying the building with worried eyes. "I'm not positive, but I think Melvin is responsible, Agnes Armstrong's nephew."

"Bingo. Seems we're thinking along the same lines. Come on." Taking her hand, Nick walked with her across the construction yard along a path that led into the entrance of the building. Kicking aside pieces of masonry and other debris in their path, he guided her across the huge open area where a massive stone fountain occupied center stage. Inside, it was almost eerily quiet. And vacant. Most of the men in Nick's crew had fanned out on the construction site to look for Paige. Others were still at work on the upper level.

"Wait here," Nick said, urging her toward the low ledge surrounding the fountain. "I'll feel better knowing you're not wandering around.

I've scoped out areas most likely to be booby-trapped, but better safe than sorry.''

Still standing, Rachel shot him a warning look. "Don't start, Nick."

"Think of—"

"The baby!" she finished, rolling her eyes.

"Exactly!" Nick said. "If Melvin is orchestrating the accidents, he's proven he isn't particular about who gets hurt. Why put yourself—and the baby—at risk?"

"He's orchestrating delay, Nick, that's the key. As part-owner, he gets money for any delay attributable to the architect or the contractor. The details are spelled out in the contract."

"Yeah, I arrived at the same conclusion when I reread the contract."

She put both hands on her hips. "And when did you plan to share this information with me?"

"Not before I made a thorough search of the site and the building, which I haven't had time yet to complete. Once I 'shared' it, I knew nothing would keep you away from here, Rachel."

"So you just kept me in the dark! It was my choice to make, Nick." Rachel waved a hand in agitation. "Oh, we don't have time to hash this out. We really have to find Paige!"

"Right. So sit and let me do just that." This time she didn't resist as Nick urged her down on the low ledge of the fountain. Touching the deep frown between her eyes, he said in a less forceful tone, "Try not to get too agitated, okay?"

"You're pushing it, Nick."

Shaking his head, he began to back away, then suddenly he stepped close, lifted her chin and kissed her on the mouth, hard. "Good girl."

Before she could recover, his long-legged stride had taken him across the building and Rachel was left with a mix of emotions—fear for Paige's safety, surprise at Nick's kiss, irritation, confusion and oddly beneath it all, a curious joy. God knows why, she thought. It was hardly a secret that Nick was sexually attracted to her.

Unable to sit still, she jumped up and began pacing at the base of the gigantic fountain. Although the extravagant creation had been fun to design, Rachel had no interest at the moment in admiring the result. She was circling it when she heard a small sound.

Pausing, she searched for the source. Then, as her gaze moved up the thirty-foot tall stone structure, she saw Paige clinging to the top boulder, white-faced and scared.

"Paige! My God, how did you get up there?"

"I climbed. I had to rescue this little bird," she said, lips trembling. Cupped in her hands was a small, bedraggled bird. "I saw him and I knew he was hurt, so I had to get him. Now I'm too scared to climb down. I'm too scared to even *look* down!''

"Don't look down," Rachel ordered quickly, trying not to show her own panic. "Stay very still right where you are. I'll send someone for Nick and he'll climb up and get you."

"S-some of these big rocks are real wiggly, Rachel."

Oh, God. The stone base for the fountain had been set in place only a week ago. Several days were required to properly cure the mortar holding the tons of rock in place. Until then, the massive structure couldn't be considered stable. But nothing should be moving, not even slightly.

"Two rocks already fell off behind me," Paige informed her. Before Rachel could caution her, the little girl turned to point out the damage and dislodged more stone. It hit the concrete floor with a crash that shook Rachel as much as Paige. To her horror, two huge boulders which shaped the path of what would be cascading water, suddenly shifted with an ominous groan. She held her breath, praying they would stay put. At this point, any more movement, even another wiggle, could bring the whole thing down. Even uncured mortar was relatively stable. What could have happened? Was this Melvin's work, too?

She looked around frantically for some-body...anybody. But no one was in sight.

Rachel's heart was in her throat. She found the spot where Paige must have climbed the structure and looked up at the child. "Paige." Her tone was low, but urgent. "Don't move. We won't wait for Nick. I'm coming up there. I'll hold out my hand. When we touch, I'll help you climb back down."

"What about the baby bird?"

Rachel closed her eyes. "Paige. You'll have to leave the bird up there. Nick will use a ladder to get it later."

"No! It'll die."

"Okay." This was no time to argue. Rachel took a breath. "I've got an idea. Put it in your pocket. You've got a pocket in your shorts, haven't you?"

"Uh-huh."

"Then do it. Carefully. And hurry."

"He might get squished."

"Do it, Paige."

"Okay." Meekly, Paige stuffed the baby bird into her pocket.

Rachel was already on her way up, having no problem finding toeholds. The problem was the instability of the entire structure. The fallen stones may have displaced others. She could only pray this side held up until she could rescue Paige.

At the top, she quickly unbuckled her hard hat and passed it to the little girl. "Put this on, Paige. You see how it fastens, don't you?"

"Uh-huh."

Two interminable minutes passed while Paige set the hard hat on her head and fastened it. Then Rachel held out her hand. "Okay, Paige, we're gonna be fine. Turn around—not too fast! Now, I want you to stick out your legs just as if you were coming down a ladder. I'll show you where to put your feet to have a nice toehold. Trust me, okay?"

"O-okay. But be careful not to hurt the baby bird, Rachel."

Already one small foot was waving wildly, seeking a toehold. Rachel caught it and wedged it into a snug crease between two boulders. Then she did the same with the second foot. And again and again, the whole time shielding the child with her body and they descended. With fifteen feet still to go to the floor, Rachel's foot slipped when a stone shifted and the whole structure shuddered.

"Don't move."

Nick's voice. Rachel went weak with relief.

"Both of you, keep your hands and feet where

they are," he said. *"Don't move.* I've got a ladder."

"We're scared, Nick," Paige said, her small voice trembling.

"I know, honeybun. But try to be brave and do as I tell you. I'll have you both down in no time."

"I hope the baby bird's okay in my pocket."

"Don't ask," Rachel muttered, sensing Nick's confusion. Right now, she simply tightened her arms around the little girl's waist and prayed the wobbly structure would hold one more minute.

The most welcome feeling in the world came when Nick's arms closed around her. Trembling with relief, she made a soft sound. "We're not there yet," he told her quietly, his mouth close to her ear. "Be still while I give you my hard hat."

"But Nick, what about—"

"Rachel." No arguing with that tone. With the safety helmet fastened, he said, "Now. I want you to do exactly as you instructed Paige. I'll guide your foot to the first rung of the ladder, but keep your arms tight around her and try not to disturb any more stones. Got that?"

"Yes."

For a moment, Nick simply savored the feel of Rachel's warm, soft body safe in his embrace while his heart thundered in terror. The next few seconds were crucial. Both Rachel and this little girl were in dire peril. The baby, too. His baby, his child. His second chance.

Suddenly Nick realized that he'd finally accepted the deaths of Michelle and Joey. In spite of all he'd suffered, he could now move on.

And Rachel was the reason.

Balanced on the ladder with his arms around her, he knew with absolute certainty that if the fountain collapsed and Rachel was taken from him, then he would be lost forever.

He was suddenly flooded with emotion so intense that it nearly took his breath away. He couldn't go through that again. Dammit, he *wouldn't* go through that again! Without thinking, his hold tightened about her as if by the sheer force of his need he could keep her and this young girl safe. He wanted a life, a real life. He wanted a wife and she had to be Rachel. He wanted their child. He wanted a home and a mortgage and two cars, not one, in the garage. He wanted it all again. But it came with risk, bone-chilling, terrifying risk. There was no escaping that. Still, he wanted it.

His men waited at the foot of the ladder, tense and anxious, but ready to follow his lead. There would be nothing they could do if the stones began to fall. And nothing he could do. He took a deep breath and pressed his face for a moment against Rachel's hair and inhaled the sweet scent of her.

"I love you, Rachel."

"Oh, Nick..." Her response came, hushed and joyful. "I love you, too."

He waited another heartbeat, let her words settle deep inside in a place that had been too long empty, and then he said, "Okay. Ready, you two?"

"Yes!" Rachel whispered.

"Me, too," said Paige in a small voice.

"Then here we go."

It was when he had guided Rachel's foot to the first rung of the ladder that the topmost boulder suddenly shifted as stone and mortar separated and the whole structure shuddered. And then tons of rock were in motion. Men's shouts mingled with the terrifying rumble and groan as the boulders broke free. Buried pipes ruptured, spewing wild jets of water. Counting on Rachel to hang onto Paige, Nick wrapped his arms hard about her and with a powerful, desperate lunge, he kicked free of the ladder. In the thunderous crash, he remembered curling his body around Rachel and Paige. Next, there was exploding pain and a blinding splash of white light. And then nothing.

Chapter Eight

RACHEL AND PAIGE escaped unharmed in the collapse of the fountain, but only because Nick had shielded them with his body. All three probably owed their lives to the quick action of Nick's crew in pulling the ladder to safety while they were still on it. But in the shower of stone that had rained down as they fell, Nick himself had no protection since he'd given his hard hat to Rachel. For her, the twenty minutes that he lay unconscious had been terrifying.

He was finally brought around by the EMTs, who had arrived within a few moments of the frantic 911 call. Wisely, they'd ignored Nick when he balked at going to the hospital. Nobody could force him to stay, however. As soon as he had the results of the X rays and found he had no concussion, he decided to check himself out.

Rachel was still shaken. She'd been joined in the ER by Miranda, who overheard Nick dismissing the trauma resident's caution. He admitted to a killer headache, but declared that if he slept in any bed other than his own that night, it would be Rachel's. Miranda had blinked at that, causing Rachel to hustle her back to the waiting room where she promised a full explanation in the morning.

She should have known there would be no stalling Miranda.

"Paige, darling, I am so thirsty," Miranda declared, rummaging in her purse for change. Resting beside Paige in a box scrounged from the nurse's station was the wounded bird that had caused all the ruckus. "Be a sweetheart, sugar. Go get me a cold drink, please."

Paige studied mother and daughter with a knowing look. "You want to talk private stuff, huh?"

Miranda tweaked her ponytail and winked. "Clever girl."

Taking the change, Paige shot a mischievous look at Rachel. "Okay, but if I don't get to hear it, be sure and make her tell you the *special* thing Nick said to her when we were stranded on that ladder."

Rachel closed her eyes. "Paige…"

"I'm outta here," the little girl said, skipping off. "Watch my bird!"

When Rachel looked, Miranda was regarding

her narrowly. "What did he say and why would
he think he'd be welcome in your bed, Rachel?"

Rachel sighed, glancing back to the treatment
cubicle in the hope that Nick might rescue her
one more time. "I've been trying to find a good
moment to tell you something, Mother. But it's
just so…difficult. It's…embarrassing, actually."

"Never put off a sticky duty," Miranda said,
as if she were never guilty of that sin.

"I'm pregnant," Rachel said baldly. "And before you jump to the wrong conclusion, it's
Nick's baby, not Jared's."

"You're kidding," Miranda said. For once,
Rachel had managed to confound her mother.

"What's wrong with this picture?" Rachel
asked dryly of no one in particular. Then, struggling to contain a smile, "I think I've finally
shocked you, Mother."

"Then give me a minute!"

"To compose a motherly lecture?"

"No lecture, darling," Miranda said. Then
reaching up, she kissed Rachel and hugged her
hard. "I'm tickled! I won't even press you for
details, provided you plan to do the right thing."

Rachel felt a rush of affection for her irrepres-
sible mom. And some chagrin upon recalling
Miranda's reaction months ago when she'd announced her engagement to Jared. Miranda had

been gracious, but too, too polite. Rachel had returned to her office afterwards with an odd letdown feeling. None of that today!

"If you mean marriage, Mother, probably."

"Probably?"

"Well..." Rachel spread her hands in a wry shrug, "it's complicated." She was enjoying shaking up her mother a little for a change.

"He asked you?"

"And then reneged," Rachel said wickedly.

Miranda was beginning to enjoy herself, too. "This is payback, isn't it?" she asked, regarding her daughter shrewdly. "For all that nagging I've done. For trying to loosen you up. For wanting to shake some fun and some sense into you!"

"Could be, Mom," Rachel said, still smiling.

"Okay, one more question and Paige and I will leave you two to whatever plans you have for the rest of your lives."

"Hah!"

"What did Nick say when you were stranded on the ladder?"

Rachel's smile went soft with joy. "He told me he loved me."

"Didn't I say it?" Miranda crowed, grinning. "I always liked him best."

IN THE CAR, Nick settled back against the headrest of the passenger's seat after reluctantly allowing Rachel to drive.

"Let's go home, sweetheart."

Home. Rachel let the word sink like a sweet song into her heart. "My place or yours?"

He rolled his head to look at her. "Yours. I want to make love on that frilly bed again."

Smiling, she turned out of emergency parking and headed for Westheimer. "The doctor said you're supposed to take it easy for twenty-four hours."

"After we make love I'll think about sleeping." Reaching over, he splayed one hand wide over her tummy. "How's our baby?"

"He's fine. Couldn't be better."

"Good." Nodding, he settled back again. "I've got a lot to tell you, Rachel."

"About the accident?"

"That and more." Again he was looking at her. "About being on that ladder and discovering suddenly what was at stake. But it can wait until we get home." His tone went deep, sending her senses tingling. "Where I can touch you and hold you when I tell you again how much I love you."

Rachel looked at him before turning her eyes back to the road. "Are you sure? Sometimes people do or say things in a stressful situation that they back away from later."

"Like my first proposal?"

"It happens, Nick."

He reached over and stroked the side of her cheek. "I don't want to propose to you in a car, Rachel. This time I want to do it right, okay?"

"Okay." Entering the I-610 ramp, she headed southwest. "Oh, I forgot. Jared called while you were in the ER." She smiled. "He said he wasn't surprised you didn't have a concussion. He thinks it would take more than a huge boulder to do that."

Nick grunted, but without affront. "His way of saying I'm hardheaded and stubborn."

"He loves you. And he admires you."

He looked at her. "Come again?"

"It's true. And he was pretty shaken over your close call. He blamed himself. Said if you hadn't been distracted by assuming responsibility for his bad behavior, you would have figured out what Melvin was up to sooner."

Nick smiled slowly. "I don't know about that." He slipped his fingers beneath her hair and began caressing her neck. "It's hard to stay mad at him when things are turning out so fine."

What he was doing now felt fine, too. She really should make him stop, considering the interstate traffic whizzing by them at the speed of light. "Nick…"

With a soft chuckle, he moved his hand from her neck to her thigh where it rested, feeling heavy and warm and possessive. She would just take her chances, she decided, falling in behind a huge semi.

"Jared said to tell you he'd heard from Agnes Armstrong," she remarked in a breathless voice.

Nick's hand stilled. "What'd she say?"

"That her nephew was at the police department, accompanied by his lawyer. Seems he decided to turn himself in...after a conversation with Agnes."

"Jared isn't representing him, is he?"

"No, Jared considers any defense of Melvin a conflict of interest. Anyway, Agnes apparently forced Melvin to admit that he'd paid some thugs to sabotage the project, not to shut it down, but to cause delays, just as we both suspected. Jared ran the number on the penalties—paid out by the contractor and architect to the owner. They're in the six-figure range, Nick."

"Greedy bastard," Nick growled. "And stupid, too."

"Right on both counts." Nearing her exit, Rachel signaled to change lanes. "Why didn't you mention you'd had a conversation with Jared when I was telling you about my suspicions?"

"There wasn't time to go into that, Rachel.

With Paige missing, every second counted. But just so you'll know, I've been checking the crew and I found a couple of guys who had falsified their applications. Both had access to the site and could have tampered with the equipment. When I questioned them, they denied everything, of course. They quit before I could fire them. As for the collapsed fountain, I bet we'll find that the mortar mix was altered.''

"That is so incredible," Rachel murmured.

"And criminal. I needed Jared, as a lawyer, to read the contract, which he did. He decided on his own to talk to Agnes.''

"He must have worked his usual magic," Rachel said dryly, "since she wasted no time confronting Melvin. Just one more thing, Nick…'' She signaled to enter the gates of her complex. "If we're ever to collaborate again as architect and contractor, I'm giving you fair warning. I want to be fully informed from day one until the keys are handed over to the owner.''

"Yes, ma'am." Nick's hand had found its way to a more intimate place. "But I reserve the right to disagree, sweetheart.''

"Protecting me again," she said, but her tone lacked force. It was hard to be exasperated when she felt such melting pleasure. Pulling into her driveway, she somehow managed to stop the car without crashing into something.

"Yeah, protecting you, Rachel," Nick said softly. He reached to gently stroke her cheek. "Because that's the way a man cares for his woman. Because I love you and I want you safe. Because you're carrying my child. Because I want to marry you."

Disarmed and aroused, Rachel searched his face. "You said you weren't going to propose in a car."

He gave a short laugh, leaned over and pulled her close enough to kiss. "Then let's go inside where I can do it the right way."

ONCE INSIDE, NICK fell into Rachel's bed, not to make love to her, but to wait for his pain medication to kick in. In spite of his big talk, his headache forced him to take a couple of the pills prescribed by the ER resident. He was asleep in thirty seconds.

Rachel went into her bedroom two hours later to check on him. She'd taken a shower, changed into a silk kimono and fixed a light meal in case Nick awoke hungry. At the door, she stopped short. He should have looked ridiculous sprawled on the white eyelet and satin trappings of her bed, but he didn't. He looked gorgeous and sexy.

Tanned and utterly male. Moving closer on tiptoe, she sank onto the bed beside him.

Tenderly she sifted the dark hair away from the bandage circling his head. He could have been killed today. Her heart stumbled at the thought. As it was, she'd been given a gut-wrenching scare. She wouldn't easily forget that feeling.

Was this the emotional pitfall that Nick feared? Maybe. Probably. Her hand drifted to his chest, warmed by the life and vitality beneath firm muscle. She prayed he'd gotten beyond it. When you loved someone, risk was a given.

Nick stirred and caught her hand as she started to pull away. "Don't stop now, sweetheart."

She went breathless at the look in his eyes. "Did I wake you?"

"I'm not complaining."

She smiled. "How's your headache?"

"What headache?" He brought her hand to his lips. "Crawl in here with me and I'll prove I don't have one."

Rachel wasn't sure what possessed her at that moment, but without giving herself time to reconsider, she stood up. Her fingers went to the sash of her kimono and pulled it loose. Watching her, Nick was suddenly stone-still as she let the silk slip from her shoulders and fall in a whisper to the floor.

As if in a trance, Nick rose slowly on one elbow. Everything male quickened in him while his heart raced like a runaway train. She had lovely breasts, he thought, nipples dark and peaked with arousal. He put out a hand and touched her, then he leaned forward, caressing with tongue and fingertips. Her sighs signaled to him her pleasure and, with both hands at her waist, he drew her closer, his mouth skimming down her midriff to kiss the place where their child nestled. Pressing his lips to the soft swell of her tummy, he wanted to smile, but found it beyond him.

"Ah, Rachel...what are you trying to do to me?"

Pulling her onto the bed with him, he laid her back against the frilly pillows. Before covering her with his body, he simply savored the sight of her, flushed and expectant. Then lowering his head, he kissed her neck, her chest, her breasts.

They'd been intimate once before as only a man and a woman having sex could be, but their intimacy that night had not extended to this exquisite sensual exploration. Tonight Nick took the time to make slow, sweet love to her. Tastes and scents and touches became a feast of carnal delights.

Rachel was ready and panting with need when Nick pulled her beneath him. With eyes dark and intense, he positioned himself to enter her. Her hands were pressing on his back, nails nipping to urge him on. With a groan, Nick drove himself smoothly and deeply inside her.

For a moment in time they were suspended, lost in the exquisite pleasure of it. He bent then to kiss her, blending lips as well as bodies, and this time there was heightened awareness and meaning. The memory of their first time together would always be with Rachel. Maybe she'd fallen in love with him that night, incredible as that seemed. And when he spilled himself deep inside her, Rachel knew without doubt she loved him now with all her heart.

"How's my baby?" Nick's hand lazily caressed her tummy.

Turning her lips to his warm neck, she whispered, "Fine. Happy. Growing."

"I love you, Rachel."

Lifting her gaze to his, she went breathless at the intense look in his eyes. His touch was warm and comforting. Loving. "I love you, Nick."

"I never thought I'd say that to another woman in this life. But I mean it from the bottom of my heart. I don't know what I was thinking

to believe I'd be able to have you in my life, yet
keep you at a distance.''

"Love doesn't work that way, does it?''

"Uh-uh.'' His hand, moving over her skin,
was suddenly still. "Shows how screwed-up a
man's thinking can be when he's falling hard.''

"I was crushed when you suddenly seemed to
back away.'' She shook her head. "It felt as if I
was being jilted for the second time. It was awful.''

"I'm sorry, sweetheart.'' He shifted, scooting
down until they were face to face. "I'll make it
up to you, I promise. Starting this weekend.''

"This weekend?''

"Yeah. That's the soonest we can get blood
tests and a marriage license.'' A second or two
ticked by. Rachel's hand on his chest moved idly
back and forth. Finally, Nick tipped her chin up.
"Rachel?''

Eyes dancing, she plucked smartly at some
hair and made him wince. "Okay, is *this* a proposal?''

He laughed. "The time is right.'' He nudged
her suggestively. "The setting is good.'' He suddenly rolled them over until she was sprawled on
top of him. "What do you think?''

"I think it's a proposal.'' Smiling softly now,
she let her fingers roam over his face and hair,

before lingering on his lips. "And the answer's yes. How could I say anything else?"

Nick pretended to be incredulous. "Easy! You haven't agreed with much I've said in the past few weeks."

Her eyes fell to the enticing mat of hair on his chest. Leaning forward, she kissed the spot at the base of his neck. "I promise to try and be more agreeable."

Nick gave a small nudge, grunting with satisfaction when she moaned. "Show me, sweetheart. Show me right now."

BORN TO WED
by Gina Wilkins

Chapter One

SASHA GREGORY WAS being smothered by satin and lace, strangled by strands of pearls, buried beneath boatloads of silver-wrapped presents. Everywhere she looked in her cozy little apartment were reminders of the wedding scheduled to take place in exactly fourteen days—her own.

The invitations had gone out weeks ago. The church and pastor, flowers and candles, musicians and caterers were all arranged and confirmed. Everything was ready for the social event of the season—everything except the bride.

She'd just gotten home from work on this Friday in June, the first evening she'd had to herself in almost longer than she could remember. Between meetings with the wedding consultant and assorted contractors, showers and parties, dinners and receptions, she'd hardly had a chance to even think during the past weeks. And, of course, there were the usual demands on her time by her career as an account executive in her father's long-established, solidly successful advertising firm.

She really needed some quiet time to think.

Her telephone rang—for about the sixth time since she'd walked in less than half an hour earlier. As she had with the others, she let the answering machine pick it up.

"Sasha? Are you there?"

Sasha recognized the voice. Jill was one of her bridesmaids, a longtime friend. And Sasha simply didn't have the energy to deal with her tonight.

"Okay, you must be out. Listen, call me when you get a minute, okay? We still haven't decided if you want all the bridesmaids to wear the same color lipstick for the wedding. If we are, we need to get together and try some on—see which colors look best on all of us, you know? Oh, and I saw Patty Louden this afternoon. She said she'd love to have lunch with us before the big day, if you can fit it in. Anyway, call me, okay? Bye."

Sasha buried her face in her hands. Lipstick? Who could think about lipstick? Sasha was trying to decide if she was about to make the biggest mistake of her life!

The telephone rang again. This time it was her fiancé's deep, rich voice that drifted through the answering machine speaker.

"Sash, it's Alan. I guess you're at one of your tea parties or whatever. I just wanted to let you know I'm going to be pretty busy at work for the next couple of days—you know, clearing the calendar so we'll be free for the honeymoon. I'll probably work all weekend. If you need me, leave a message and I'll get back to you, okay? Er...love you,'' he added, the words a bit rushed. "See you later.''

She lifted her head, very slowly, and stared at that machine as if it would reveal the face of the man she'd agreed to spend the rest of her life with. A man she had known since she was in diapers. A man whose body she knew as well as her own.

A man who suddenly seemed like a stranger to her.

And she panicked.

Half an hour later, she was on her way out the door, a hastily packed suitcase in her hand, a vague message left on her mother's answering machine so no one would declare her a missing person. Sasha needed to do some very serious thinking. And she knew she wouldn't be able to do it here.

LATER THAT EVENING, Sasha unlocked the door of the lakeside vacation home her parents had co-owned for years with her fiancé's family. It had begun to rain during her drive, and she had gotten soaked during the short dash from her car to the front porch. She shook raindrops out of her thick, red-gold curls as she stepped into the main room of the house and set her suitcase down with a sigh.

It had been a while since she'd been here last, she thought. Memories assailed her when she locked the door behind her and turned on the lights. The four-bedroom, two-bath house was old, but sturdy, furnished practically and durably, spacious enough to comfortably accommodate two families whenever they'd chosen to vacation together—which had been often during Sasha's childhood.

Sasha's father and Alan's father, longtime friends and business associates, had bought the place together years ago, when Sasha was an infant and Alan a toddler. Alan's sister, Amy, hadn't even been born yet the first time the two families had spent a leisurely week here. Since then there'd been too many summer vacations and long holiday weekends to count.

Sasha trailed her fingers over the big, round oak table where they'd enjoyed so many conversation-spiced meals, so many laughter-enhanced board games. In the living room, they'd sat around the television set and viewed countless ball games and family videos. They'd spent innumerable hot, lazy afternoons on the long, screened back porch lined with rockers. Down the path, past a picnic pavilion and barbecue pit, was the boathouse in which Alan's family stored a powerful ski boat and Sasha's parents kept a big party barge.

The Gregorys and Westcotts had been such good friends for so very long. For as far back as she could remember, everyone had agreed that Sasha and Alan were a perfect match.

They'd resisted for years, stubbornly going their own ways, regarding each other more as cousins than potential life partners. They'd played tag and touch football together, spent many hours swimming in the lake and chasing fireflies on the lawn, argued, tussled and chattered together, but they'd never even practiced flirting with each other during their formative years.

And then something had changed. And Sasha, at twenty-seven, had somehow found herself engaged to thirty-year-old Alan, their blissfully happy mothers busily choosing colors, ordering flowers and selecting menus. They had probably even named their grandchildren, Sasha thought with that smothering sensation that had been hitting her more and more frequently as the wedding date approached.

From force of habit, she stashed her suitcase in the bedroom she usually occupied while in residence here. In years past, she'd slept in one of the twin beds in that room and Amy Westcott, two years her junior, had taken the other. Alan had been given a room to himself, and their parents had taken the other two bedrooms.

When the families vacationed here after the wedding, Sasha would be sharing Alan's bed, something they hadn't done while their families were around.

It was just past eight o'clock, Sasha had skipped dinner, but she wasn't hungry. She found a canned juice in the refrigerator and carried it back to the main room, trying to decide how to fill the hours that lay ahead of her. She briefly contemplated sitting out on the screened porch to listen to the rain, but decided that would only depress her more. She chose, instead, to lose herself in mindless entertainment. She opened the video cabinet and selected a video at random, inserted it in the player, and huddled on the big leather sofa beneath an afghan her grandmother had made years ago.

By midnight, she had watched two movies filled with action, romance and adventure. When the music swelled and the credits rolled on the second one, she found herself sniffling and wiping her eyes, wondering how it must feel to be loved so desperately—more than life, itself—by one of those dashing, romantic movie heroes.

She was marrying a practical, predictable, routine-bound young banker. A very nice guy, she assured herself hastily. Handsome, successful, responsible, dependable. She loved him—of course she did—she'd known him all her life. But was she *in* love with him? Or was she only marrying him because everyone expected her to?

She was so confused.

She almost put in another video. But it was late and she was tired and she wasn't up to any further comparisons between those exciting, glamorous fictional romances and her own relationship with Alan. She changed into comfortable pajamas and crawled into bed, pulling the covers over her head as if to hide from a future that held too many questions and far too few answers.

Amazingly enough, she fell asleep almost immediately.

Something woke her a short time later. She opened her eyes and blinked, wondering if the noise had been part of her unsettling dream or something outside. The wind had picked up, so it could have been nothing more than a tree limb brushing against the house. Nothing to worry about, she assured herself, rolling over in the bed and snuggling more comfortably into her pillow.

Another sound came from the front porch, bringing Sasha straight upright in the bed. Someone was out there!

She told herself she was overreacting. It was probably nothing. Just a noise—creaking wood or something. Maybe a stray dog or cat, huddling under the porch to get out of the rain. She was perfectly safe in this vacation home, which was surrounded—though not very closely—by other lake houses that were usually occupied on weekends. Not every weekend, of course.

The local police frequently patrolled this area, she reminded herself. After a few break-ins a couple of years ago, security had been stepped up. She'd heard of no problems since. She'd always felt safe here, though this was the first time she'd actually come alone.

Someone rattled the front door.

She leapt out of the bed, her mind racing. The only telephone in the house was in the living room. Could she make it to the phone before the intruder got in? She groped for a weapon, her fingers closing around a can of hair spray. She'd heard it could be aimed at the eyes...but then what?

She hoped she wouldn't have to find out.

She tiptoed out of her bedroom and as quickly as possible across the living-room floor. Her hand was hovering over the telephone when the front door flew open, letting in a gust of wet wind and a large, dripping male.

Terrified and furious, she spun, pointed her hair spray, and shouted, "Get the hell out of here, jerkface!"

"What the…"

The man staggered backward, his hands flying up in automatic self-defense. An overnight bag crashed to the floor.

Her jaw dropped when she recognized the trespasser. *"Alan?"*

"Jeez, Sasha, you just about gave me a heart attack."

She hit a light switch, revealing his handsome, rain-streaked face, framed in wet, dark hair. He stared at her in apparent bewilderment.

"What are you doing here?" they asked in perfect synchronization.

Sasha planted her fists on her hips, the hair spray can still clutched in her right hand. "You *followed* me here! You had no right to do that."

"What are you…?"

"All I wanted was a couple of days. Just a couple of days. Is that too much to ask?"

"Well, I…"

"Marriage is a major step. Especially when two people have known each other all their lives and their families have been best friends forever and if anything goes wrong it will be…well, catastrophic."

She saw a muscle flex in Alan's jaw. "I know. I…"

"So why can't you give me a couple of days to think about this? To decide if I'm really doing the right thing? Why did you have to follow me?"

"Sasha, I didn't…"

Maybe it was the fear she'd just experienced that had loosened her tongue. Or maybe the weeks of worry leading up to this point. Whatever the reason, Sasha couldn't seem to stop her harried rush of words. "I have to be honest with you, Alan. I was already questioning whether I should marry you. But you following me here like this shows a disturbing, controlling side of you I haven't seen before. If you think you can just…"

"Dammit, Sasha, I did *not* follow you here. If I'd known you were here, I'd have gone somewhere else. The truth is, I came here to do some thinking of my own."

She blinked, then studied him uncertainly. "You did?"

He nodded grimly. "I'm not at all sure I want to marry you, either."

Chapter Two

SASHA MUST HAVE stared at Alan for a full two minutes before she hastily closed her mouth and pushed her chin high. Alan wasn't sure he wanted to marry *her?* Of all the nerve!

"You have doubts about getting married?" she repeated, just to make sure she'd heard him correctly.

He nodded.

"Then why did you propose to me?" she almost shouted at him, both her ego and her temper flaring.

"I didn't!" he roared back. "I don't even remember when we decided to get married. It seemed like one minute we had agreed to see a movie together, and the next minute we were picking out china patterns and our moms were naming our kids."

"Well, of course you proposed," Sasha argued, though she spoke more quietly now.

"When?" He looked as though he genuinely wanted to hear the answer.

"When? Um…" She tried to recall the exact moment. She remembered the movie he'd mentioned. It had been just over a year ago. Finding themselves with nothing better to do—and no one else to do it with on that particular evening— they had decided to see a critically acclaimed new film together. Afterward, they'd had dinner and enthusiastically dissected the plot. Alan had taken her home, and had almost whimsically kissed her at the door.

The kiss had been dynamite, catching them both unprepared.

A week later, they'd attended a charity event together at the country club. No one had seemed in the least surprised to see them together. Before the evening ended, they'd jointly received several more invitations.

She remembered those events very clearly. But she'd couldn't quite recall a proposal.

Had it been the first night they'd…? No, not that night.

Christmas Eve? No, they'd already been engaged by then. He'd given her the two-carat diamond ring to formalize the engagement, not to initiate it.

When *had* he proposed?

She looked at him blankly. "I don't remember."

"Neither do I. It just...happened."

"I—" Sasha didn't know what to say.

Alan shoved a hand through his wet hair. "Yeah."

"Oh, my God." Sasha sagged as the full meaning of their conversation sank in. They were two weeks away from a huge, expensive extravaganza of a wedding—and neither of them wanted to go through with it. "What are we going to do?"

Rubbing his hand wearily over his face, Alan sighed. "Let's get some sleep and talk about it tomorrow. I'm too tired now to think clearly."

Sasha was suddenly exhausted, herself—physically and emotionally. Alan was right. Two o'clock in the morning was no time to discuss something like this. No time to make life-altering decisions.

"I'm...um...sleeping in my old bedroom," she said.

"I'll take mine." He bent to pick up the overnight bag he'd dropped when Sasha had confronted him.

He took a step toward his bedroom, then glanced back at her. "By the way, if someone *had* been breaking in, just what were you planning to do? Style his hair for him?"

She glanced down at the can in her hand and flushed. "It was the only weapon I could find."

"I see. Good night, Sasha."

"Good night, Alan."

She closed herself quickly into her bedroom. For a moment, her finger hovered over the lock. But that, she told herself, was unnecessary. Judging from the look on Alan's face when he'd left her, he'd probably lock *his* bedroom door.

NOT SURPRISINGLY, ALAN didn't sleep particularly well. Of all the rotten luck. He'd come here to be alone, to think. He'd impulsively decided to spend a couple of days in quiet solitude, resolve everything in his head, and then return to his upcoming nuptials with no one being the wiser about his fleeting doubts.

He couldn't possibly have known that he would find Sasha here, confronting doubts of her own.

He hadn't realized Sasha had been feeling as railroaded and powerless in this engagement as he had. She'd certainly hidden it well. He had thought that she'd been pushing the marriage as avidly as either of their mothers. That she'd been perfectly content with the prospect of marriage to a wealthy, successful, up-and-coming bank executive. But then, he really hadn't seen much of her during the past few weeks, he remembered now.

It was startling—and a bit ego-bruising—to learn that Sasha hadn't been as pleased and complacent as he had assumed.

Why on earth *wouldn't* she want to marry him? Just what was so bad about him, anyway? There were plenty of women who would have considered him a great catch. It was just that none of the ones who'd indicated their availability to him had seemed as compatible and comfortable to him as Sasha had.

Lately he'd begun to wonder if maybe their relationship was just a little *too* comfortable. He was marrying his best friend—but was that enough?

Not that their physical relationship had been dull, he acknowledged. Even when he'd been a young man determinedly resisting his family's matchmaking, he'd been aware of how attractive Sasha was. Her wavy mane of red-gold hair, big blue eyes and slender, well-toned figure had always appealed to him, though he'd managed to resist her until that first powerful kiss a year or so ago. And in bed—well, knowing each other so well definitely had its advantages there.

But he'd begun to wonder if maybe a bit more mystery would benefit their relationship. How could there be any mystery when they'd seen each other in diapers?

He rolled over in the bed, pulling the covers over his head and willing himself to sleep. The last image in his mind before he finally fell into a restless doze was the unfamiliar, furious expression on Sasha's face when she'd aimed her hair spray at him and called him a "jerkface."

She would hate him if he said it, but she really had been kind of cute.

SASHA WAS ALREADY in the kitchen, a cup of coffee in her hand, when Alan stumbled in the next morning. His dark hair was tangled, his eyelids heavy from apparent lack of sleep. There was a pillow crease on his right cheek. He wore a white T-shirt with denim shorts, and his feet were bare. Sasha found herself hastily gulping coffee as a wave of pure lust hit her. She burned her mouth and scowled, blaming the discomfort on Alan.

It really wasn't fair of him to look so delicious this morning, when he knew she was in the middle of a crisis.

She reminded herself that he wasn't at all sure he wanted to marry her. Maybe he didn't find her as attractive as she found him. Perhaps he didn't look at her in the morning and find his knees going weak, his mouth dry. And wasn't *that* unfair?

He headed straight for the coffeepot and poured himself a cup. Only after he'd downed a third of it did he speak, his voice still gruff from sleep. "Morning."

"Good morning," she replied rather stiffly, drawing her pink terry-cloth bathrobe more tightly around her.

He made an effort to tame his hair by running a hand through it as he took a chair across the table from her. "Did you, er, sleep okay?"

"Yes, fine, thank you." She glanced at the dark hollows beneath his eyes. "Did you?"

"Oh, sure. Great," he lied through his pretty white teeth.

"I found some waffles in the freezer, if you're hungry."

"I'll just have coffee for now. Thanks."

Sasha nodded and sipped her own coffee, more cautiously this time. She wasn't particularly hungry, either.

For several minutes, they drank their coffee without speaking, carefully avoiding each other's eyes. It was so quiet she could almost hear her own heartbeat. The silence and tension finally became too much for her. She set her mug on the table with a thump that made Alan start.

"The rain has stopped," she said.

He eyed her questioningly. "Yes. Looks like it's going to be a nice day."

But she hadn't been initiating a discussion of the weather. "You shouldn't have any trouble driving now. If you leave within the next half hour, you'll be home for lunch."

His movements very deliberate, his eyes narrowed with a frown, Alan set down his cup. "What makes you think I'm leaving?"

"You have to," she insisted. "I told you, I need some time to myself. I want to take today and tomorrow to rest and think."

"Exactly my own intentions."

Her throat began to tighten. "I can hardly relax and think if you're here with me."

"Then go back to your place. If you leave now, you can be home by lunch," he added, not quite openly mocking her.

Sasha knew exactly how difficult it would be to find time for herself at home. Between the telephone ringing every few minutes and her mother and friends showing up on her doorstep, and dozens of details nagging to be handled, Sasha would be lucky to find even a few minutes of peace. "If I could think there, I wouldn't have come here," she said logically.

"So stay," he said with a shrug.

"You'll go?"

"No. I came here to get away from the phone and the fax for a few days. I'm staying."

"You left a message on my machine saying you were going to work all weekend," she accused. Funny, she'd never known Alan to lie to her before. Had there been other occasions she hadn't known about?

He had the grace to look momentarily sheepish. "I brought my computer," he muttered. "I can work here."

"You can work at home."

His jaw squared stubbornly. "But I'm not going to. I have as much right to be here as you do."

"Darn it, Alan..."

The telephone rang, cutting into Sasha's angry words.

Neither Alan nor Sasha moved. They stared at each other across the table as the phone rang again.

"It can't be for me," Alan said. "No one knows I'm here."

"I don't want to talk to anyone."

He shrugged again. "So let it ring."

She made it through one more ring before she ran into the living room to make a grab for the phone. "Hello?"

Doris Gregory burst into speech the moment she heard her daughter's voice. "Sasha, what are you doing there? Don't you know how many things you need to be doing this weekend?"

"They can just as well be dealt with next week," Sasha answered. *If ever.* "I'm tired, Mother. I need a rest."

"You can have a nice break *after* the wedding, when you and Alan are sunning on a beach in Maui. What's everyone going to think with you running off like this so soon before the wedding, hmm?" She answered her own question before Sasha could speak. "They're going to think you're getting cold feet, that's what."

"Well, er..."

"And what's Alan going to think? At least tell me you discussed this with him. You didn't just disappear without telling him, did you?"

"Yes, but..."

"Oh, Sasha, he'll be worried sick. You're all alone at the vacation house—what if someone breaks in? Have you thought about that?"

"Actually, I..."

"This is just too irresponsible of you. Your father and I are going to drive there this afternoon to talk some sense into you."

Just what she needed, Sasha thought with a swallowed moan. Whatever had made her think this would be a place to be alone and undisturbed? And why had she felt it necessary to let her mother know her plans?

"Please don't come here, Mother."

"I insist. I won't sleep a wink knowing you're there alone in this condition. It's obvious that something's bothering you, so…"

"Alan's here."

Doris hesitated, then asked, "What did you say?"

"Alan's here. He's staying all weekend."

"Well, why didn't you say so? I realize you and Alan have hardly had a chance to see each other the past few weeks. It's quite naughty of you," she added with a giggle, "but if you wanted a little time to yourselves, I certainly understand—though, of course, this isn't the best time for you to be gone. But never mind. I'll carry on here the best I can without you. If I need to ask you anything, I know where to reach you. Get some rest, dear, and we'll get busy again on Monday. Give Alan my love."

"I will." Sasha couldn't believe how quickly her mother had changed her tune. Just because Alan was here, suddenly everything was hunky-dory.

A moment later, she hung up the phone, turned and glared at Alan, who was standing in the doorway where he'd probably heard every word she'd said. "Okay, you're staying."

"Fine." His expression was impossible to read.

"Fine." She hoped he didn't expect her to entertain him. "I'm going to get dressed and then go for a walk. Alone."

He picked up his coffee cup again. "Knock yourself out."

She didn't even know him in this mood, she realized, staring at him out of the corner of her eye as she passed on the way to her room. Just who was this good-looking, enigmatic stranger? And what had he done with her agreeable, so-predictable fiancé?

Chapter Three

AFTER DRESSING IN a T-shirt, shorts and sandals, and pulling her hair into a quick ponytail, Sasha let herself out the back door and walked down the path to the water. She didn't see Alan; he was probably locked in his room with his computer.

It was a beautiful late spring day. The night's rain had cleaned the air and the grounds, leaving the sky a crisp, rich blue and the tree leaves a bright, emerald green. Churned by a distant boat motor, the lake water lapped at the shoreline and thumped against the boat dock that was still in a state of partial repair—a project her father and Alan's had started nearly a month ago and still hadn't finished. Birds called out overhead, circling the water in search of breakfast.

It was the kind of day Sasha usually reveled in. This morning, she was only passingly aware of details. Her thoughts were focused on the dilemma of what to do about her upcoming wed-

ding to a man who swore he'd never proposed to
her.

She buried her face in her hands and moaned.
How could they go through with this when both
of them were so uncertain? Yet how could they
not go through with it when everything was so
far underway?

How would they ever tell their mothers?

She was half-seriously considering throwing
herself into the lake when something cold and
wet touched her ankle. She jumped, gasped, and
looked down to find a small, scruffy dog
crouched at her feet, shivering and whimpering.
The poor thing was matted and filthy, obviously
a stray. It gazed up at her with sad, moist brown
eyes.

Sasha's heart melted.

"You poor baby. You look so hungry. Do you
want something to eat?"

Encouraged by Sasha's tone, the dog crept
closer. Sasha knelt very slowly and held out her
hand. The dog sniffed and then began to wiggle
its back end.

"Come on, then," Sasha said, straightening.
"Let's find you something to eat."

She moved toward the house, then looked over
her shoulder at the dog, who sat still, watching
her uncertainly. "Well? Come on."

The dog took one step, paused, then trotted close at Sasha's heels to the house. Sasha opened the back door into the kitchen. "After you."

The dog cocked its head, took a step over the threshold, then looked up at Sasha as though making sure it correctly understood her instructions. Sasha urged it inside, shut the door behind them, then walked straight to the sink, where she filled a bowl with water and set it on the floor. "Here, you drink some of this while I find you something to eat. Surely there's something here in the freezer suitable for a dog. Hmm. There are a couple of steaks...two pounds of hamburger...what's this? Yuck. Looks like one of Mother's frozen casseroles. Trust me, you *don't* want that, no matter how hungry you are. Oh, here we go."

She pulled out a package of frozen all-beef franks. "I prefer turkey dogs, myself, but you'll probably like these. Just let me open them and stick them in the microwave..."

"Sasha? Who are you...good Lord, what's that?" Standing in the kitchen doorway, Alan stared in dismay at the filthy mutt sitting at Sasha's feet, gazing adoringly up at her.

"It's a stray. He looked so sad and hungry, I couldn't just send him away."

"It's filthy. And it smells."

"I'll give him a bath after I feed him." The microwave chimed, and Sasha pulled out the plate of warmed wieners. She began to cut them into bite-size pieces.

"He could have fleas. Worms. Rabies."

"He doesn't have rabies." Sasha knelt to set the plate in front of the dog. The dog sniffed the food, licked its lips, then looked at Sasha as though asking for permission. "See what nice manners he has? Go ahead, fella, you can eat it."

The dog took a tentative bite, then attacked the food with eager greed. Alan stepped closer. "Are you sure it's a he?"

"Well, I haven't looked," she admitted. "With all that hair, it's hard to tell at first glance. He's quite a little butterball to be so hungry-looking, isn't he?"

Overcoming his initial distaste, Alan knelt by the dog, patted it carefully, then satisfied that it wouldn't object, he ran his hand along its bulging belly. "It's not a he," he said a moment later. "It's a she. And she's very pregnant."

Sasha felt her eyes go round. "Are you sure?"

"Obviously, I'm no doggie obstetrician. But that would be my guess."

"Heavens. What are we going to do with her?"

Washing his hands in the sink, Alan lifted an eyebrow.

Sasha cleared her throat. "I meant, what am I going to do with her."

"I'd say a bath is the first priority."

But the dog had other ideas. She waddled to the door, then stood there looking expectantly at Sasha.

"I think she wants out," Sasha said unnecessarily. She opened the door and watched as the dog trotted out to the grass and briskly answered nature's call. And then it returned, entering the house again as if she'd lived there for years.

Sasha laughed. "She's housebroken, at least. She's really a little sweetheart, isn't she?"

"She's obviously been someone's pet. I wonder if she got lost or was abandoned?"

"Who would simply abandon a helpless little animal?"

Alan's eyebrows rose higher. "You've obviously never spent much time at animal shelters."

"Have *you*?"

"I spent six weeks working at a humane society for a Boy Scout community service project when I was in high school. More animals are abandoned than they can ever find homes for."

"Well, this one will have a better chance of

finding a good home once she's clean," Sasha said briskly, heading for the linen closet.

By the time she'd located some old towels and carried them into the bathroom, Alan was already there. He held out a plastic bottle of doggie shampoo. "The label says this kills fleas."

Sasha looked at him curiously. "Where did you find that?"

"Mother left it here. It's the kind she always used on Weebo."

Weebo had been the Westcott family pet for many years, and had been included on nearly every family outing. The little gray poodle had died recently, to the dismay of his longtime owners.

Sasha began to fill the tub. "I hope she doesn't mind getting wet. In her delicate condition, I'd like to keep this as easy as possible."

But the dog gave her no resistance when Sasha lifted it carefully into the tub. Using the hand-held shower head, she wet it down, then began to work up a lather.

"Yuck," she said. "The water's getting really nasty."

Standing in the doorway, his arms crossed over his chest, Alan watched her. "You surprise me."

"Why is that?" she asked absently, soaping the dog's floppy ears.

"I wouldn't have thought you'd have wanted anything to do with a filthy stray mutt. You never particularly liked getting your hands dirty."

"Well, I couldn't just leave the poor thing out there to starve. And I don't mind getting my hands dirty occasionally," she added, guessing at his meaning. "I just don't like getting fish goo all over them. I could never understand the attraction of your favorite pastime."

"Second favorite pastime."

There was no expression on his face when she glanced over her shoulder, suddenly flushing warmly. She turned her attention quickly back to the dog, telling herself Alan probably hadn't meant what she'd automatically assumed.

Finally reassured that the dog was as clean as she was going to get, Sasha let the water out of the tub—wrinkling her nose at the mess left behind—and dropped a towel over the shivering, wet animal. Alan stepped forward to help her lift the dog out of the tub. They worked together in silence to rub her dry.

Sasha sat back on her heels to study the results of their efforts. Dirty white would always be the dog's predominant color, with patches of brown and black scattered at random over her body. She would win no beauty contests, but there was something very appealing about her funny little face.

"If she's lost, do you think her owners might have left a message with the local animal shelters?" she asked.

"I suppose it's possible." But Alan didn't sound particularly optimistic that anyone was looking for their canine guest.

"I'll call and check. But before I do anything else, I have got to clean this tub."

Alan glanced at his watch. "It's nearly noon. I'll run into town and get some dog food. Want me to pick up burgers or Chinese or something while I'm out?"

"That sounds good. Thanks. I'll call the animal shelter while you're gone—oh, and the local newspaper office. Maybe someone listed her there as missing."

Sasha thought the look Alan gave her as he left was slightly pitying—as though he thought she was deluding herself. She knew what the odds were against finding the dog's owner. But she had to try. Surely someone had a home for such a sweet-natured, well-mannered little mutt.

She didn't quite know why she'd fallen so hard, so quickly for the little dog. She wasn't usually a "dog person." But something about the dog's sad, lost eyes had touched her, reached a part of her that sympathized. Maybe it was because she could all too vividly identify with being anxious and lost, uncertain what her future was going to bring. She knew exactly how it felt to long for a safe haven.

HIS ARMS LOADED with packages, Alan returned an hour later. He found Sasha sitting on the sofa watching an old movie on TV, the dog sleeping contentedly in her lap.

"Any luck finding her owners?"

Sasha shook her head. "As far as I can determine, no one's reported missing a mixed-breed dog that matches this one's description."

"So what are you going to do with her?"

"I don't know. I suppose I'll take care of her tonight and decide what to do with her tomorrow."

Tomorrow was Sunday, the day both Sasha and Alan planned to return home. Sasha had several decisions to make during the next twenty-four hours or so, Alan mused. The fate of a stray dog was the least of her problems.

"I brought food," he said, setting his packages on the coffee table. "Kibble for the mutt, barbecue for us."

A gleam of interest appeared in Sasha's eyes. "Barbecue?"

He nodded. "I've had so many fancy gourmet meals lately that I was in the mood for some real, solid food. I've got barbecue pork sandwiches, cole slaw and baked beans. Peach cobbler for dessert."

Sasha's tone sounded studiously nonchalant when she said, "That doesn't sound bad."

"Let's eat, then."

Sasha prodded the sleeping dog. "Come on, Molly, Alan's brought lunch."

Alan lifted his eyebrows. "Molly?"

Her cheeks pinkened a bit. "I had to call her something. And she looks like a Molly."

"If you say so." Alan was startled by how quickly Sasha had bonded with the shaggy little dog. He'd never seen her exhibit much interest in pets before.

It occurred to him that maybe he didn't know Sasha quite as well as he'd thought, no matter how many years they'd been acquainted. Could it be, he wondered, that there were things he hadn't bothered to ask because he simply assumed he already knew the answers? And could it be that Sasha didn't know him quite as well as she'd thought for the same reasons? Maybe, in this case, knowing each other for so long had prevented them from knowing each other very well.

Because that seemed like too much of a riddle to handle on an empty stomach, he pushed the questions to the back of his mind and followed Sasha—and Molly—into the kitchen.

Chapter Four

SASHA QUICKLY SET the kitchen table while Alan filled two glasses with the iced tea she'd made while he was gone. They sat down to eat with the sound of Molly munching in the background.

Sasha watched broodingly while Alan snapped his paper napkin and laid it precisely over his lap. He then took his knife and cut his sandwich into neat, identically sized quarters. He had ladled coleslaw onto the right side of his plate, baked beans on the left. None of the food touched. Alan picked up a wedge of sandwich, bit into it neatly, then set it down exactly in its original position. Next, she predicted, he would take a bit of his coleslaw, then a bite of beans, a sip of tea, and another bite of sandwich. And so on, counter-clockwise around his plate, until he'd finished his meal.

As he dipped his fork into the coleslaw, Alan noticed her watching him, her own meal untouched. "Is something wrong with your food?"

She shook her head and picked up her sandwich, which she had broken raggedly in half. "It looks good."

He nodded and took a bite of his beans. "It is good." After a sip of his tea, he picked up his sandwich again, glancing at the corner of the room where Molly was still chowing down. "She seems to like her food."

"I'm sure she has learned not to be picky."

He was already dipping into his coleslaw again. "Have you decided yet what you're going to do with her?"

"No, not yet." She watched him take a bite of baked beans.

"You know, of course, that my place has a no-pets rule." He reached for his tea glass.

They had planned all along to move into Alan's apartment after the wedding, since his place was considerably larger than Sasha's. She'd already given notice on her lease.

"I know," she said grimly, watching him take another neat bite of his sandwich. She didn't want to think now about where she or the dog would be living two weeks from now. "Don't you *ever* eat clockwise around your plate?" she asked in a sudden burst of irritation. "Or take two bites of something before moving to the next item?"

He faltered, his eyebrows rising. "Excuse me?"

She pushed her plate away, the meal only half eaten but her appetite gone. "One bite of every dish, counterclockwise around your plate. When you eat ice cream sundaes, you eat the cherry first, then the whipped cream, then the topping, then the ice cream. You finish each layer of a strawberry shortcake before moving to the next layer. It drives me crazy."

"I didn't realize my eating habits were so annoying to you." His voice was chilly.

"They're so...predictable," she complained. "Just like so many other things you do."

"Such as?"

"The way you read the newspaper. You first stack it in the same order every time—news first, then business, then sports, then entertainment, then the rest. After you finish each section, you fold it, set it aside, then wipe your hands on a tissue before picking up the next section."

"I don't like newsprint smudges on my hands," he said stiffly.

"And the way you get dressed in the mornings. First you floss twice between every tooth. Then you brush every inch of your mouth, rinse, and then brush every inch again. Then you shower—shampoo your hair twice, wash the right side of your face, then the left, your right ear, then your left, your right arm, then your left, and all the way down.''

On a roll now, she forged on, unable to hold in observations that had been nagging at her for weeks. ''You shave the right side of your face first. You put your right arm in your sleeve first, your right leg in your pants, your right foot in your sock and then your shoe. You put your money clip and nail clippers in your right front pocket, then your change and penknife in your left front pocket, then your wallet in your right back pocket, then your handkerchief in your left back pocket. And then you recheck everything before you leave your apartment. Twice.''

His expression was thunderous, his voice icy. ''At least *I* don't have to go back inside half a dozen times every time to retrieve things I've forgotten.''

She lifted an eyebrow, realizing that he'd just struck back. ''I beg your pardon?''

''Every time we try to go someplace, I have to wait because you forgot your lipstick. Or your contact case. Or your jacket. Or your checkbook. Or maybe your...''

''I get the picture,'' she cut in through clenched teeth.

But now *he* was on a roll, obviously as bothered by her quirks as she was by his. "How many times have you locked your keys in your car? How many times have I arrived at your apartment to find that you've forgotten to lock your door, so that just anyone could walk in? Can you blame me for being obsessive about double-checking everything when you're so absent-minded?"

"Absentminded?" She slapped her hands on the table and stood, leaning toward him for emphasis. "Just because I don't have more chore-ographed routines than the Dallas Cowboys Cheerleaders, that doesn't mean I'm absent-minded!"

Very slowly, he rose to face her. "Did you or did you not leave me waiting two hours at the airport last month because you forgot to pick me up? And wasn't it you who forgot and left a skillet on a burner when you left for work one day? If your smoke alarm hadn't miraculously had working batteries, and if your neighbor hadn't been home to call the fire department, you might have burned the whole place down."

"I've made a couple of mistakes," she admitted angrily. "Everyone who isn't as obsessively perfect as you are makes a mistake every once in a while. But I'm not an idiot. I graduated with honors from the university, and I'm the most pro-

ductive and successful account executive at the
ad agency.''

"I didn't call you an idiot. I called you absentminded. There's a difference—which you
would realize if you would put a lid on that infamous temper of yours long enough to think
about it.''

"My temper? *You're* making aspersions about
my temper? You—who's been known to yell
loud enough to rattle windows when you're
mad?''

"I do *not* yell!'' Alan shouted.

Molly whined and cowered beside her food
bowl.

"Now look what you've done.'' Sasha rushed
to comfort the distressed dog. "It's okay,
sweetie,'' she crooned. "He's just very loud
when everything doesn't go exactly his way.''

Alan stood so stiffly he could have had a poker
taped to his spine. "Aren't you fortunate to have
identified all my flaws before you made the mistake of marrying me? You could have been stuck
with me, my annoying routines and my terrible
temper for the rest of your life.''

Her lower lip quivered, but Sasha kept her
gaze focused on the little dog. "Yes, I suppose I
am fortunate.''

"And so am I. I would hate to think that everything I did drove my wife crazy."

He turned and stalked out of the room before she could reply. Her eyes burning, Sasha swallowed around a huge lump in her throat. It was the first real quarrel she and Alan had had since the summer when he was fifteen and she was twelve. She and his then ten-year-old sister had teased him after spying him kissing Shelly O'Connor. He'd gotten so mad at them—especially at Sasha. His fragile teenage ego had fueled his temper, causing him to lash out loudly. Sasha had stood toe to toe with him, yelling back until their parents had interceded and sent them to separate rooms.

Swiping at her infuriatingly damp cheek, she mourned the loss of her lifelong friend more than the loss of the stranger who had been her fiancé.

ALAN DIDN'T KNOW why he stayed at the cabin after his quarrel with Sasha. If he'd had any sense, he'd have packed up and left rather than hanging around for more of the tension hovering between them—or more of her criticisms of him, he thought bitterly.

So he had a few deeply ingrained habits. So he liked his life to be planned and organized. So he'd been accused more than a few times—usually by his younger sister—of being a "control freak." That didn't make him a total jerk, did it? He had plenty of other things going for him. There were still a good many women who would have been interested in him, quirks and all. Just because he hadn't been particularly interested in any other woman in a very long time didn't mean he had to live like a monk now that Sasha had dumped him.

He grimaced as the unpleasant term crossed his mind. Closing the lid to his laptop computer— which he hadn't been able to concentrate on, anyway—he stood and began to pace his bedroom. A couple of hours had passed since he'd stormed out of the kitchen, and he'd been sitting in here sulking ever since. No, not sulking, he corrected himself quickly, knowing that was the term Sasha would have used. Deliberating. Trying to come to terms with the new direction his life had suddenly taken.

Sasha didn't want to marry him. Apparently, she found him too…predictable, he thought with a scowl. Their engagement was over. They were no longer lovers. He wasn't even sure they were still friends.

He rubbed his chest, trying to massage away the heavy ache centered somewhere around his heart. He would get over this, he assured himself.

He hadn't been absolutely convinced he wanted to go through with this marriage, anyway. It would just take him a little time to adjust. He'd gotten into the habit of having Sasha in his life and taken for granted that she would always be there.

He really should leave. Staying here with her was a mistake. She'd be perfectly all right here without him. He should go home, start making plans, try to decide how to go on with the rest of his life now that his wedding plans had been derailed.

He winced and scrubbed a hand over his face, feeling his head suddenly start to ache. Oh, God. Now he had to tell his mother.

He had just reached for his overnight bag when he heard Sasha call his name. "Alan? *Alan!*"

The urgency in her voice made him drop everything and run.

Chapter Five

SASHA WAS CROUCHED in one corner of her bedroom when Alan found her. The little dog lay on the carpet at her feet, whimpering.

"Sasha? What's wrong?"

Sasha looked up at him with huge, distressed eyes. "I think something's wrong with her."

He knelt beside her, studying the shivering dog. "It looks like she's about to have her puppies."

"Ohmigod. Are you sure?" A renewed note of panic had crept into Sasha's voice.

"Relatively," he answered, laying his hand on the dog's straining side. "Pretty sure, actually."

"Ohmigod. What are we going to do?"

"I suppose we're going to make sure she's as comfortable as possible."

"And then what?"

"Then…we let nature take its course."

Sasha stared at him. "That's *it*? Shouldn't we take her to a vet or something? Surely there's an animal hospital or a…"

"Sasha, dogs don't usually go to a hospital to have their puppies. She's perfectly capable of dealing with this herself."

"What if something goes wrong?"

"We'll take care of it," he assured her. "Now how about finding something to use for bedding? Old towels, maybe."

"I'll be right back." She dashed out of the room as if the dog's very life depended on those old towels.

Alan couldn't help chuckling at her panic. Sasha had never handled medical situations well. Cool as a cucumber in even the most stressful business crises, she had been known to pass out cold at the sight of blood. He remembered the time when he'd fallen off the top step leading down to the boat dock and had busted his head on a rock. He'd bled profusely, but hadn't been seriously injured, not even suffered a concussion. Sasha had nearly gone into hysterics. It had taken her parents and his to convince her that he would be all right—and that had been when they were kids who swore they didn't even like each other.

He knew her so well, he thought, nostalgia bringing a renewed ache to his heart.

She returned with enough towels to provide comfort for a half dozen pregnant dogs—and their owners. "Now what?"

"Now," he said, putting the memories and their present convoluted relationship out of his mind, "we stay out of her way."

"Ohmigod."

Alan reached out to take her hand. "She'll be all right, Sasha. She's a tough little survivor."

She clung to his hand without even seeming to notice what she was doing. "She's so small. What if...?"

"She'll be fine," he repeated, and hoped he knew what he was talking about.

By the time Molly was cuddled up with her three puppies some time later, both Alan and Sasha were frazzled. The pups had been born without a lot of fuss, and everything had been cleaned up again. Molly handled the entire ordeal with much more equanimity than either of her human assistants.

"I'm exhausted," Sasha proclaimed, wiping her brow with the back of one hand. "But, Alan, aren't they sweet?"

He looked doubtfully at the damp, nearly bald, wrinkled little creatures nudging blindly against their mother. "They're...little."

"They're precious." Sasha tenderly patted Molly's head. "You did good, sweetie."

"I don't know about you, but I'm starving,"

Alan announced, relieved that the whole thing was over.

Sasha looked startled. "You're hungry? After watching *that*?"

He couldn't help laughing at her expression. "I can't say it was the tidiest procedure I've ever watched, but it's all a very natural process. Molly came through it just fine, and so did her pups. So, yes, I'm hungry—even after watching *that*."

Sasha wrinkled her nose, thought for a moment, then smiled ruefully. "I think I'm hungry, too."

"Why don't we go out for dinner?" he suggested, encouraged that they seemed to be getting along again. Even if the engagement was over, he would like to believe he and Sasha could salvage something of their lifelong friendship.

"Go out?"

"Yeah. There's not much food in the kitchen, since neither of us brought groceries. We can go to Minelli's for pasta and salad, if you like," he suggested, naming her favorite local restaurant.

She bit her lip in indecision. He wondered if her hesitation was due to her reluctance to share another meal with him or a general unwillingness to go out. "What about Molly and the puppies?" she asked, motioning toward the dozing family.

"We won't be gone long. They can rest while

we're out. Or if you'd prefer," he added a bit reluctantly, "I'll go for takeout again." It wasn't that he was unwilling to go fetch food, but the last time he'd done so he and Sasha had ended up yelling at each other across the kitchen table. They were much less likely to quarrel in public.

Sasha seemed to come to a similar conclusion. "All right. If you're sure Molly will be okay, Minelli's pasta sounds good."

Alan nodded, wondering just how awkward the meal would be with so many uncertainties hanging between them. But they couldn't just ignore the past twenty-four hours, he thought grimly. They had issues to discuss and decisions to make. As little as he looked forward to that conversation, Alan knew they had to get it over with soon.

The wedding date was less than two weeks away.

SASHA SUSPECTED THAT Alan had suggested going out to avoid another unpleasant scene like the one at lunch. She didn't blame him; it had gotten ugly. And she was well aware that she'd been the one to start it. She'd been feeling guilty about it ever since.

It had been unkind of her to criticize his little habits. It wasn't as if any of them were all that

bad. They had just gotten on her nerves
lately…as nearly everything had. Of course, it
hadn't been necessary for Alan to attack her in
return. As she had pointed out to him, just because she wasn't obsessive about checking and
double-checking everything she did, that did *not*
mean she was absentminded!

But she wouldn't get mad again, she vowed,
setting her hairbrush down after freshening up for
dinner. She would be calm, relaxed, rational, ma-
ture. No more personal criticisms, she promised
herself. She would merely point out that the
doubts they'd both been struggling with this
weekend meant they had to take a long, hard look
at whether they should go through with this wedding.

Not that she thought there was any real doubt
about the outcome now, she thought a bit glumly.
Alan had already been wondering if he really
wanted to marry her. He'd been aware, even
more than she had, that their engagement had
come about more because of other people's ex-
pectations than their own. He didn't even remember proposing to her. After the things she'd said
to him at lunch, he must be relieved that it all
seemed to be coming to an end.

As for herself…she didn't know exactly what
she was feeling, she thought, pushing a hand

through her hair in a dispirited gesture. But sadness seemed to be in the forefront of her tangled emotions.

"Sasha? Are you ready?" Alan called from the living room.

"Coming," she replied, lifting her chin and forcing a placid expression onto her face. She stopped to pat Molly on the way out of her room. "We won't be long, sweetie. You and your babies get some rest and we'll decide what to do with you all later, okay?"

And wasn't *that* a joke, she asked herself ruefully as she moved toward the bedroom door. She was promising to settle Molly's future when she didn't even know what was going to happen in her own!

Alan was waiting at the door, looking impatient. "Ready?"

She nodded and tucked her purse beneath her arm. "I'm ready."

"Have you forgotten anything?" he asked, and then winced when he realized what he'd said. It was something he always asked her before they left together, a habit he'd acquired long ago. Yet in light of the quarrel they'd had at lunch, the question seemed to have an all-new meaning. "I—er—"

"It's okay," she said, letting him off the hook. "I have everything I need."

He opened the door, avoiding her eyes. "We should go. Minelli's gets crowded Saturday nights."

She had just taken a step toward the doorway when the telephone rang. Alan looked at her then, both of them going very still. The phone rang again.

"Should we let it ring?" she asked.

He grimaced. "I wish I could say yes. But it's probably your mother. If you don't answer, she'll worry."

She knew he was right. As little as she wanted to talk to her mother just then, she knew if she didn't answer, she was likely to find her parents on the doorstep before the evening was over. Sighing, she picked up the phone. "Hello?"

"Oh, there you are. I was beginning to worry. I hope I'm not...interrupting anything?"

"No, Mother, you aren't interrupting anything. Alan and I were just leaving for dinner at Minelli's. We were on our way out the door when the phone rang, as a matter of fact."

"Then I won't keep you. I just need a quick answer from you. Can you be available for a final fitting on your wedding gown Monday afternoon at four? The seamstress has been unable to reach you, so she called me, instead. She's concerned that you've been putting it off too long, especially if there are any adjustments to be made.''

Sasha could feel her stomach tightening. ''Um—I really don't know, Mother. I'll have to get back to you on that.''

''Now, Sasha, I know you hate fittings, but you really can't put this off any longer. I know you don't have your calendar there with you, but surely whatever you have scheduled can be shuffled. This is important.''

As if her work responsibilities were *not* important, Sasha thought in frustration. ''I really can't give you an answer now. You'll have to tell her I'll call her when I get back.''

Doris must have heard something in her daughter's voice, though Sasha had tried to keep her emotional turmoil masked. ''Sasha, dear, is something wrong? Are you and Alan having any problems?''

''I...'' Sasha didn't want to lie to her inconveniently perceptive mother, but she wasn't ready to discuss the likely cancellation of the wedding, either. ''Mother, could I call you tomorrow? Alan's waiting for me.''

''I'm worried about you, Sasha. You've been acting so oddly during the past couple of weeks. And the way you ran off this weekend without any warning, and you've been so reluctant to talk to me—well, I can't help worrying that something's going on between you and Alan. Have you quarreled? Are you having a disagreement about something? Because if so, we—''

"I'll call you tomorrow. I promise," Sasha said, and then quickly hung up the phone.

Alan was watching Sasha's face when she joined him. "You didn't tell her you've been having second thoughts?"

"I think you and I should come to a mutual agreement about what we're going to tell our parents."

He nodded, his expression unrevealing. "Good idea. It's going to be…difficult."

She swallowed. "Yes," she whispered, suppressing a shudder.

"Let's go eat," Alan said with an abruptness that suggested he didn't want to think about that right now any more than Sasha did.

They didn't discuss their plans during dinner. Though the subject hovered between them, neither would be the one to broach it. They talked about the birth of Molly's puppies, about a major contract Sasha had just acquired at the ad agency, about Alan's irritation with his car, which had a recurring transmission problem. Anything to avoid talking about their engagement, or nonengagement, whichever it happened to be at the moment.

Sasha noticed during the meal that Alan was eating a bit awkwardly, toying uncharacteristically with his food. "Is something wrong with your food?"

He flushed and fumbled with his fork. "Er...no...I was just..."

Sasha suddenly realized what he'd been doing. He'd been trying to vary bites of his meal, rather than his usual meticulous counterclockwise rotation. Great. She had made him so self-conscious about eating that he couldn't even enjoy his meal.

He was probably incredibly relieved that she would be out of his life soon, only to reappear at the occasional, unavoidable family get-together. That thought was so depressing she promptly lost her appetite. It was the second meal that day she hadn't been able to finish. If she kept this up, she wouldn't have any trouble at all losing that extra five pounds she'd gained during a series of fancy business dinners with her new client.

"Do you want dessert?" Alan asked, noticing that she'd pushed her plate away.

"No, but feel free to have something if you like."

"I don't really want anything else." Alan, the

man who almost never turned down dessert, set his napkin down and signaled for the check.

"I'll pay for dinner," Sasha said quickly. "You bought lunch."

Alan gave her a look that could have fried bacon. "I'll pay."

Oops. It seemed that she'd accidentally tripped over his ego. It was probably still a bit out of joint because she'd admitted she'd been having doubts about the wedding. She conceded the mini-debate over the check because she didn't want to quarrel with him at the moment. They had enough of that sort of thing still ahead of them.

Chapter Six

IT WAS STARTING to drizzle when Sasha and Alan left the restaurant. By the time they got back to the cottage, the rain was coming down in earnest. Sasha couldn't help glaring up at the dark clouds and cursing them for their lousy sense of irony.

There was no umbrella in the car Alan had rented while his own was in the shop. "Sit tight and I'll run inside and get one for you," he advised, pulling up as close as he could to the house, which did not have a garage or carport.

"You'll do no such thing." She reached for the door handle. "I won't melt in a little rain."

It wasn't a little rain. It was a *lot* of rain. And by the time she and Alan were safely inside, they were drenched. Sasha could feel her blue T-shirt and khaki shorts clinging to her, and her hair was dripping around her face. Yet she couldn't help laughing when she looked at Alan, who was as wet and bedraggled as she was. "We look like drowned rats."

He chuckled and reached out absently to

smooth a wet lock of hair away from her face.
"You do not in any way resemble a rat," he
informed her. "You look as beautiful wet as you
do dry."

He lowered his head, a familiar gleam of intent
in his eyes. And then he went still, as both of
them realized at the same time that people who
were about to get unengaged didn't generally
stand around kissing each other.

It had seemed like such a natural moment for
a kiss, Sasha thought wistfully. Only forty-eight
hours ago—before her impulsive dash to the cottage, before they'd both confessed doubts about
marriage, before Alan admitted he'd never really
proposed to her—this cozy moment would have
led to much more than a kiss. Already her mind
was filled with images of drying him off with her
own body, pushing her hands through his
lustrous wet hair, licking the raindrops from his
skin. She had never had any doubts about their
compatibility in bed, where his meticulous thor-
oughness was a definite asset.

But things had changed between them now,
maybe irrevocably. And Alan was obviously no
longer comfortable kissing her just because he
liked the way she looked wet. He dropped his
hand and stepped back. "Er—I'll go dry off,"
he muttered, moving toward his bedroom without

looking back at her. "You'd better check on the dogs."

She'd actually forgotten about the dogs for a moment. Biting her lip, she nodded—though she knew he wasn't looking at her—and moved toward her own bedroom. Only when she was closed inside with Molly and the puppies did she allow herself to shed a few tears for the kiss that hadn't been—and the ones that would never be.

ALAN'S BED SEEMED unusually uncomfortable that night. Hard. Lumpy. Empty. But he finally managed to drift off—only to be brought straight upright by a clap of thunder loud enough to rattle the windows—and everything else in the house. Moments later there was a sizzling flash of lightning, followed by another boom of thunder. Rain hammered against the roof, accompanied by a tapping sound that could indicate small hailstones.

They were in the middle of a rousing summer thunderstorm, he realized. And Sasha was utterly terrified of thunderstorms. Had been since she was a small child.

He rolled out of bed and moved toward the doorway, then hesitated before stepping out of the room. He was wearing nothing but a pair of boxer shorts. And while Sasha had seen him in his underwear plenty of times—even before they'd ever considered becoming lovers—now he found himself self-conscious about his state of undress.

Cursing beneath his breath, he snatched the jeans he'd worn earlier off the chair where he'd left them neatly folded and stuck his legs into them—first the right leg, then the left, he thought defiantly. He zipped them, but didn't bother with the snap, or with a shirt. All he was going to do was check on her and make sure she was all right, he told himself as lightning illuminated the living room, followed almost immediately by a clap of thunder and another sustained flash of lightning. Maybe Sasha was sleeping through the storm.

He opened her door as quietly as possible, peeking inside, prepared to slip back to his own room if she was, indeed, sleeping. But lightning lit up the room long enough to show him a huddled, shivering lump in the middle of her bed. She had the covers pulled over her head and he saw her jump when thunder crashed again.

Putting their personal problems aside, he moved toward the narrow bed. "Sasha?"

The bundled form shivered again. "I'm fine," she said, her voice firm, even though it showed a slight tendency to squeak. "You can go back to your room."

He sat on the edge of the bed and rested a hand on what might have been her shoulder. Even through the covers, he could feel her trembling. "Sasha."

"I'm a grown woman, Alan," she said with a stiff dignity that was negated somewhat by the muffling effect of the bedding drawn over her head. "I can handle a thunderstorm just fine by myself."

Knowing her pride would compel her to argue all night, he took the matter out of her hands and dragged her, bedclothes and all, into his lap. He had to scoot toward the middle of the bed to keep from falling off the edge. Even as she muttered a protest, Sasha burrowed into his arms, burying her face in his shoulder when thunder rattled the windowpanes again, accompanied by an intensifying of the rain and wind.

"Quite a storm going on out there," he commented unnecessarily, keeping his voice measured and even.

She nodded. "I really am okay," she insisted one more time. "I know it's only a thunderstorm."

"You've never liked them."

"No," she admitted. "I've been afraid of them all my life—no matter how hard I've tried to get over it."

Holding her snugly against his chest, Alan thought back to a little strawberry blond girl screaming for her mother when lightning had lit up the summer night skies. And he remembered an afternoon when he'd been about thirteen, when their parents had been trapped on the other side of the lake by an unexpected thunderstorm, leaving Alan in charge of ten-year-old Sasha and eight-year-old Amy.

Amy had played with her dolls, totally unaffected by the storm raging outside. Sasha had been a mess. She'd whimpered and shivered until Alan had finally sat her on his lap, awkwardly patting her back until the storm passed. He'd promised her then that he would protect her, that he wouldn't let the storm hurt her. He felt just as protective of the intelligent, competent woman in his lap now as he had toward that frightened little girl so long ago.

It was only natural for him to care about her, he assured himself, his cheek resting against her tangled curls. He'd known her all his life. Even if it turned out they weren't meant to be married, he still had strong feelings for her. He supposed he loved her like a sister.

That noble thought almost made him snort aloud in self-derision. Whatever his feelings were for Sasha, there was nothing brotherly about them, he thought, shifting in discomfort. He sure as hell didn't get this hard and achy when he hugged his sister!

A hard gust of wind slammed against the house, causing Sasha to cling more tightly and Alan to think a bit uneasily about the massive oak on the west side of the house. His dad had been muttering for a couple of years that they needed to have that big old tree trimmed back before a falling limb took out part of the roof, but no one had seemed in a hurry to follow through. If the oak remained intact through this storm, Alan was going to insist that his and Sasha's parents do something about the tree before the next storm proved one too many.

His thoughts were jerked abruptly away from the tree when Sasha's fingernails dug into his bare shoulder in response to another chaotic blast from outside. "Careful, honey," he murmured, easing her nails out of his skin. "You're taking hide."

"I'm sorry," she moaned, her face still buried in the crook of his neck. "I hate this. I really hate this. It makes me feel so stupid."

"Don't." He stroked her head, her shoulders, her back, smoothing away the tangled bedclothes, letting his warmth soak through her thin nightgown. "It's a big storm—enough to make lots of people nervous."

Her cheek rested against his bare shoulder. She sighed, her clenched muscles slowly relaxing beneath his soothing ministrations. "Thank you for never making me feel like an idiot about this."

"I don't think you're an idiot—about anything," he assured her.

Sasha sighed again, and finally lifted her head. "Don't be so nice to me tonight," she said with a slightly crooked smile. "I don't have all my defenses in place."

He smiled faintly, one hand toying with a curl at the side of her face. "You don't need defenses against me, Sasha."

Lightning illuminated her face, revealing her expression, which looked a bit wistful. "Don't I?" she asked, her voice so soft he barely heard her over the din of the storm.

"No," he muttered, his gaze focused on her soft, vulnerable mouth. "Not tonight."

Another clap of thunder. Another powerful gust of wind. Sasha trembled in his arms—and he was completely unable to stop himself from lowering his mouth to hers. "It's all right," he murmured against her lips. "I won't let the storm hurt you."

They were the same words he'd used when

they were children. But the way his body reacted
to having her in his arms now made it clear that
he hadn't thought of her as a child in a very long
time. His mouth closed over hers, and he kissed
her as he had grown accustomed to kissing the
woman who'd seemed destined to become his
wife. Her taste was so familiar to him. He knew
every centimeter of her mouth. Every inch of her
body. Every nuance of her voice.

He'd believed he knew her every whim—until
she'd run away from home for the weekend in
sheer panic at the thought of marrying him. Until
she'd told him that the way he ate "drove her
crazy"—as well as the way he showered, the
way he dressed, and who knew what else.

Disturbed by his thoughts, he lifted his head.
But when Sasha reached out to draw him back
to her, he didn't resist. She needed him now to
help her hold off the storm—and he needed her
to calm the storm inside him. Maybe they both
needed to be together one more time before de-
ciding whether to stay together for the rest of
their lives.

Maybe it was only rationalization, but it
worked well enough to allow him to slide into
the bed with her. He rolled so that she was lying
beneath him, her short nightgown bunched high
on her thighs. He slid his hand from her knee up

the smooth expanse of skin to her panty line. She moaned softly—whether from the caress or in reaction to the storm's renewed fury, he couldn't have said.

Her hands clenched at his shoulders, then slid slowly, lingeringly downward. Over his chest, her thumbs pausing to circle his nipples. Down his abdomen, fingertips tracing each rib. To his waist, where she dipped beneath the loosened waistband of his jeans.

He shuddered, burying his face in her throat. It was different this time. Maybe it was the storm. Maybe the uncertainty of their future together. But there was a new edge of desperation to his hunger, an undercurrent of urgency to his desire. He wanted her. Burned for her. And he didn't want to think now that this could be the last time he would have her.

Sasha pushed impatiently at his jeans, urging him to remove them. Her legs tangled with his, her hips undulating in temptation and invitation. Even as Alan helped her shove the jeans out of the way, he wondered if it was only fear of the storm driving her, a need for distraction from the wind and thunder. Had she concluded that there was enough between them to keep them together—or was this her way of saying goodbye?

She dragged his mouth to hers, her hands buried in his hair. He thrust his tongue between her parted lips. *Mine,* he found himself thinking with a fierceness that was new to him. For one more night, at least, she was his.

The storm raged outside while their passion raged inside. And by the time the storm was spent, so were they.

Sasha fell asleep on Alan's chest. Still breathing raggedly, Alan tucked her into the crook of his shoulder, one hand cupped protectively at the back of her head. *Mine,* he thought again. *Mine.* And then he, too, allowed sleep to overcome him.

Chapter Seven

IT WAS BARELY dawn when Sasha and Alan were awakened by Molly, who politely but insistently expressed a desire to go outside. Disoriented, Sasha blinked and frowned as Alan's face came into focus. He lay very close to her on the narrow twin bed, his bare skin just brushing hers beneath the tangled covers. His feet were probably hanging off the end. They'd never shared a twin bed before, but they had managed very well.

Her eyes widened as she woke enough to realize fully what had happened the night before. "Oh," she whispered, her cheeks heating. "I—"

Molly whined again, gently thumping the bed to remind them of her presence, and her need to go out. "I'll take care of her," Alan murmured, sliding from the bed and reaching for his jeans. "Go back to sleep."

But even if Sasha's mind hadn't been whirling with questions and confusion, there was no sleeping through the noisy whining and whimpering the puppies set up when they realized their mother's warm body was suddenly missing. Ruefully, Sasha climbed out of bed and patted the three blind mutts, trying in vain to soothe them until Molly returned.

She felt like doing a little whining and whimpering of her own.

What, exactly, had happened last night? One minute she'd been cowering beneath the covers, waiting for lightning to strike the house and burn it down, or for a particularly violent wind to bring a tree through her roof. The next minute she'd been in Alan's arms, no longer caring if the storm blew her away.

She couldn't help wondering what their lovemaking had meant to him. Had he simply been offering comfort while at the same time taking pleasure for himself? Had he been trying to repair their relationship, to remind them both of the good things they had going for them? Or had he considered it one last, intimate interlude before they went their own ways—a way of bringing closure to their engagement?

She didn't know exactly how she felt about any of those possibilities. She only knew that charity was one thing she absolutely did *not* want from Alan.

A rustle from behind her was the only warning she received when Molly and Alan returned.

Composing her expression, she watched as Molly settled back onto the bedding where she was immediately and enthusiastically greeted by her newborns. Alan knelt beside Sasha. ''They didn't like her leaving them, I take it.''

''Not a bit,'' she agreed, her voice still husky from sleep. She ran a finger along the soft back of one tiny puppy. ''What breed do you suppose they are?''

Alan chuckled. ''Heaven only knows.'' He lifted one absently and glanced beneath it, ignoring its wiggling. ''Male,'' he commented, then reached for another. ''Female. And...female. Two girls and a boy.''

''I'll have to find homes for them. D'you suppose your parents would like another dog?''

He looked doubtful. ''I'm not sure Mother would be willing to replace her purebred, champion-line poodle for a little mutt, but I suppose we could ask her.''

We, he'd said. Habit, or statement of intent?

She patted Molly one more time, then rose. ''You haven't had much sleep,'' she said, noting that Alan looked a bit hollow-eyed. ''Maybe you should go back to bed.''

He smiled faintly and shook his head. ''I couldn't go back to sleep now. I'll go start a pot of coffee. Maybe look for something for breakfast.''

"I'll make breakfast,'' Sasha offered quickly. ''After all, I'm the reason you…well, you didn't get much sleep.''

His mouth curved into an enticingly crooked smile. ''My pleasure,'' he assured her.

She felt her cheeks flame. Glumly, she looked down at her bare feet. ''I feel like such an idiot about last night.''

Any trace of humor had vanished from his voice when he answered after a pause. ''Why, exactly, do you feel like an idiot?''

"It was just so…stupid,'' she muttered. ''I can't believe I didn't have more self-control than that.''

She risked a quick peek at his face, which now looked grim. ''You're really upset about this, aren't you?''

"Well, of course I am,'' she almost snapped, her embarrassment making her defensive. ''I'm a grown woman, for Pete's sake. I should know better.''

For some reason, Alan was beginning to sound annoyed. ''C'mon, Sasha, it isn't as if it hasn't happened before.''

"What does that have to do with anything? I should have outgrown that sort of thing a long time ago. Just because I had a weakness as a kid, doesn't mean I have to let it make a fool of me now.''

He blinked. ''What the hell are you talking about?''

''About my stupid, irrational fear of thunderstorms. What do you *think* I'm talking about?''

He looked momentarily abashed. ''I...er...''

''I've spent years trying to get past this stupid hang-up, yet I still find myself cowering under the covers every time there's a crack of thunder. It's ridiculous and humiliating.''

Alan shook his head, his expression clearing. ''Stop worrying about it. It's no big deal.''

''It's stupid,'' she repeated in a grumble.

''Sasha, it's okay. So you've got a thing about thunderstorms. Everyone's afraid of something.''

''You're not,'' she muttered beneath her breath.

His eyebrow lifted. ''What did you say?''

She raised her chin and said it more clearly. ''I said you're not afraid of anything. You never have been. Even when we were kids.''

He shook his head in apparent disbelief. ''You're wrong, you know.''

She made no effort to hide her skepticism.

''Why do you think I'm so...obsessive, I think

you called it? It's because I'm afraid of forgetting something important. Of screwing up.''

She ran a hand through her hair, smoothing the tangles with her fingers. ''I can't imagine you ever screwing up anything.'' She could have added that she'd always been a bit intimidated by his perfection, but she saw no need to be quite *that* candid.

''I screw up all the time,'' he said, his voice grim again. ''I would say the situation you and I have found ourselves in is evidence enough of that.''

A screwup. Was that how Alan viewed their engagement? And what had last night been to him? Just another lapse in judgment? Sasha looked quickly away, before he could read the disappointment on her face. ''I'll go start breakfast. You'll have time for a shower, if you want one.''

He reached out to her. ''Sasha...''

She skillfully avoided his hand by walking across the room to retrieve her robe and slip into it. ''I'll call you when it's ready.''

He didn't try again to detain her as she left the room, but Sasha was aware that he watched her as she walked out.

ALAN BUTTONED HIS shirt and tucked it into the waistband of his jeans. His hair was still damp from the shower, but he didn't bother to dry it. He was in a bit of a hurry to get to Sasha in the kitchen. The way they had parted in the bedroom bothered him—made him think he must have said something wrong. Screwed up again.

Like the way he had misunderstood her when she'd talked about feeling like an idiot about last night. She'd been talking about her fear of storms, while he had thought she'd been talking about...well, something else entirely, he thought with a wince.

Was that it? Had *she* misunderstood when he'd said their current predicament was an example of his occasional errors in judgment? Hadn't she realized he was referring to the fact that they'd both felt compelled to escape to the vacation house because they'd been too confused to talk to each other? Didn't she know he blamed himself for that lack of communication, for letting things escalate almost beyond their control? Now they had a chance to set things right—if they could both just sit down and talk rationally about what they wanted.

He knew what he wanted. Now he had to find out if Sasha felt the same way.

"I was just about to call you," she said when he walked into the kitchen. "Breakfast is ready."

She'd made pancakes from the box of just-add-water mix their mothers kept in the refrigerator, and she had thawed and cooked link sausages from the freezer. Cups of coffee and glasses of orange juice prepared from frozen concentrate sat beside each plate.

"Looks good," Alan said, taking his seat.

"I just used what was available." She cut into her own short stack of pancakes. Alan noticed that she hadn't made eye contact with him since he'd entered the room.

"We need to talk," he said, picking up his fork.

She hid behind her coffee cup. "Maybe we should wait until after breakfast before we start a serious conversation. I'd like to shower and dress first."

He didn't want to put this off, but he could tell from looking at her that she wasn't ready for a discussion about their relationship. Maybe she was hungry, or maybe she just wanted to be showered and dressed before they talked. He knew enough about women to understand that she would feel at a disadvantage with him showered, shaved and dressed while she was still in her nightgown, her hair still tousled from sleep.

Looking at her over the rim of his coffee cup, he wondered if he should tell her that he thought she looked beautiful in the morning. But then he decided maybe he should just keep his mouth shut. Women were funny sometimes, always trying to find deeper meaning or hidden motivation in the simplest statement.

"All right," he said, instead. "If that's what you prefer."

She nodded and stuffed another bite of pancake in her mouth. Alan didn't try to make any further conversation, but concentrated, instead, on his own breakfast—taking a bite of his pancake, a bite of sausage, a sip of juice and a sip of coffee, and then repeating the cycle. Yes, he knew what he was doing, and knew that it was probably driving Sasha crazy...but, hell, this was who he was, he thought with a touch of defiance. Take him or leave him.

Defiance fading, he found himself hoping that Sasha would decide to take him.

Chapter Eight

SASHA DIDN'T LINGER over breakfast. Leaving Alan to clean the kitchen, since she had cooked, she hurried into her room to shower. She had hardly looked at him throughout the meal, and hadn't spoken more than a half dozen words to him. She simply hadn't known what to say.

The words he'd spoken earlier had kept repeating in her mind all through breakfast, keeping her so preoccupied she could hardly concentrate on anything else.

"I screw up all the time," he had said. *"I would say the situation you and I have found ourselves in is evidence enough of that."*

She couldn't bear the thought that Alan regarded their engagement as a huge mistake, one that he blamed himself for making.

She spent a long time in the shower, letting the hot water pound against her stress-knotted muscles, cravenly postponing the inevitable discussion with Alan. When the water ran cold, she reluctantly climbed out of the shower and toweled off, tied on her robe, then dried her hair before leaving the bathroom.

She was startled to find Alan waiting in her room. She wasn't ready for this, she thought on a quick flare of panic. Whatever he had to say, she didn't want to hear it when she was still wearing nothing but a bathrobe. She needed to be dressed. Mentally prepared.

He rose quickly from a kneeling position when she entered. "Sorry," he said, looking a bit flustered. "I was just checking on the pups."

With a measure of relief, she realized that he hadn't actually been waiting for her. That he wasn't going to immediately launch into that "discussion" they'd both been avoiding. And she couldn't help smiling that he'd been drawn back to the puppies. Alan was showing a soft spot where Molly and her babies were concerned—which only endeared him more to her.

"How are they?" she asked, automatically tightening her sash as she approached him.

"Noisy," he said a bit ruefully, motioning toward the squeaking, squirming trio. "Molly must have the patience of a saint."

Holding her robe closed with her left hand, Sasha knelt to pat Molly's fuzzy head. "Hey, there, sweetie. Are you hungry? Thirsty?"

"She ate a little while you were in the

shower,'' Alan said. ''I—er—puppy-sat while she was gone. The little mutts sure hate it when she leaves, don't they? You wouldn't believe the way they whined and howled.''

Sasha chuckled. ''They may be tiny, but they certainly know how to express their displeasure.''

''I'll say. Heaven only knows how demanding they'll be when they actually get their eyes open.''

Giving the puppies each one last pat, Sasha rose, stumbling just a little when her robe tangled around her ankles. Though she immediately regained her balance, Alan reached out to steady her, anyway. ''You okay?''

She nodded, vividly aware of his hand on her shoulder, even though a layer of terry cloth lay between his palm and her shower-damp skin. ''I'm fine, thanks. Um…I'd better get dressed now.''

It was a hint for him to leave the room. He either missed it or ignored it. Instead of moving away, he lifted a hand to run his fingertips along the curve of her cheek. ''Your skin is still flushed from your shower,'' he commented softly. ''It's almost as pink as your robe.''

She felt her color deepening, which had nothing at all to do with her shower. Alan's thumb slid across her lower lip. She felt it quiver, and knew he was aware of her reaction, as well.

He lowered his head to nuzzle her hair, then her flushed cheek. "You smell so good," he murmured. "Like sun-warmed peaches."

"It's—" She cleared her throat, shaken by the words which—coming from Alan—were almost poetic. "It's a new shampoo."

"I like it." His lips dragged lightly across her cheek, then moved against her mouth. "It makes me…hungry."

She felt her eyelids going heavy. Her hands lifted reflexively to rest against his chest. "Alan…"

"Sasha." Her name was a warm brush of air against her moist, parted lips. "Let me taste you."

She melted into him.

He tasted her very thoroughly. Savoringly. Sasha reached up to cup his face between her hands, holding him. The first time Alan had kissed her, she'd reacted as she had never responded to another man's embrace. That had not changed in all the kisses that had followed.

Yes, there were things about Alan that annoyed her—just as there were things about her that irked him. But maybe she'd been letting her uncertainties about his true feelings exacerbate the minor irritations. If she were convinced he loved her as she wanted and needed to be loved by the man who would be her husband and the father of her children, she could overlook the small, human imperfections—just as she hoped he could overlook hers.

He dragged her suddenly against him, his hands biting into her hips, holding her against the rigid evidence that whatever else he felt for her the physical attraction was very real. "Sasha," he muttered, "I want you. I want you very badly."

It wasn't exactly what she needed to hear—but it was certainly a step in the right direction. "I want you, too," she whispered. "But—"

"We'll have that talk," he promised gruffly between kisses. "Later, okay?"

Reaching down to the sash of her robe, she loosened it quickly. "Later," she agreed, letting the robe slip from her shoulders.

Alan caught his breath, then slid his hands up her sides to her breasts. Cupping them gently, he lowered his head, drawing one taut nipple into his mouth and then the other, repeating the ministrations until Sasha was trembling and clinging to him, aching for a more intimate connection.

He drew her to the bed and she followed eagerly, divesting him of his clothing along the way. This wasn't just lust, she thought as she pressed him to the bed and draped herself over him. Her feelings for Alan were strong. Complex. Powerful. But were they returned in the same way? Was he deeply, passionately in love with her, or merely fond of her in addition to physically attracted?

She kissed his strong, stubborn chin. And then his throat, where his pulse hammered beneath his skin. His broad, sleek chest. She trailed a series of quick, open-mouth kisses from one flat, brown nipple to the other and then downward, making his stomach contract sharply beneath her mouth. And then she moved lower, making him groan.

She didn't know whether she could make him love her, but she had no doubt that she could make him want her. If only that could be enough. But she knew, even as the thought crossed her mind, that it would not be enough for long. At least, not for her.

It wasn't long before he drew her back up to him, kissing her with a roughness that was unlike him—but delighting her with its urgency. "Now," he said, gripping her hips and urging her to him.

"Now," she agreed, rising over him.

He joined them with one quick, hard thrust that took Sasha's breath away. It returned with a gasp when he began to move beneath her. And then it left her again in a strangled cry when she exploded around him.

Moments later, Alan groaned and stiffened, signaling his own release. And then he collapsed beneath her, holding her tightly against his chest.

Sasha buried her face in his throat, struggling to catch her breath. What if this was the last time? The question popped unbidden into her mind, making her shiver in dread. Misreading the signal, Alan snuggled her more tightly against him, murmuring her name.

She clung to him with a sudden desperation. Just the thought of never being with Alan again left a painful, hollow feeling inside her chest. This wasn't just affection. She loved him. Funny, but she hadn't realized how much she loved him until this weekend, when she'd had to face the very real possibility of losing him.

She knew now that she hadn't been running from her fears of not loving Alan enough to marry him. She'd been afraid that he hadn't felt the same way about her. That he was planning to marry her only because everyone seemed to expect him to.

She still didn't know exactly how Alan really felt about her. And until she did, she couldn't be confident about what the future held for them.

IT TOOK A WHILE for Sasha and Alan to fully recover from their lovemaking. Molded together on the twin bed, they dozed for a time, allowing their breathing and pulse rates to return to normal. They were pulled out of bed again the same way they had been before: Molly requested a trip outside.

Alan sighed. "We're going to have to put in a doggie door," he muttered.

Sasha saw no need to remind him they'd be leaving later that day—presumably taking the doggie family with them. "I'll let her out."

But Alan was already reaching for his clothes. "I'll let her out. I'm getting used to it. You can try to figure out a way to get dressed and puppysit at the same time."

She nodded. "I'll meet you in the living room. As you pointed out earlier, we need to talk."

Alan looked back from the doorway. "Yes," he agreed somberly. "It's definitely time for us to talk."

Sasha gulped and reached for her clothes as he followed the impatient dog down the hallway.

Sasha took the time to put on a little makeup before she left the bedroom. Eyeshadow, blusher, a sweep of mascara. Even a touch of lip gloss. Not that it mattered now what she looked like, but it gave her a bit of confidence she badly needed.

"Okay, Molly—and kids. Here goes," she said, trying out a shaky smile. "Wish me luck."

Molly wagged her tail. The puppies scrunched more tightly against their mother and ignored Sasha completely.

Alan was pacing the living room when Sasha joined him. Not a good sign, she thought, pushing her hands into her pockets. And he was wearing a deep frown—another bad omen.

She swallowed. "Alan?"

He turned, his expression clearing only marginally. "You look nice," he said, gesturing a bit awkwardly toward her khaki slacks and the bright red shirt she'd donned for courage.

Since flowery speeches had never been Alan's forte, Sasha had learned to take what she could get. He wouldn't have said it if he hadn't meant it, she reminded herself. "Thank you."

"You—uh—want anything? A soda or something?"

He seemed uncharacteristically hesitant, almost nervous. Which, of course, made Sasha worry all the more. "No, I'm fine."

He nodded, looking grim again. "Then why don't you sit down. Get comfortable."

She perched on the very edge of a chair, her

back ramrod straight. She was hardly comfortable, but it was the best she could do at the moment.

Alan remained on his feet, legs spread, shoulders squared, his chin set at a determined angle. This was the way he looked when he had something rather difficult to do, and he wanted to get it over with quickly and efficiently, Sasha recognized. "I've been thinking," he announced abruptly. "About our engagement, I mean."

She nodded. And waited.

He took a deep breath. "There's really no reason for us to end it now, is there? We've had a chance to talk and spent some time together, and now we know where we stand. Everything has been planned and arranged for months. There's no need to cancel those plans now. We might as well go ahead and get married."

Chapter Nine

SASHA NEARLY FELL off her chair. She stared at Alan, wondering if she could have possibly mis-understood him. "Excuse me?"

He tugged at his collar, as if he were wearing a too-tight tie rather than an open-throated polo shirt. "I'm sure you heard what I said. I think we should stay engaged. Go ahead with the wedding."

"I heard you. I'm just not so sure the words made any sense to me." Sasha rose slowly to her feet, gaping at him in open disbelief. "Did you just imply that after spending the weekend together we now know where we stand?"

"Well, yeah. Sure." He cleared his throat again, then continued. "Before this weekend, neither of us knew the other was struggling with doubts. We were both disturbed because we felt that we were facing our concerns alone. Now we've brought it all out in the open—which is what we had to do before we could go on with our plans," he added. "It's good that we've had this time to work out our problems."

Either he was being incredibly dense, or he had no idea what their problems really were, Sasha thought, baffled as always by the workings of the masculine mind. "Alan, we haven't *solved* anything! We haven't had a real talk this weekend. We've hardly talked at all. We've admitted we had problems, but we haven't actually done anything about them."

He frowned again. "How can you say we haven't talked? We've determined that it was bothering both of us that we didn't feel we'd made a solid, conscious decision to get married. We both felt a bit railroaded into this engagement by our well-meaning families and friends. Now we can say we've discussed it and have agreed that getting married is the best thing to do. So there's no further question that the decision was ours, or that it was mutual."

Fists on her hips, Sasha felt her "infamous temper," as Alan had called it, beginning to simmer inside her. She could not believe the presumption he was displaying at this moment. Though Alan had always had a slight tendency toward arrogance, she hadn't expected it from him today. "*Do* we both agree it's the best thing to do?"

"Why not?" he said with a breeziness that shot her temperature a few degrees higher. "We get along very well, for the most part. We each have a few eccentricities that bug the other, but what married couple doesn't have a few things like that to overcome? And you have to admit that in some areas, we get along *very* well," he added with a tentative smile probably meant to charm.

It didn't. Sasha hadn't been this mad at Alan since he'd put a frog in her bathing suit when she was nine. She'd pushed him off the dock into the lake then. She wished there was a large body of water available now.

"Let me see if I have this straight," she said, her voice cold enough to freeze blood. "You and I get along pretty well, considering everything, and we're dynamite in bed, so hey, we might as well go ahead and get married."

He grimaced. "That isn't exactly what I..."

"After all," she forged on, "the plans are already underway. Just think how messy and unpleasant it would be to call things off at this late stage."

He set his teeth, a sure sign that she was trying his patience—as if she cared. "Sasha, you're overreacting. If we could just talk logically about this..."

"But I'm *not* logical, remember? I'm temperamental and unpredictable and 'absent-minded.' It's a wonder I've been able to get along as well as I have on my own for so long. Heck, I'd be a fool not to marry you so you can take care of me."

"Now, dammit, I never said…"

She cut him off with a sharp, flat movement of her hand. "Never mind. I think you made yourself clear."

"Are you saying you don't agree with me? That you still aren't sure getting married is the right thing to do?"

"That's exactly what I'm saying."

Alan studied her for a long moment, his eyes hooded, his expression unreadable. "I guess you've made up your mind, then."

"Yes," she said softly, "I guess I have."

She'd made up her mind that she wouldn't settle for a marriage of convenience. A practical, carefully calculated union of two close-knit families. She wouldn't be a wife who was regarded with tolerant affection or resigned patience. She wouldn't be married because it would be too much trouble to change their plans at this late date.

At some point during the past year, or maybe at some point during the past two days, her feelings for Alan had changed from the love of friendship to a deeper, stronger, utterly terrifying emotion. She thought of the way he'd helped her take care of a filthy, homeless dog. The calm, steady manner in which he had supervised the birth of Molly's puppies. The way he'd held Sasha through the storm, without once making her feel foolish about her fears. The spectacular lovemaking they had shared in her narrow little bed.

She loved him. Passionately. And if Alan didn't feel the same way about her, she refused to break her heart struggling futilely to change him. When he looked at her, she was afraid he still saw the little girl he'd grown up with. Maybe he would never truly see the woman she had become.

She lifted a hand to her chest, knowing her heart was already broken. But maybe—just maybe—she could salvage some of her pride, if she could just hold on a little longer.

If Alan was suffering from anything more than irritation, it didn't show in his expression. "So the engagement is over."

"Yes," she whispered, glancing at the diamond still resting on her left hand. "I'm afraid it is."

Alan shoved a hand through his hair. "You're sure this is what you want?"

It wasn't what she wanted. But he hadn't offered what she really wanted—his heart. "I'm sure it's the right thing to do," she amended.

"We could have had a good marriage, Sasha. We have so much in common. So many of the same goals. Values."

He hadn't mentioned love. "I'm sorry. It isn't enough."

Her words seemed to hit him like a slap. He turned away from her, his movements stiff. "Then I suppose you're right. We might as well end it."

She nodded miserably.

After a moment, he sighed. "It's going to be ugly."

"We'll handle it." She was thinking about moving away, maybe changing her name. That would certainly be easier than facing her mother, or Alan's.

"I'm sorry it worked out this way."

Her eyes burned, but she refused to shed the tears that threatened. "So am I."

Alan drew a deep breath. "What should we do first?"

"I...I suppose we should tell our families."

He almost shuddered. "Er…yeah. We should tell them."

"They'll be…upset."

The muscle in his cheek jumped again. "I think it's safe to say that's an understatement."

She nodded and rubbed her chest again. It was easier when they were shouting at each other, she thought dimly. That hadn't hurt as badly as this cool civility. "They'll get over it."

Though he looked a bit doubtful, he nodded. "Probably."

"I, um, still have to find homes for the dogs," she murmured, unable to think quite clearly about anything beyond that afternoon.

Alan frowned as if he was a bit surprised that she'd brought the dogs up at that particular time. "Yeah, I suppose. Though heaven knows who you'll find that will want them."

She couldn't even think about parting with Molly and the puppies right now. It just seemed like another goodbye she wasn't ready to say. To keep herself busy, to keep from looking at Alan—maybe to hold back the tears—she checked the time.

Almost noon. She wasn't sure she could take another stilted, painfully polite meal. Maybe she should just leave now, before she lost all remaining shreds of her dignity and begged Alan to love her.

Feeling as if she were moving in slow motion, she slid the diamond ring off her left hand, which felt strange and empty without it. "You'd better take this back," she said, holding it out to him, proud that her hand was relatively steady. "Maybe you can…maybe you can sell it or…or something," she finished lamely.

The thought of some other woman wearing her ring made her want to break things. The thought of Alan ever giving another ring to another woman made her want to scream. But she couldn't keep this one. Every time she looked at it in the future, she would see a symbol of broken dreams and a shattered heart. Maybe it would be easier if she didn't have a visible reminder of how foolish she had been.

As if she would ever need to be reminded.

Alan looked at the ring as though it would explode if he touched it. "Keep it. I don't want it back."

"Please," she whispered. "Take it. I—I don't want it."

He'd given it to her for Christmas, without a great deal of ceremony, in front of their families. She'd thought at the time that she might have liked a bit more romance with the giving of the beautiful ring. Now she understood that romance had been the missing ingredient in their relationship from the beginning. A diamond, for all its beauty, was only a rock. She needed so much more.

It would have saved them both a lot of grief if she'd spoken up much sooner about what she'd really wanted Alan to give her.

After a long pause, Alan took the ring and slipped it into his pocket, his face hard. "If this is what you want," he repeated dully.

"It—" She choked and turned away.

The rattle of the doorknob was the only warning Sasha and Alan had before the door flew open and two worried-looking couples rushed in. Sasha whirled, stared, then groaned and buried her face in her hands. This was all she'd needed to top off one hell of a day, she thought in despair.

Their parents had arrived.

Chapter Ten

ALAN STOOD FROZEN in the center of the living-room floor, wondering what in hell his and Sasha's parents were doing there. He recognized the expression on his mother's sturdy, square-chinned face. It was the terrifying look she got when she'd decided something was wrong in the family and it was up to her to fix it. It made him want to turn and run.

"What in the world is going on with you two?" short, stocky Iris Westcott demanded impatiently, glaring at her son. "Doris called and carried on this morning as if the world was coming to an end."

"Something's wrong," thin, jittery Doris Gregory pronounced gravely, wringing her hands, her eyes narrowed on her daughter's bent head. "We need to know what has happened so we can help you."

Alan gave his father a how-could-you-do-this-to-me? scowl, to which Noel Westcott responded with a helpless shrug mimicked by Sasha's father, Ernest Gregory. "There really was no need for you all to come running here today."

"Does that mean Doris is wrong? You and Sasha *aren't* having problems?" Iris demanded, daring him to lie to her.

"We...uh..." He faltered, unable to bring himself to make the announcement that was sure to bring chaos to the room.

Doris seized the awkward moment triumphantly. "I knew it!" She rounded forcefully on her daughter. "Alexandra Marie Gregory, what have you done?"

Sasha dropped her hands, looking up indignantly. "I haven't done *anything*!"

"You see, Doris, I tried to tell you we shouldn't barge in here," Ernest complained. "The kids probably just had a few things to work out between them before the wedding. You and Iris are always blowing things out of proportion."

"We know our children," Doris sputtered.

"And we know when we're needed," Iris added.

The two longtime friends often finished each other's sentences.

"I haven't heard either of the kids say much of anything yet," Noel commented. "Seems to me that if they'd wanted help, they'd have asked for it.''

"Exactly," Alan agreed.

Doris suddenly made a grab for Sasha's left hand. "Why aren't you wearing your engagement ring?"

Sasha looked toward Alan. He met her eyes, knowing they were both in perfect accord for at least that moment. They both wished they were anywhere else but here.

He watched as she took a deep breath. And then she broke the news in a firm, flat voice. "Alan and I aren't engaged anymore, Mother. We've called off the wedding."

The reaction, after a long moment of stunned silence, was every bit as bad as Alan had predicted. All four parents started talking at once, ranging from maternal cries of dismay to paternal pleas for everyone to remain calm.

"How could you break the engagement less than two weeks before the wedding?" Iris demanded, throwing up her hands. "Don't you *know* how hard Doris and I have worked?"

"What have you done, Sasha?" her mother wailed. "How could you chase away a man who would make such a wonderful husband and father? A man you've known and cared about all your life?"

Alan had to wince at that. Sasha obviously cared for him in some ways, but as she had pointed out, it hadn't been enough. When it came right down to it, he simply hadn't measured up. Hadn't been what she wanted.

It hadn't seemed to occur to her that she was exactly what *he* wanted. That he couldn't imagine ever wanting another woman now. That losing her was the most painful experience of his life.

She was looking at him again, her expression sad and oddly pleading. He wished he knew what she was silently asking from him. Maybe there would be one more thing he could do for her before they went their separate ways.

The parents were still babbling. Tears poured down Doris's face. Ernest patted her shoulder, looking as though he shared Alan's wish to be elsewhere. Noel was beginning to look angry, as if he wished he could still order Sasha and Alan to their rooms until they decided to be reasonable and do what they were told.

"What can we do to fix this?" Doris demanded. "What's gone wrong?"

Sasha shook her head. "There's nothing you can do, Mother. Not this time. Alan and I have made our decision."

"You're the one who blew it, aren't you?"

Doris asked in resignation. "I knew when I heard your voice on my answering machine that you were going to do something foolish. You came running here and poor, dear Alan followed you to talk sense into you, but it didn't help."

"Alan's a good man," Ernest told his daughter in a father's worried voice. "Solid. Steady. He can support you and take care of you."

Alan could hardly believe his ears. "Are you firing her from the ad agency, Ernest?" he asked, taking a protective step toward Sasha.

Taken aback, Ernest shook his head. "Of course not. She's the best damned account executive I have on staff."

"Then she's perfectly capable of supporting herself. She doesn't need me to take care of her."

"Thank you," Sasha murmured, edging a bit closer to him so he could hear her.

"She's *too* career obsessed," Doris accused her husband. "You've been grooming her from the time she was little to take over the business someday and you forgot to remind her how important it is to save time for a family. Is the ad agency going to be there for her when she's tired? Or sad? When she's old and alone?"

Twenty-seven-year-old Sasha blinked and Alan could tell she was dismayed at being prematurely relegated to a lonely old age.

"It isn't *my* fault that she can't seem to keep a guy," Ernest said defensively. "Alan's the best of the long line she's dated, and I've said so, but I can't make them stay together."

"We'll never have grandchildren," Doris moaned. "I'll have to call all our friends and tell them the wedding's off."

Alan was beginning to get defensive on Sasha's behalf. What kind of family support was this? Her engagement had just fallen apart, which had to be stressful for her, even if her heart wasn't broken. Her parents should be giving her moral encouragement, not blame and grief.

"Sasha will not end up old and alone," he said clearly. "She's a beautiful, intelligent, fascinating woman who can have any man she wants. I was just the wrong one for her, that's all."

Sasha looked at him in apparent surprise, her eyes suddenly overbright. He was shaken by the hint of tears he saw there. She hadn't seemed inclined to cry earlier, when she'd torn him apart by giving back his ring, he couldn't help thinking.

"Alan's right—for once," Iris announced brusquely. "Sasha is an ideal young woman. I considered myself very fortunate to have her for a future daughter-in-law. It's obviously Alan's fault that the engagement is over."

Alan's jaw dropped. *His* fault? Now, wait a minute...

Noel nodded glumly. "The boy always was impossible to please. Everything has to be just so. Always has to have things his way. I've warned him that a lot of people won't put up with his demanding ways, but I guess he didn't listen."

"But, Alan didn't..." Sasha began, only to be interrupted by Iris's mournful agreement to her husband's assessment.

"Alan demands perfection. He wants to control everything around him, and I'm sure Sasha grew tired of him trying to change her to suit him."

"I never tried to change Sasha," Alan defended himself. "I wouldn't *want* her to change, in any way. But..."

"I don't know where we went wrong," Iris bemoaned to the room at large. "He'll end up one of those lonely, grouchy old bachelors, following a precise daily routine and worrying about dust and germs."

"Mom!" Alan protested, not sure whether he was more insulted or indignant. With parents like his and Sasha's, he seethed, who needed enemies?

"That's terribly unfair," Sasha piped in, taking yet another step toward Alan, ending up close to his side. "Alan is a very special man. He'll find someone someday that he…that he can truly love. And she'll be a very lucky woman to have him."

Alan's eyes narrowed again on Sasha's face. The things she'd said, the little break in her voice—was there any chance that Sasha was under the mistaken impression that he wasn't in love with her? "Sasha…"

"I knew it!" Iris said. "It *is* Alan's fault. You're just too demanding, Alan. It's true that Sasha has her little oddities, but nobody's perfect. If you had any sense, you would overlook her little…well, flaws."

Doris's chin lifted. "*Her* flaws?" she repeated, turning to the other woman.

Iris nodded glumly. "You know, her flightiness. That scatterbrained way of hers. I knew Alan would have a little trouble dealing with it, since he's such a perfectionist, himself, but I thought he'd find a way."

"Sasha is not scatterbrained. She's creative. Something Alan, with his accountant's mentality, probably doesn't quite recognize."

Iris frowned. "His accountant's mentality? I'll have you know my son can be very creative when he chooses."

"He certainly doesn't choose to be very often," Doris snapped. "I knew there would be times when Sasha would get a bit...well, bored with Alan's set ways, but I thought she could entertain herself for the most part."

"Now, Doris," Noel interceded, trying for a measure of calm, "you have to admit Sasha tends to go off on odd tangents. That's not a criticism, I love the girl, myself. I guess it comes from being a pampered only child."

"Pampered?" Ernest scowled. "I've had the girl working at the agency since she was twelve. She's earned her position there, let me tell you. And she's damned good at it. She'd hardly be a top-notch account exec if she was 'scatterbrained.' If your boy hadn't been so indulged in his persnickety ways, he'd realize he needs Sasha to shake him out of his dull routines a bit."

"My son is not dull!" Iris added. "There are plenty of women who'd be thrilled if he looked at them."

"We have never 'indulged' Alan," Noel agreed. "We've recognized that he's a man who knows what he wants and knows how to go about getting it. We're proud of him for that."

As the debate escalated in both noise and intensity, Alan turned to Sasha. "Could we step outside?'' he asked, his voice barely audible above the din.

She heard him, and nodded. No one seemed to notice when they slipped out the back door.

Alan led Sasha down to the water, which lapped softly against the shoreline and the boat dock. A breeze rustled leaves over their heads, and a fish jumped with a splash out in the middle of the lake. The peaceful sounds were pure heaven compared to the storm raging inside the house.

Alan cleared his throat, glanced at Sasha, then stalled for a moment with a dry comment. ''It's no wonder you and I have our, uh, quirks, with both of us having such weird parents.''

Her quick laugh was as wry as his tone. ''They really are weird, aren't they? Do you think they'll ever be friends again?''

''Oh, yeah. It isn't their first fight. Won't be their last.''

''I would hate to think that our situation had ruined a friendship that has lasted for so many years.''

''Sasha, could we forget about our parents for a minute?'' Alan asked, unable to wait any longer to speak out. He knew he was taking a major risk, that he was in danger of being shot down for the second time that day, but he couldn't help himself. This was too important to give up without making at least one more effort. "There's something I need to ask you. Something I should have asked you a long time ago."

He watched as she seemed to steel herself. The way she drew inward, as if in self-protection, twisted his heart, while at the same time it gave him a modicum of hope that he was reading her correctly.

Damn, he hoped he wasn't screwing up again.

"What is it you want to ask me?"

In answer to her wary question, he reached out to take her hands in his. Her fingers were so cold. He cradled them tenderly in his palms to warm them.

He drew a deep, bracing breath. "Alexandra Marie Gregory, will you do me the very great honor of marrying me?"

Her hands jerked in his, but he didn't release her. Her face bleached of color, her eyes going wide and distressed. "Alan, you—"

"I didn't really propose to you before," he cut in quietly. "I was so arrogant and foolish that I let us drift into an engagement without ever making it clear to you that I am deeply, madly in love with you. That I have been since the night I kissed you after our first movie date—or maybe I've been in love with you all my life."

Tears welled in her eyes, one spilling over to trickle pitifully down her pale, soft, right cheek. ''You're only saying that because...because...''

''Because it's true,'' he finished when she choked. ''Because it's always been true. I told you I loved you when I gave you that ring.''

''I know,'' she said with a little sniff. ''But...''

''But I didn't make you believe it,'' he said regretfully. ''I made it sound casual and superficial, and I don't blame you for doubting me. But I know what I feel, Sasha. I love you as I have never loved another woman, as I will never love anyone again. And if you don't feel the same way, it will rip my heart out.''

''Oh, Alan.'' Her fingers curled tightly around his. ''I love you so much it's been tearing me apart. I was so afraid you were only marrying me because our families wanted it so badly. I couldn't bear to think that was all we had between us.''

Sheer relief flooded through him so powerfully it almost weakened his knees. It was all he could do not to crush her hands in his as he drew her toward him. When he thought of how close he'd come to losing her because of his own blind stupidity...

He paused suddenly, remembering. Releasing

her left hand, he reached into his pocket with his right and pulled out the diamond ring she'd given back to him earlier. "I gave this to you in front of everyone last time," he said gravely. "I didn't let you know how much it meant to me to see it on your hand. This time I want to place it on your finger in private. With all my heart."

She smiled shakily and held out her left hand.

He paused just before sliding the ring onto her finger. "You won't change your mind this time?" he asked, needing to be sure. "The wedding is still on?"

She met his eyes steadily. "You really love me? Even if I am forgetful and temperamental and impulsive? Our family connections have nothing to do with the way you feel about me?"

"I love *everything* about you," he answered firmly. "And if you can overlook my dull, obsessive ways, I'll spend the rest of my life convincing you of the way I feel about you. I would love you if I'd met you only yesterday. It has nothing to do with our families, and everything to do with the woman you are."

"You aren't dull and obsessive," she defended him loyally, casting a quick, defiant look toward the house. "You're...prudent. And I love you."

He laughed, slid the ring on her finger, and

then pulled her into his arms for a long, heated kiss. Only Sasha, he thought, could make the word "prudent" sound like an accolade.

"I love you," he told her between kisses. "I love you. I love you."

He would tell her until she never had reason to doubt him again.

Breathlessly, Sasha laughed and eagerly returned the kisses, sheer joy shining from her eyes.

Epilogue

THEIR PARENTS WERE waiting when Sasha and Alan walked hand in hand back into the living room of the vacation house. Though they were no longer yelling at each other—to Sasha's relief—there was a definite chill in the air. Her parents and Alan's stood stiffly at opposite sides of the room.

Doris rushed forward before Sasha had a chance to say anything. "My poor baby," she crooned. "I'm so sorry we pushed you into something that was making you unhappy. I don't want you to worry about a thing, you hear? I'll take care of canceling everything so you won't have to bother with it."

"No, mother, I—"

"I'll cancel the rehearsal dinner and the arrangements for the honeymoon trip," Iris said quickly, unwilling to be left out now. "Alan, dear, you should take some time off work. Maybe go with your father on a fishing trip or something. I'm sure the stress of all this has been difficult for you.''

''But, Mom, we—''

''We'll have to return all the gifts, of course,'' Doris said with a regretful sigh. ''Even that gorgeous Waterford bowl Aunt Agnes sent, which was so unlike her since she's normally such a tightwad. But, still, it has to be done and I'll have to call the caterer and the…''

''Mother…''

''Mom…''

They were totally ignored as their mothers continued to take turns listing all the people who would have to be notified that the wedding was off.

Alan looked ruefully at Sasha and then lifted two fingers to his mouth. A moment later a shrill whistle split the room.

Sasha almost laughed when their parents fell silent, looking at Alan as if he'd lost his mind.

''Now that I have your attention,'' he said, squeezing Sasha's right hand. ''There's something you should know.''

''Alan and I are engaged,'' Sasha announced, smiling broadly as she lifted her left hand to display the flashy ring she wore there. ''He just asked me to marry him.''

The announcement was greeted with blank silence.

"I—um—don't understand," Iris said after a moment. "You mean you've made up? You've decided not to end your engagement, after all?"

"No. She means we've begun an all-new engagement," Alan said with a crooked smile. "And this time, it was entirely our idea. We love each other, and we want to be married—no matter how our families feel about it."

Doris lifted a hand to her temple. "You children are giving me a headache. Why don't you make up your minds?"

Ernest and Noel looked at each other and smiled wryly.

"They aren't children, Doris," Ernest said. "That's what they're trying to tell us, I think. They're adults, and they know now what they want. And it's time for us to stand back and let them handle their own affairs."

Noel nodded and stuck out his hand to his son. "Congratulations, boy. I hope you and Sasha will be very happy together."

"Thanks, Dad. I know we will be."

Sasha noted that their mothers still looked a bit dazed and bewildered. She gave them both a smile of sympathy. "Alan and I really do appreciate all the hard work you've done on our be-

half, Mother, Iris. We love you both. In fact,"
she added, breaking into a smile as a sudden
thought occurred to her, "we'd like the two of
you to have a small gift in appreciation."

She glanced up at Alan, who was looking at
her with loving curiosity. And then she turned
back to their bewildered mothers. "How would
you each like an adorable puppy?"

Alan laughed, then pulled her into his arms for
a kiss. And Sasha kissed him back with the happy
conviction that he was kissing her because he
wanted to, because he loved her—and not because their families expected him to.

TO HIRE AND TO HOLD
by Margot Dalton

Chapter One

PEOPLE CROWDED THE tenth-floor room, clutching folders and briefcases. The instant Lee stepped amongst them, she realized her clothes were all wrong.

And no wonder, she thought, heading toward the nearest vacant chair. She'd gone and listened to her sister again. When was she ever going to learn?

"Look, you're applying for a job in television," Moira had told her airily, as if she knew everything there was to know about the media. "So you have to look the part, right? Creative but competent, and with just a bit of an artistic edge."

Though she sounded like an image consultant or fashion designer, Lee's younger sister actually spent her days teaching chemistry to junior high school students. From what Lee could tell, Moira mostly taught them how to perform lab experiments that flared up and set the ceiling on fire.

"An artistic edge?" Lee had asked. "What does that mean?"

"It means you need to have a certain look. Arty but not too wild, creative without going over the edge. Able to take charge but remain attractive. Let's see what I've got here...."

They'd finally settled on one of Moira's long patterned skirts, black rayon splashed with big russet flowers exactly the same colour as Lee's hair. Moira added woven leather sandals and a high-necked cotton blouse, also russet.

When Lee was dressed, Moira had stepped back in her paint-stained overalls, frowned thoughtfully and pronounced the look "almost perfect," then offered a pair of gold hoop earrings the size of bracelets.

"No," Lee said, rebelling at last. "I don't want to wear those great big hoops. How about these?"

She rummaged through her own meagre jewel case and held up a pair of jade cameos.

"Oh, all right." Moira had relented, tossing the gold hoops aside with obvious reluctance. "I guess the jade matches your eyes. I wish we could do something about all those freckles on your nose, though. Hey, you want some of my Pan-Cake makeup?"

"No, I don't."

"And we'll leave your hair loose on your

shoulders," Moira said as if her sister hadn't spoken. "It's so shiny and pretty, Lee. Just like fire."

"Sure, okay," Lee muttered. "Whatever."

Anything to get away from the woman.

On the bus to her interview in downtown Seattle, she'd finally taken a scarf from her handbag and tied her hair back at the nape. That, at least, made her feel more like herself.

But now as she sat in the anteroom gripping her leather folder and awaiting the most important job interview of her life, Lee knew that her look was all wrong.

The other people in the room, presumably applying for similar jobs, could be divided into two classes. The younger men and women weren't dressed up at all. They stood around idly, looking comfortable and bored in their khaki pants, T-shirts and runners. These were the ones who'd recently graduated from media programs and fine arts courses, and who still serenely believed their youth and genius alone would be enough to land them high-paying jobs in the field of their choice.

And, Lee thought sadly, looking down at her worn folder, they were probably right.

The other group was more like her, mostly people in their late twenties or older. They seemed tense and anxious, reviewing their employment files and qualifications as they waited to be called. But none of them wore long skirts and sandals. This group was dressed in power suits, vests and pinstripes, wingtip shoes and spectator pumps.

Lee found herself falling somewhere between the two groups, with no idea where she really belonged.

The story of my life, she thought ruefully.

All at once she became aware of a male posterior, denim clad, moving close to her shoulder. She drew away, startled, then looked more closely. This was beyond doubt, a very shapely example of its type, in clean faded jeans topped by a leather belt. Muscles flexed and bunched nicely beneath the soft blue fabric.

"Oh, hey, sorry to crowd you," a muffled voice said above her head. "I didn't realize anybody was sitting in that chair."

Belatedly, Lee realized the man was doing something mechanical to a photocopy machine.

"Okay, that's what we want," he muttered, as the machine whined, sputtered, and spit out a couple of sheets of paper which he gathered into a manila folder. The man slung on a tweed sport jacket that rested over the back of the adjoining chair, then turned to stand in front of her.

He wore a black T-shirt tucked into his jeans and had muscular tanned arms. His jaw was square and handsome, his face bright with amusement. He had dark curly hair, not too long, and shrewd brown eyes.

Lee stared up at him, her polite smile stiffening in shock and disbelief.

At the same time, the cheerful look vanished from his face. He looked around as if seeking escape, but the chair beside Lee was the only empty one in the room. He settled into it with obvious reluctance.

She was vividly conscious of tiny, irrelevant details, like a new scar on his upper lip and some weathered creases around his eyes that hadn't been there six years ago. At this close range, the familiar scent of him, buried deep in her memory for so long, was almost too appealing to bear.

"Hi, David." Lee cleared her throat. "What...what are you copying?" she asked to fill the awkward silence.

His jaw tensed and a muscle jumped in his cheek, but his voice was calm enough when he answered. "One of my employer references. The machine was jammed."

"So you fixed it? Just like that?"

He looked down at his square, capable hands. "I can fix anything."

"I know," she said.

David Clementi had always been able to fix anything. Except...

"So I guess you're here to apply for a job, too?" she asked.

"Just like everybody else," he said curtly. "This is a terrific opportunity."

"The new station..." Again her voice caught, but she forced herself to continue, for all the world as if they were simply a couple of acquaintances making polite conversation. "It's going to be really high-tech, and it's...so far away."

"I'm not a bit worried about high-tech," David told her. "And Spokane is a great place to live."

She could tell that he was beginning to recover his equilibrium. He extended his legs comfortably and interlaced his fingers behind his head. The tweed jacket fell away to show a lean waist and hard flat abdomen.

Lee tried not to stare, but she could feel her mouth go dry, and her heart beginning to pound.

After all these years, the man's mere presence was enough to destroy her.

"You look...really good," she ventured at last. "How have you been?"

"Fine," he said. "Just fine."

Despite his offhand manner, she could hear the anger in his voice, and see how tensely he gripped the papers in his hands.

So he'd never forgiven her. Well, no wonder, Lee thought miserably.

"I tried to call you a couple of times after…" She stared at her sandals and nerved herself to continue. "But you'd just disappeared," she said. "Nobody knew where you were."

"I went to Australia for a few years. I had a good job at a television station in Sydney."

"Why did you come back to Washington?"

"Family troubles," he said in a short tone that made her reluctant to ask for details.

"I see."

"So what kind of job are you applying for?" he asked after another painful silence.

"Copywriting, production, scriptwriting…it doesn't really matter. I just need a job."

"Why are you wearing that getup?" he asked abruptly. "You look like a gypsy. I guess your taste in clothes must have changed."

Her cheeks flamed with embarrassment and a bracing touch of annoyance.

"This outfit was Moira's idea. She said I should look arty and creative, but competent."

"That sounds like Moira, all right." He smiled, his lips curving with a brief touch of warmth that made her pulse race again. "What's she doing these days?"

"She's going to Bolivia with her boyfriend to work in the peace corps. They'll be leaving in just a couple of weeks."

He was examining her so closely that Lee had

to force herself not to shift in the chair like a nervous child who'd been called to the principal's office.

"What about you?" she asked, trying to sound casual and conversational. "What are you applying for?"

"Same thing as always." He frowned and glanced idly around the room, as if talking to Lee O'Connor was the last thing in the world he wanted to be doing. "Sound mixing, booth and board work, edits. I'm still the guy they call when the machines aren't working."

"Yes, you always have been."

Lee felt a wave of inexplicable sadness. She took a deep, shaky breath, trying to steady herself.

People all around them were now being summoned to the interview rooms, and it was only a matter of time until her name was called.

"Do you know anything about these people?" he asked, not looking at her. "I mean the Martlow family."

"Well, I know a bit." She searched her memory. "They've grown from one little station in Bellingham to a media chain all across the northwest. And I've heard," she added wistfully, "if you can get a job with the Martlows, they pay really well."

"Are you married?" he asked suddenly. "If you are, nobody told me about it."

Lee glanced up at his hard tanned jaw, then looked down again at her hands, clenched tightly in her lap.

"No," she said, her cheeks flaming. "I'm... not married."

David arched an eyebrow briefly but showed no other sign of emotion. "Well, the Martlows prefer to hire married employees," he said. "Did you know that? In fact, most of these college kids here in this room don't even stand a chance."

"Married?" She stared at him. "Why?"

David sat back and cast a glance around at the thinning ranks of applicants. "It's some kind of management quirk," he said without expression. "Apparently Edna Martlow believes married people are more stable, less likely to move or have sick days or get involved in drugs and all the other stuff that Edna and her husband don't approve of."

Lee looked down morosely at her gaudy flowered skirt. "That makes sense, I guess."

There was another long, tense silence.

"So," she said at last, "I guess you're... married now, are you?"

"No, I'm not. And a whole lot of people have told me I won't be able to get a job offer from these people because of it."

"You're kidding. You mean they don't even consider hiring single people?"

Lee stared at him again, her cheeks draining of color. For a moment she was so worried that she even forgot about the incredible awkwardness of running into him like this.

"But that kind of discrimination isn't even legal, is it?" Lee's anxiety mounted. "I really need this job! I've already been laid off, and Moira's going to be leaving in..."

She fell silent, biting her lip.

David Clementi watched her with a look of sardonic amusement that made her want to hit him.

"Why are you applying for the job, then?" she muttered at last. "What's the point, if they don't hire unmarried people?"

"During my interview," he said calmly, "I plan to tell them I'm married but my wife and I are having a lot of problems. I'll say we're working on the relationship, trying hard to hold things together. Then if I get offered the job and turn up next month in Spokane on my own, I can say it just didn't work out."

"But that would be lying, wouldn't it? I always thought..." Her voice faltered, but she forced herself to continue. "You were never the type of person to tell an outright lie."

"No," he said bitterly. "I was the guy who

always told everybody the truth and tried hard to keep my promises. And what did it get me? Tossed away like an old shoe, practically on my wedding day.''

"David," she whispered, "You don't understand. Right after it happened, I..."

"Look, let's not talk about all that, okay?" He made a dismissive gesture. "It happened six years ago. I got over it."

Well, I didn't, Lee thought miserably, smoothing the fabric of her skirt over her knees. *I never got over it....*

"I'm a pretty moral person," he was saying. "I don't drink and drive, I don't cheat on my taxes, and I'm good to my mother. If I tell these people I'm married in order to get myself a good job, and I fully intend to be a terrific employee, who gets hurt?"

"So if what you do isn't hurting anybody," Lee asked slowly, "you believe it's not wrong?"

"That's what I believe."

She pondered this approach to morality. "It just doesn't sound like you," she said.

"You don't know me," he told her coldly. "And you never did, or you couldn't have treated me the way you did."

The words hurt almost unbearably. "David, I told you, breaking our engagement wasn't..." She paused awkwardly. "There were...things going on in my life. I asked for a little time, but you just went off to Australia.''

''After I asked for an explanation, remember? And you wouldn't even give that satisfaction.''

''I wanted to. I really did, but my mother said…''

But at that moment, David's name was called. Lee watched as he got up and headed for the interview room. He was tall and lithe, with an easy stride that made the cramped waiting room seem even smaller.

She waited for him to turn and glance at her, maybe even give her a smile to ease the tension between them. But he strode into the interview room without looking back.

Lee settled into the chair, pressing her palms to her hot cheeks, trying again to breathe deeply and stop the noisy pounding of her heart.

She was called to her own interview before David came back, and realized after entering the suite beyond the anteroom that applicants were being questioned in at least two different groups.

Edna Martlow herself presided over Lee's interview, plump and majestic in a navy blue suit and ruffled white blouse, with gray hair and eyeglasses secured by a gold chain around her neck. Three other management types, two men and a woman, sat with Edna at the table while her husband Wilbur popped in and out, obviously commuting between the various interview rooms.

Wilbur Martlow was small and cheerful. Hands clasped behind his back, he rocked on his toes and made chirpy noises like a balding cricket. Lee liked him at once, and wished he'd been questioning her instead of the imposing Edna.

She'd never been interviewed by an employment panel before, and found herself increasingly anxious as she opened her folder and laid out her résumé along with examples of a few successful advertising campaigns she'd created at her previous jobs.

Edna put her glasses on and studied the documents with thoughtful pursed lips, then handed them on to the others. She left no doubt that she was in charge of the interview, though the other three also tossed out occasional questions, assessing Lee's level of experience and professional knowledge.

At last Edna folded her hands on top of Lee's college transcript, removed her glasses and looked directly across the table.

Now that Lee was a little less nervous, she understood that Edna Martlow wasn't really intimidating at all, just competent and brisk. Her eyes twinkled warmly, and despite the executive clothing, she looked like somebody who might enjoy putting on an apron and whipping up a batch of cookies.

"So, Letitia," she said.

"Lee. That's what most people call me."

"Well, Lee, your professional qualifications certainly seem to be in order. Let's talk for a few minutes about personal issues, shall we?"

Lee nodded.

"What can you tell us about yourself?" Edna smiled kindly. "Do you have any hobbies?"

"Well, I like oil painting, hiking, writing fiction, and all kinds of sports. I play fastball in a women's league, just for fun although we get pretty competitive. And I've been volunteering for the past four years as a tutor for kids having trouble in high school."

"An excellent charitable activity," Edna said approvingly.

"I really like working with kids."

Edna Martlow jotted something in her notebook. "Do you play any musical instruments?"

Lee shook her head. "My sister Moira got all the musical talent. I can't carry a tune to save my life. But I still love listening to music."

"What kind?"

"Jazz, soul, blues, semi-classical…I have really varied tastes."

"Do you have any pets?" one of the other interviewers asked.

"The building I live in doesn't allow pets. But I love animals. I grew up on a small farm east of the city," Lee said. "We had goats and a few pigs."

"So if you could have a pet, what would you choose?" This was from the second man, sitting at Edna's right elbow.

Lee wondered if there was a correct answer to this question, or if they were just making conversation to see how she responded.

"A dog," she said after some thought. "But not a big one. I'm afraid of big dogs."

"You've been at your current job for...almost five years," Edna said, glancing down at the résumé. "Why do you want to leave?"

"The station is downsizing and going to an all-news format. There won't be as much need for creative script work. We're all being laid off."

"So at our new station, you would be seeking a position in production?"

"I can do any kind of writing or commercials," Lee said. "But I love working on video production."

"We're looking for somebody experienced enough to head up a department dealing with mini-documentaries, local interest features, that kind of thing."

Lee's heart thudded with excitement. "Oh,

that would be…'' She bit her lip, trying not to sound too eager. ''I'd really love a job like that.''

''And the salary would be… Just a minute. Calvin, do you have that schedule of pay and benefits?''

One of the other interviewers handed over a sheet of paper and Edna studied it briefly. When she read off the annual salary for the head of the production department, Lee felt briefly dizzy, almost lightheaded.

It was more than twice her present income, an unheard-of amount.

And for the kind of work she loved more than anything…

''Now, about your personal situation.'' Edna watched her closely. ''I assume you're married. As a company we believe very strongly in family values. In fact,'' the woman added, ''we find that we fit best with employees who are in long-term domestic arrangements.''

Her gaze was meaningful, almost challenging. Lee gripped her ringless hands under the table while her life flashed before her eyes.

Years of Sunday school in stuffy rooms, a childhood mostly devoted to an earnest effort to be a good little girl, the heart-wrenching pain of breaking her engagement to David Clementi six years ago, and then Moira's casual announcement last month that she was getting married and moving out of their shared apartment, leaving Lee with a rent she could never afford...

And now this dream job.

She thought about David's handsome tanned face as he said that if something hurt nobody, it couldn't be called wrong.

For the briefest of moments she remembered the plans they'd made all those years ago as they rocked together in the porch swing on his mother's lawn, holding each other dreamily, kissing and cuddling. They were going to live in a big old house with a shady verandah, and have four kids and two dogs.

David had always wanted lots of children, and so had she...

At the sweet unbidden memories, pain slashed through her like a knife and tears stung in her eyes.

"Lee?" Edna Martlow was asking.

Lee took a deep breath. "Yes," she said hoarsely. "I'm...I'm married."

She glanced around, half-expecting a bolt of lightning to cleave the ceiling and strike her dead on the spot. But nothing happened except that Edna Martlow gave her another warm, approving smile.

"How does your husband feel about moving to Spokane if we decide to offer you this job?"

"Oh, he...he doesn't mind at all," Lee said.

"He'd be happy to move if it meant I could have a wonderful job like this."

"So he's supportive of your career?"

"He's wonderful," Lee said, suddenly reckless.

If she was going to invent a husband, he might as well be a good one.

Edna smiled, looking warm and motherly. "That's good to hear. It's always nice to meet a young couple who are happily married."

"Yes, we're very happy. My husband and I share everything, and support each other in whatever we do. I couldn't imagine living without him. He's just the most wonderful man I've ever known."

By now, it hardly even felt like lying. Lee could almost see this marvellous husband, though his status and occupation remained blurry. His face, though, still looked a lot like David Clementi's.

But not so cold and sardonic, Lee pondered with a little shiver. David never used to be that way. He was always warm and cheerful in his younger days. But that had been before she...

Lee gathered herself together with a little start when she realized Edna Martlow was concluding their interview.

The sense of euphoria began to fade as soon as she got up and gathered her papers, muttering an awkward thanks. By the time she stumbled from the room and rushed through the outer waiting area, she was utterly appalled at what she'd just done. Tears stung behind her eyelids and choked her throat when she recalled those bald-faced lies.

David Clementi stood in the hall, waiting for an elevator. He glanced casually at her flushed cheeks. "Is something wrong?"

Lee shook her head and punched the button for the lobby, then gripped her arms, overtaken by a sudden chill.

The car arrived and they rode down together in stiff silence.

"I take it your interview didn't go well?" he said at last.

"Oh, it was great," she told him bitterly. "You should see the kind of salary they're offering, and for a full-production supervisory position. It's the job of a lifetime."

"So what's the matter?"

She looked up at him, seeing his face through a blur of misery. "I did what you said. I panicked and told them I was married."

"So did I." The elevator stopped and they walked out into the lobby together. "What's so bad about that? I told you, it's a victimless crime. And besides, the Martlows have no legal right to discriminate based on marital status."

"But what if I got the job?" Lee asked in rising panic. "I'd have to turn it down, or else everybody's going to know I lied."

"Do you think they'll offer you a job?" He leaned against a marble pillar, watching her.

Lee turned away to kick aimlessly at the brass trim edging the carpet. "I doubt it. There must be applicants more qualified than I am. And probably," she added grimly, "those other people aren't all big liars."

He grinned at her obvious distress. Lee wanted to kick him instead of the carpeting.

He took a pen and notebook from his jacket pocket and jotted something down. "Well, if you get offered the job, that's my number."

Lee grabbed the paper without looking at it and jammed it into her leather folder as David started to walk away.

"Why would I call you?" she called after him. "What does that have to do with anything?"

He paused, then turned. "Think about it, Lee. What if we both get offered employment with Martlow Enterprises?" The grin broadened but didn't touch his eyes, which remained hard and watchful. "We'll just have to get married, won't we?"

"Married? To you?" She gaped at him. "You've got to be joking."

"Why not? It sounds to me like a great plan.

You can call and beg me to marry you. It'll get you off the hook.''

"David, that's not a bit funny," she told him, suddenly furious.

"I think it's a hell of a lot funnier than what you did six years ago. Maybe this time," he added, the grin vanishing, "you'd have enough at stake not to walk out on me."

Lee watched, stunned and speechless, as he strode across the lobby and out through the glass entry doors.

Chapter Two

LEE FINISHED UP her last week at her old job, then watched as Moira flew around their shared apartment, packing and sorting her belongings.

After six years of an amiable relationship that had endured all through college, Moira and her boyfriend, Colin, had finally made their decision to enter the peace corps. Now, at the end of the school term, they were preparing to put their belongings in storage and head down to South America where they intended to teach local children how to read and help the villagers dig water wells.

Lee thought it was all very romantic and generous, and she was genuinely proud of her sister. But she did have occasional moments of panic when she wondered what was going to happen to her.

"You could always go live with Aunt Charlotte until you get a new job," Moira suggested as she tossed books into a cardboard carton.

"Not on your life," Lee said.

Their aunt lived in a sagging, moss-covered old house on Mercer Island with three flatulent basset hounds. The last time Lee visited, Charlotte had forced her to eat all the creamed cauliflower on her plate before being served dessert.

"Well, you could always move in with a friend," Moira said. "Hey, do you think I'll need a winter coat in Bolivia?"

"I'm sure you will. And your boots, too," Lee said. "All my friends are in relationships," she added, staring at her own neat pile of packing boxes, a stark contrast to Moira's wild clutter.

Obviously touched by the bleakness in Lee's tone, Moira crossed the room to hug her sister. "Poor Lee," she whispered. "I'm sorry, honey. Have you decided on anything at all?"

Lee forced a smile. "Oh, don't worry about me. I'll be just fine. I'm looking on this as a..." Her voice caught briefly, but she forced herself to go on. "It's kind of a nice holiday. I don't have to get up every day and go to work, and in a few more days I won't even have an apartment to clean."

"So what will you do for now?"

Lee shrugged. "You know what I'm doing. I'll put my stuff in storage, rent a room by the month at a hotel somewhere and keep looking around for a job. After I've got work again, I can find a place to live."

Moira studied her anxiously, gripping a pair of fur-lined winter boots in her arms. "And you'll really be okay?"

"Of course I will," Lee said. "I have my savings to live on. Remember how you used to tease me all the time about saving for a rainy day? Well, guess what, it's raining."

Moira hesitated, looking unconvinced. "Maybe you'll still be offered that job in Spokane."

"Not a chance. It's already been three weeks since they had the interviews. And besides..."

"What?" Moira asked.

But Lee shook her head and turned away.

She'd never told anybody except David Clementi about her shocking behavior at that interview, and she fervently wanted the whole humiliating incident to stay in the past and be forgotten.

MOIRA AND HER boyfriend went away near the end of June, with a suddenness that left Lee feeling dizzy and bereft. She had two more days to use the apartment, and she was sleeping on an air mattress surrounded by books, with everything else she owned now packed into boxes or stored at her aunt's house.

Rain fell beyond the window as she sat gloomily on the floor in the whispering silence, hugging her knees and pondering her fate. It was midafternoon on a weekday but she wore jogging pants, an old plaid shirt and fleecy socks, and had spent most of the day doing the *New York Times* crossword puzzle.

I should be out looking for work, she thought restlessly. *This is so crazy. I need a place to live, a steady income, some kind of structure in my life. I can't...*

The buzzer sounded, announcing a package. Lee let the delivery man upstairs and signed for a courier envelope. She wandered into the barren kitchen and used the only remaining knife to open the envelope, then stared in shock and disbelief.

The envelope contained a job offer from the new television station in Spokane. Lee had been chosen for the position of head of the production department, at a salary that once again made her mouth go dry and her heart pound with excitement.

Affixed to the job offer was a personal letter from Edna and Wilbur Martlow, welcoming her to "the family of Martlow Enterprises" and offering any assistance they could to help Lee and her husband get settled in Spokane. Lee's attendance at her new job was required before July 15th if possible.

"And," the letter concluded, "we will also

want your husband's name, age and social security number so we can add him to our generous schedule of medical benefits. Thank you for your prompt attention to this, and we look forward to working with you."

"Oh, no," Lee wailed, sinking to the floor with her back against one of the kitchen cabinets, clutching the letter in her hands. "Oh, hell!"

Her mind began to work feverishly, trying to come up with a solution, but she could see no possible way out of this mess.

She would simply have to decline the job offer.

Lee rolled her head against the cupboard door, trying not to cry because if she ever gave way to tears, she feared she'd drown in self-pity. But the dark tide of misery rose up and threatened to overwhelm her.

Suddenly she caught sight of her leather folder on the counter. Moving stiffly like a woman caught in a nightmare, she got up and walked over to rummage through the folder, taking out the scrap of paper with David Clementi's phone number.

It wouldn't hurt to call him, she told herself, reaching a shaking hand toward the phone. She could just express courteous interest and ask if he, too, had been offered a job.

Then she remembered his look of sardonic

amusement at their last meeting and drew her hand back.

For a long time, Lee wavered in an agony of indecision. At last, feeling reckless and despairing, she took a deep breath and dialled the number.

"Hello?" he said, answering on the second ring.

"David? It's Lee."

"Hi." Instantly his voice turned cold and expressionless.

"I just wondered if you..." She swallowed hard. "If you got a job offer from the Martlows."

"It came this morning." He paused so long that she began to shift nervously on her feet, twisting the phone cord. "You too, I assume?"

"Yes, the courier package just arrived. It's..." She took a deep breath. "It's such a great job, exactly what I've always dreamed of."

"Well, that's nice," he said. "I'm very happy for you."

Silently, Lee cursed his deliberate obtuseness.

"But you know I can't accept it," she said, "because of that lie I told. I'm supposed to supply them with my husband's name and his ID."

"I know you are," he said. "I got pretty much the same letter."

"So what are you going to do?"

"Well, I haven't quite decided yet." She could hear the amusement in his voice. "Do you have any suggestions, Lee?"

The rotten so-and-so. David Clementi was enjoying this, she realized. He wanted to see her squirm and beg for his help.

Well, she wouldn't give him the satisfaction. Not in a million years.

"No," she said coldly. "I really don't have any suggestions for either of us. I certainly wouldn't want to do anything I would regret later. We lied and I guess we'll just have to pay for it, that's all."

"But what are you…"

"Goodbye, David."

She hung up before he could say anything more. But her brief surge of anger soon passed, leaving her feeling lonely and miserable again.

Lee stared bleakly at the phone for a while, then wandered back into her empty living room and stretched out on the air mattress, burying her head in her arms.

SHE WAS AWAKENED from a troubled sleep sometime later by a knock at her front door.

Probably Mrs. Buchanan from down the hall, needing to borrow a toilet plunger again.…

Lee heaved herself to her feet, wondering if she could remember which box Moira had put the plunger in. She trudged to the door and flung it open, then gaped in astonishment.

David Clementi stood in the hallway, wearing jeans and a white polo shirt. His curly hair and broad shoulders glistened with raindrops.

"How did you get up here?" she asked.

"The doorman is a friend of mine. We go to the same gym."

"No kidding," she said grimly. David Clementi had always been the kind of man who had friends everywhere.

"You look terrible," he said, examining her closely. "Have you been sleeping?"

"I look terrible?" She glared at him. "What happened to that whole sermon about how telling lies is okay if it keeps from hurting people's feelings?"

He grinned, looking distinctly unrepentant. "That's right, you look especially beautiful today. So can I come in?"

"No," she said, trying to close the door.

But he inserted a foot in the opening. "Come on, Lee. You called me, remember? I know what kind of trouble you're in."

With a gesture of defeat, she opened the door and let him into the apartment. David looked thoughtfully at the mountains of packing boxes.

"You were pretty confident about getting this job, weren't you?"

"No, I wasn't the least bit confident. I have to move because I shared this place with Moira and now she and her boyfriend have gone to South America. I could never afford the rent on my own. Especially," she added bitterly, "since, as of last week, I'm also unemployed."

He hesitated near a stack of boxes.

"You can sit on that one if you like," Lee said, waving her hand. "It's full of books. The furniture is already gone."

"Where?"

"Mostly to an auction house, except for a few pieces stored in my Aunt Charlotte's basement."

"I always liked Aunt Charlotte." He settled onto one of the boxes, looking as casual as if this were a normal social call.

"I know," Lee said wearily, lowering herself onto her air mattress and staring out the window again. "And I think you're one of the few people in the world she's ever approved of."

He watched her for a moment, his face unfathomable. At last he reached into his breast pocket and took out a sheet of paper with an official-looking stamp, handing it to her. Lee unfolded the paper and glanced through the wording, then stared at it blankly.

"This is...but this..." Her hands began to shake, making the paper rattle. "David, this is a marriage license."

"Yes," he agreed. "That's what it is, all right."

"And it's got..." Still dazed, she examined the paper. "It has our names on it. Yours and mine."

"Quite a sight, isn't it?"

"But this is..." Still dazed, she sat opposite him on one of the boxes filled with books. "This is the craziest thing I ever heard in my life."

He leaned back and crossed his arms. "Why is it crazy? We're both going to Spokane to work for the same company. You need a husband to save you a lot of embarrassment. It wouldn't hurt for me to have a wife when I arrive, since I've already told them I do. We could get married, supply them with the vital information they need, and have a legal divorce by fall. They can hardly fire us for getting divorced."

Lee stared at him, her eyes wide. "You're out of your mind."

He ignored her. "That license is valid any time we decide to use it."

"But how could we..." She wondered if this was some kind of bizarre nightmare and she'd be waking up soon. "I can't believe we're having this conversation."

"Ask me to marry you," he said.

"What?"

"Just say it. 'David, will you marry me?'

Think about it, Lee. With that one sentence, you can solve all your problems.''

He was right, of course. But she could never say those words. Not while he was obviously getting so much enjoyment from her predicament.

''Come on, you know you have to do this,'' he said reasonably. ''What choice do you have?''

''I could tell the Martlows how I lied,'' she said, grasping at straws. ''They obviously like my qualifications. Maybe if I was completely honest with them, they wouldn't...''

Her voice trailed off lamely and she looked down at the crisp new marriage license in her hands.

David watched her with shrewd, dark eyes, waiting impassively.

Lee struggled with herself, casting about for some acceptable option, her thoughts scurrying back and forth like a rat in a trap. At last she took a deep, shuddering breath and gritted her teeth.

''David,'' she muttered with painful reluctance, ''will you...oh, hell.''

''Say it,'' he told her.

Lee fought back tears of humiliation. ''Will you marry me?''

HE DROVE AN expensive sport-utility vehicle with a ski rack on the roof and a mountain bike attached to the rear door. The van was filled with camera equipment and various kinds of sporting gear, including badminton rackets and baseball gloves.

Lee glanced into the back, then over at his aquiline profile. "You still lead a busy life."

"I like being active."

The rain drummed on the roof, beading on the side windows and trickling across the windshield in heavy rivulets while the wipers maintained a steady, soothing rhythm. It was like being in a cave, surprisingly cozy and safe. And it made David seem very close to her, as if they were the only two people in the world. Again she was conscious of how good he smelled.

He headed for Bellevue and pulled off down a side street, parking in front of a big old house with gables and dormers, set well back behind rows of maple trees.

A small plump woman stood on the brick walk. She wore rubber boots, a yellow raincoat and a broad-brimmed plastic hat, and held a white poodle on a leash. The dog sniffed a peony bush, then lifted its leg daintily.

"Good boy, Chipper," the woman said, bending to pat his fuzzy topknot. "Hello, David."

"This is my landlady, Maybelle Schwartz," he said to Lee. "Maybelle, this is Lee O'Connor, the girl I'm going to marry."

Maybelle beamed and enfolded Lee in a wet hug. "Well, that's wonderful news! David's the best man in the whole world," she told Lee solemnly. "Just the best. And I should know, because he's been my tenant for a long time. I hate to think he's moving."

"But we're really not..." Lee began, appalled by what was happening to her.

"Come on." David took her arm and drew her toward the door. "We'll get soaked if we stand around out here. See you later, Maybelle."

"Come downstairs for a drink!" the woman shouted after them. "We have to celebrate!"

"Okay," David called back, pausing on the verandah and searching for a key. "As soon as we can, Maybelle."

Inside the house he took Lee up an oak staircase to a second-floor suite that had a rounded living room with a brick fireplace and leaded glass windows.

However, the place was stripped of furniture and filled with packing boxes, just like Lee's.

"What a lovely suite," she said, hugging her arms and chattering nervously. "You must hate to leave. I've always loved these... Oh my goodness!" she added, jumping a little as a huge black dog appeared in one of the arched doorways and eyed her with menacing intent.

"That's my dog, Hulk," David said. "Hulk, come and meet Lee."

The big dog paced into the room, still watching Lee with unwavering yellow eyes. He sank down near one of the packing boxes and began to gnaw his front paw with teeth that looked like sharpened piano keys.

"What is he?" Lee asked with horrified fascination. "A Doberman?"

"No, Hulk's a rottweiler. He weighs eighty-three pounds."

"He seems...well behaved," she ventured.

"Well, he should be." David was rummaging through a box. "He's been to obedience school three times."

"Why?"

"He flunked out the first two times. Once for nipping at the instructor, and once for fighting with other students."

Hulk continued to watch Lee steadily. Avoiding the big dog's gaze, she moved away and examined a couple of paintings leaning against the far wall while David rummaged in a box.

"You don't have any pets," he said. "Do you?"

"Our building didn't allow pets."

"That's good," he said cheerfully. "Because Hulk would eat them."

At the sound of his name the dog's ears rose

briefly, then lowered. He rested his muzzle on massive forepaws, never taking his eyes off Lee.

"Here it is." David took some papers from the box. "I hadn't intended to pack this stuff away yet, but the movers came by this morning to take the desk away, and I had to..."

"What is it?" Lee asked when he paused to read the paper in his hand.

"It's a prenuptial agreement."

"A prenuptial agreement?" She forgot her nervousness over the dog long enough to stare at him in disbelief.

This time it was David's turn to invite her to sit on a packing box. "I suspected you might be proposing to me if we both got job offers," he said calmly, "so I wanted to be prepared."

He handed over the papers and she took them, still feeling stunned. The document had been composed on a word-processing program and looked surprisingly official. It laid out the circumstances of their "marriage," and contained a series of clauses designed to protect both parties.

He specified the marriage was entered into "for mutual convenience only," that both parties retained full financial autonomy and would have no claims on one another's estates upon dissolution of the arrangement, and that both parties agreed that a written statement of intent from either of them would be sufficient grounds to dissolve the marriage without further argument.

"Both parties will have equal input into all decision-making related to the partnership," she read aloud, "which will remain entirely platonic for the duration of the marriage."

She glanced at him briefly but he was staring out the window, whistling tunelessly under his breath. Lee returned to the document which included a place for both their signatures and an official witness.

"Who would ever be willing to witness this thing?" she asked.

"We could get it witnessed at the office of the justice of the peace," he said. "Or by whoever performs the marriage ceremony."

"And when would we…" Lee passed a hand over her eyes, then glanced up nervously as Hulk got to his feet and took a few steps toward her before he turned and headed out of the room, toenails clicking briskly on the polished hardwood.

"You were going to ask when we'd get married?" David asked.

She put down the papers. "This is crazy," she said. "It's totally insane."

"Look, you used to be a bright, interesting girl," he told her. "Surely you can think of something else to say besides that."

Lee glared at him. "So you honestly don't think it's crazy?"

"Of course not. I think it's very sensible. We need each other and we're entering into a short-term, mutually beneficial business arrangement. I'll help you move to Spokane and get settled, and afterward we'll go our separate ways."

When he put it that way, the suggestion didn't seem quite so ludicrous. But still...

"When do you have to be out of your apartment?" he asked.

"By Friday morning."

"So where were you planning to go?"

"To a hotel," Lee said. "I was going to send all the boxes to Aunt Charlotte's until I found a job and a place to live. But now, if I accept this position..."

The job with Martlow Enterprises was becoming more tempting with each passing moment. But she couldn't accept the position without also going through with this bizarre marriage. She was completely, utterly trapped and David knew it, damn him.

Lee's head began to ache.

He watched her closely, leaning forward on the packing box.

"Look," he said at last. "I've got all my furniture on a moving van that's parked downtown. They can swing by and pick up your boxes before they leave, and the furniture at your aunt's house, too. I'm driving up to Spokane tomorrow with a U-Haul trailer, and I already have an apartment rented up there in a nice old house by Lincoln Park. In fact," he added, looking around, "it's a lot like this place."

"You must have been pretty sure you'd get the job."

He shrugged. "Wilbur Martlow knows I'm the best video technician in the northwest. But after I checked out Spokane, I liked the place so much that I'd already decided to move there even if Martlow didn't hire me."

"And this apartment of yours...it has..." She paused, her cheeks warming painfully. "It has two bedrooms?"

"And a den," he said. "It's a nice apartment. No problem about Hulk, either, although the landlady is a cat person. She raises purebred white Persians," he added with a brief grin. "I only hope a few of her little darlings don't go missing."

Lee looked at the opposite doorway in alarm. "Surely he wouldn't."

"No way," David said. "I was just kidding. Hulk is actually a real softie."

Lee shivered, recalling those big teeth and cold yellow eyes. "So," she said at last, "you have to leave tomorrow."

"And you have to respond to your job offer," he said, "supplying all that data about your husband."

"Then we'd have to..." She clasped her hands tightly, gazing out the window at wet tree boughs tossing in the wind. "We have to do this...soon?"

"Yes, we do." David watched her with that same cool, detached expression. "Would four o'clock be all right with you?"

Chapter Three

IF LEE'S LIFE in recent weeks had exhibited a certain nightmarish quality, the rest of the afternoon was positively surreal.

At around three o'clock, she'd called to accept the job offer. By evening she had only a blurry, confused recollection of standing in somebody's downtown office in her plaid shirt and running shoes. Rain pattered against the windows as she agreed to take David Allan Clementi as her lawfully wedded husband.

The marriage was witnessed by a young woman who served as secretary to the justice of the peace. When Lee and David arrived, the woman was changing a toner cartridge in the photocopy machine. During the brief ceremony, she seemed unaware of the dark smudges all over her hands and on her cheek.

Afterward, the justice read their prenuptial agreement and looked at both of them curiously over the tops of his reading glasses.

"It's...what you'd call a modern kind of marriage,'' David said at last, breaking the tense silence that ensued.

The man shook his head but signed the paper without comment, and they left the office together as husband and wife.

Back at David's apartment building, they went downstairs to have fruitcake and a glass of sherry in Maybelle's bright, cluttered suite. The landlady hugged both of them and shed a few tears.

''This is so romantic,'' Maybelle sighed, stroking her poodle with a trembling hand. ''The two of you...just so romantic.''

Lee wanted to protest but she could see how much Maybelle was enjoying this fantasy vision of their romance, so she refrained.

''Yes,'' she murmured instead. ''It was really a...whirlwind courtship, Maybelle.''

David gave her a private salute with the sherry glass and raised an eyebrow in grudging approval. Lee's cheeks warmed as she turned away hastily to admire Maybelle's geraniums.

After they left the landlady's apartment he offered, with distant courtesy, to take Lee out to dinner, but she refused, his offhand manner bothering her more than anything.

''I've had enough excitement for one day,'' she said, anxious to get away from him so she could think about the staggering thing she'd just done. ''Especially if we're going to be leaving early in the morning." At his quizzical expression, she added, "I have some laundry that needs doing, so I'll have to turn you down. Sorry."

He nodded, looking unperturbed, and dropped her off in front of her apartment where he sat for a moment tapping his fingers on the wheel.

"Are you sure you're going to be okay?" he asked, looking as cool as a cucumber himself.

"I'm fine." Leaning into his vehicle, she faked a smile. "Thanks for everything," she said, unable to restrain her sarcasm. "It was...the nicest wedding I've ever had."

Lee slammed the door on her last word, before he could say anything further. She ran into the lobby of her building, watching nervously from the mailbox cubicle until he put his vehicle into gear and drove off through the silver curtains of falling rain.

But the rest of the evening stretched ahead of her interminably, and the raindrops were loud and depressing against the windows.

Lee moved around her apartment, finishing up the last of her packing, then called Aunt Charlotte about the furniture, and a couple of friends to let them know she was leaving. At last she had a bath and drank a mug of hot chocolate while she gloomily sat cross-legged on her air mattress.

She hugged her knees, brooding over David's motives. During their first encounter in that interview room, he'd looked as if Lee O'Connor was the last person on earth he wanted to see, ever again. Now they were married, and it had been mostly his idea.

She rolled her head on her knees, frowning, and wondered if this whole thing really was just a convenient, mutual accommodation to get both of them out of a tight spot, or if David Clementi wanted some obscure form of revenge.

Maybe he intended to punish her for what she'd done to him six years ago. He could even be planning to betray her in front their new employers, and cause her to be fired and abandoned in a strange city.

But that kind of petty viciousness had never been David Clementi's style. Even now, despite the depths of anger he clearly felt, there were times when he could be charming, even show flashes of the teasing dark-eyed lover she'd once adored.

Lee sniffled and wiped her eyes with the back of her hand, then got up when the phone rang.

"Hi," David said. "Just checking in to see what you're doing."

Lee clutched the phone and forced away the image of this man as he'd been six years ago. "I'm drinking a cup of hot chocolate," she said, "and wondering whether I should have myself committed for psychiatric assessment."

"You and me both. This is more than anybody should have to do for a new job." He sounded rueful, even a little sympathetic. Some of her wariness eased.

"Really, I'm okay," Lee said. "This is just…it's not exactly what I'd always visualized for my wedding night, that's all."

She could sense David's sudden tension, almost hear the way he controlled himself to keep from making a sharp response. But when he spoke, his voice was quiet and neutral.

"Do you want me to bring Hulk over to spend the night with you so you'll have some company? It's pretty barren in your apartment."

"God no!" Lee thought about the big dog with his cold yellow eyes. "It's nice of you to offer," she added hastily, "but I don't think so. I'll see you tomorrow, David."

She hung up before he could answer, afraid she might disgrace herself by bursting into tears.

THE TRIP FROM Seattle to Spokane was less than five hours on the freeway, traversing the scenic beauty of the Wenatchee mountains and Mount Baker National Forest before emerging onto the rugged flat prairies around Moses Lake.

Within an hour of leaving Seattle, they passed from steady rain into bright clouds that filled the sky like masses of flapping laundry pegged to the mountaintops. A fitful sun began to appear, raying down through breaks in the clouds, and touched the snow-capped peaks with long fingers of light.

"Look, the sun's shining." Lee waved a hand shyly toward the mountaintops. "That's supposed to be a good omen at the beginning of a new job, right?"

David glanced at her, then gazed out the window again, watching the landscape flow past.

She shifted to look over her shoulder at Hulk, who lay full-length on the blanketed backseat, chewing a rawhide bone. When she caught his eye, the big dog lifted his upper lip to show a bit of fang. Lee turned away quickly.

"We should probably talk about ourselves a little," she said to David. "I mean, what's happened since we..." She floundered briefly. "Because, you know, it's going to be pretty embarrassing if we're supposed to be married and we don't know the first thing about each other's recent past."

"You're right," he agreed. "What do you want to know?"

"Well...how are your parents?"

"My father died three years ago."

"Oh, I'm so sorry, David," she said with impulsive warmth. "I always liked him."

"He was a good, gentle man." David gripped the wheel and stared down the highway.

"And your mother?"

His face tightened. "She's in Portland," he said coolly. "They moved off the ranch after Dad's first heart attack, and Mom's still there."

Lee glanced at him, chilled by something in his voice, and by the bleak look on his face. "Are you going to tell her about..."

"About what?" he asked when she paused.

"This." Lee waved a hand awkwardly to indicate the vehicle, the dog in the backseat, the U-Haul trailer behind them. "Our little joint project."

He tapped the wheel with a dismissive gesture. "This isn't going to last long enough to be worth mentioning. Besides, I don't like to upset her these days."

"Why not?" Lee frowned, picturing Adele Clementi, who had always been a tall, quick-moving woman with a booming laugh, someone who found life a joyous adventure.

"She's not all that well. In fact, that's mostly why I did this."

"Did what?" Lee asked.

"Got involved in this whole marriage thing with you," David said. "Mom's medical care is getting really expensive. I had to be certain of a good job to help look after her."

Well, at least that helped to explain his motives. Lee felt a combination of relief and concern. "But your mother's really sick? I haven't…"

"How about you?" David interrupted, clearly anxious to change the subject. "Didn't I hear your parents got divorced?"

Lee nodded, staring out the window. "Five years ago. My mother's remarried and lives in Pennsylvania. I don't see her nearly as often as I'd like. And my father has really bad arthritis, but he doesn't suffer as much since he left the dampness here and moved to Arizona."

"Do you see him much?"

Lee felt a sudden chill. "Hardly ever."

David cast her a questioning glance. "Really? You and your dad were always so close."

"Things change," Lee said briefly.

"No kidding. What an understatement."

She cast him a quick sidelong glance but his profile remained utterly cold and unrevealing. Lee sighed and settled back to watch in silence as the glorious landscape unfolded beyond the windows.

Eventually David pulled off the freeway and parked at a brick-and-cedar restaurant that stood alone by the service road.

"It's lunchtime," he announced, getting out

and opening the rear door. "Come on, Hulky boy, let's go for a run."

Lee walked with him into a vacant field beside the restaurant, enjoying the sunshine and the wind on her face. Hulk loped ahead of them, hysterical with joy at being released from the vehicle. He paused frequently to scratch in the dirt and bounded from place to place, sniffing bushes and flowers.

"Just like a big kid," David said, watching the dog.

He put a hand casually on Lee's arm. Her skin burned at his touch, warming her whole body. She wondered if David even realized he was holding her, since all his attention seemed to be on the dog. As soon as she could, Lee pulled unobtrusively away from him.

They put the reluctant dog back into the van and lowered the windows a few inches, then went into the restaurant where they examined the menu and pondered their lunch choices, speaking in polite monosyllables, using the menus as an excuse to avoid looking at each other.

"I'll have a steak sandwich, medium rare," David told the waitress after they'd made their choices, "and my wife will have the chef's salad and garlic toast."

Lee's cheeks flamed with embarrassment.

"Don't *do* that," she whispered furiously after the young woman left with their order.

"Do what?" he asked.

"Don't call me your wife."

He raised an eyebrow. "Why not? It's true, isn't it?"

Lee looked down at the table, moving her cutlery around and lining it up on the napkin. "I really hate hearing you say it."

"Well," he said coldly, "like it or not, you'll have to get used to it. Everybody is going to be referring to us as husband and wife when we get to Spokane."

"I don't care what everybody else does!" she burst out, then leaned across the table and lowered her voice when she realized the older couple at the next table were watching them curiously. "But I don't like hearing *you* say it," she muttered. "It makes me feel…really uncomfortable."

He gave her one of the mirthless, sardonic grins that made her want to smack him. "Isn't this cute?" he said, raising an eyebrow. "Our very first fight."

Lee glared at him for a moment, almost too angry to speak. "You're really enjoying this, aren't you?" she muttered at last. "You've got me trapped in an uncomfortable, impossible position, and you like to watch me squirm. I would have thought such pettiness was beneath you.''

''Well, you would have been wrong,'' he said without expression, reading the wine list. ''I'm a nasty, vengeful kind of guy, Lee. Being tossed aside without an explanation can do that to a person.''

''I tried to explain, but you were gone!'' she said, and again the neighboring couple turned to stare at them with overt interest.

He turned his gaze on her fully, so dark and intent that she had to force herself not to shift uneasily on the bench. ''So why don't you explain it to me now?''

Lee took a deep breath. ''There were horrible things going on in my family at the time, and I wasn't able to talk about them. I asked you for a little time to work through it, but you assumed I was having second thoughts and went to Australia. It was all such a mess.''

''Horrible things in your family?'' he asked, looking suspicious. ''What kind of things?''

She shook her head. ''It's six years too late to talk about all this, David. I don't even want to think about it anymore.''

''What do you want, then?''

''I want to get to Spokane, secure my job and move out on my own as soon as possible so I won't be a bother to you," Lee said, still moving her cutlery around nervously on the paper napkin.

"Well, that makes two of us," he said in a neutral tone.

Lee glanced up at him. "But," she said, "I do want you to know I really am sorry for hurting you, David. I've always felt terrible about it."

Her timid apology seemed lost on him. He simply stared at her for a moment, then nodded and returned to his study of the wine list, leaving her feeling small and sad.

LEE WAS PLEASANTLY surprised to find that Spokane, which she'd never visited, was a beautiful place. The river meandered through the heart of the city, bordered by parks and hiking trails. In the southern portion where David had rented his apartment, rugged coulees and pine-covered hillsides glistened in the afternoon sun, dotted with well-kept houses.

Their apartment was on the main floor of a stately home near Lincoln Park. The mansion was well maintained and spacious, with hardwood floors, ten-foot ceilings and solid oak moldings.

Lee wandered through the empty rooms, looking around in astonishment.

"How do you manage to find such great apartments?" she asked, pausing in the kitchen doorway to watch him setting out Hulk's food and water dishes and arranging the dog's blanket near the back door.

He cast her a quick, unsmiling glance.

"I'm glad you like it. I thought you should have the south bedroom," he added, "because it has a little half bath attached."

"Thank you," she said awkwardly. "That's really generous of you to give me the nicest bedroom, especially when it's actually your apartment, not mine."

"No, it's not. We're sharing equally. Didn't you read the prenuptial agreement?"

With lithe, easy grace, David got up to fill the food dish, then put the big paper sack away in a lower cupboard. Hulk approached his dish, sniffed cautiously and began to eat, massive jaws crunching.

"When do you think the movers will get here?" Lee asked.

David glanced at his watch. "Pretty soon, they said, probably any time after three o'clock."

"Moving time is always such chaos," Lee said. "It takes Moira and me about a year before we can find stuff again."

"Not me," he said calmly. "I'm a terrific mover. By tonight you'll be all settled in, eating popcorn on your couch."

She looked at his muscular arms, the restless

energy of his body, and knew he wasn't exaggerating.

For the briefest of moments Lee allowed herself to enjoy the unaccustomed luxury of this experience. It was really nice to have somebody taking charge and helping with everything.

But this was only temporary, she quickly told herself, horrified by the wayward turn her thoughts were suddenly taking.

In a couple of months, she and David Clementi would be going their separate ways, just as they had once before, and she'd be alone again. At all times, she had to remember that.

Of course, there wasn't much danger of forgetting, she told herself grimly, when he kept reminding her at every turn.

But at least she'd have a great job and be financially secure.

And this "marriage" to her old fiancé, as stressful as it seemed at times, still gave Lee some much-needed breathing space. She would have a chance to settle in, adjust to her new responsibilities and get to know the city, before she had to start looking for a place to live.

"I've been thinking…" she began.

"About what?" he asked when she paused.

"Did it ever occur to you," she asked, stroking the satiny wooden finish of the door frame, "that the Martlows are probably going to think this whole situation is really strange?"

"What situation?" He was prowling around the kitchen, opening and closing cupboard doors, testing the hinges, pausing to check the faucet. "I'll have to replace these washers," he muttered. "Remind me to pick some up next time we go to the hardware store, okay?"

Next time we go to the hardware store.

The man already sounded as if they'd been comfortably married for decades. Lee shivered and hugged her arms, then resumed her former line of thought.

"The Martlows," she repeated. "Aren't they going to think it was a little weird, how we both went in to apply for jobs and didn't mention that we were married to each other?"

He was out of sight under the sink, sprawled full-length on the kitchen floor. Lee gazed down at his lean hips and long, denim-clad legs. Her mouth went suddenly dry and she forced herself to look away.

"Why should they think it's weird?" he asked, his voice muffled. "Lots of places have a policy about not hiring married couples. Maybe we were just trying to give ourselves the best prospects by not being completely forthcoming at the interview."

"No kidding," she muttered gloomily. "Not forthcoming. Now there's an understatement."

He emerged from under the sink and sat on the floor looking up at her steadily. "Look, you've got to quit brooding over this. We haven't done anything wrong. We're here right on time and ready to start our new jobs. We're both going to be great employees. We told them we were married people, and we are. There's nothing for you to worry about."

She hesitated, wanting to believe him.

In the backyard beyond the kitchen window, flowers bloomed in a shaded rock garden, and a couple of robins fluttered and splashed in a birdbath by the walk. The prairie sun was dazzling, a hard, clear light that turned everything to gold.

"Nothing to worry about," she repeated, watching the birds in their marble bath. "God, David, I hope you're right."

A FEW DAYS later, Edna Martlow sat on one side of a huge teak partners desk and looked across the gleaming expanse at her husband. He was riffling through a pile of invoices, his reading glasses perched on the end of his nose. Under the fluorescent office lights, his bald head shone with a dull pink glow.

She felt a flood of affection so intense that it

made her eyes mist briefly. "I love you, Wilbur," she said.

He glanced up, smiling at her over the rims of his glasses. "Now, what brought that on?"

"I don't know." Edna folded her hands on the desk, searching for words. "When we were young and starting out in marriage and business, I was such a baby. I didn't know anything about life."

"You were always a smart girl," he protested. "Smarter than anybody."

"No, Wilbur, I was an idiot. It took me years to realize what a treasure you are."

His face softened. "You really feel that way, Eddy? After all these years, and now that I've gotten old and bald?"

"I'm old and fat," she said calmly. "And I love you a lot more than when we were nineteen, Wilbur. Sometimes when I look at you nowadays, it's all I can do to contain myself."

He grinned. "Maybe we need a holiday. Let's take some time off and get away all by ourselves so you can tell me how wonderful I am."

She nodded thoughtfully. "As soon as the new station is up and running, that's exactly what we should do. Where would you like to go?"

"Well...Hawaii is a nice place. We could go back to that resort at Hanamaula." He smiled.

"You always look so pretty with flowers in your hair, Eddy."

Edna chuckled. "You're crazy," she told her husband. "Certifiably insane."

They beamed at each other for a moment, then returned to the papers on their desks.

"Speaking of happy couples," Edna said after a moment, "what do you think of this Clementi business?"

"Clementi?"

"The young couple we hired for the new station. I have their job acceptance letters here."

"We hired a couple?" Wilbur said blankly.

"We didn't know they were married to each other," Edna told her husband. "You remember, Wilbur. They're from Seattle. He's the new technician and she's heading up our production department. She used her maiden name for the job interview."

"Letitia O'Connor," he said, brightening. "The pretty redhead with the shy smile and the freckles."

"Now he remembers," Edna commented dryly.

"And those two are married? I haven't been paying much attention to the job applications."

"Yes, they are," Edna looked at the papers on her desk, "although they never told us."

Wilbur shrugged. "I suppose they thought we might have a policy about not hiring couples."

"But don't you remember what they said at their interviews, Wilbur?"

"What about them?"

Edna consulted the transcripts of the job interviews. "Lee O'Connor told us she was happily married and adored her husband. She said he was a wonderful man."

"That's nice," Wilbur said, looking pleased.

"But David Clementi told your panel that he wasn't getting along with his wife, and didn't know if the marriage could be salvaged."

"Oh dear," Wilbur said, suddenly alarmed. "Now that you mention it, I do recall him saying something like that. I just never made the connection."

"Of course not," Edna said patiently. "We had no idea at the time that they were married to each other."

"The poor girl," Wilbur commented. "Her marriage is in trouble and she doesn't even realize it. A nice-looking fellow, too," he added thoughtfully. "That young Clementi, I mean. And a very capable technician, by all accounts."

"Well, we certainly can't have their marriage falling apart as soon as they start working for us. I'd feel just terrible."

"Eddy, what are you planning? I know what it means when you get that look in your eye."

"Nothing," she said serenely. "Nothing at all."

"Now, don't you be interfering in their marriage," he warned his wife. "Whatever problems this young couple may be having, it's not our concern. We're only their employers."

"Yes," Edna agreed, thinking about Lee O'Connor's rapt, wistful expression during the job interview when she'd talked about her husband. "We're only their employers."

"I mean it," Wilbur said sternly. "No meddling."

Edna gave him an innocent glance. "I'm not thinking of meddling. I was only planning a party for the new employees, that's all. Just a simple little affair to welcome everybody to Spokane."

"Eddy, you're plotting. I can always tell."

"Oh, pooh," she said, heaving her bulk out of the chair. "Get back to work. I'll go make us some soup and toast."

While he watched suspiciously, she went around the desk to drop a kiss on his bald head, then left the room, her mind busy with plans.

Chapter Four

WHEN DAVID TOLD HER how quickly he could get settled into a new home, it had been no idle boast. With a level of energy and calm efficiency that amazed Lee, he set to work assembling furniture, mounting bed springs on mattresses, hanging artwork and hooking up the stereo equipment.

Meanwhile, Lee worked at her own jobs. She unpacked dishes and clothes, arranged plants and ornaments, and got the kitchen, bathrooms and laundry facilities set up to her liking.

She enjoyed the work so much that it was difficult not to be seduced by the pleasantness of their silent cooperation.

Moving and settling into a new apartment with Moira had always been such a stressful, nerve-jangling experience. Moira was easily distracted and never seemed to pull her own weight when there was hard work to be done. Even more annoying, she would refuse to involve herself in discussions about where pictures should be hung, or how a cabinet should be arranged.

"Whatever, Lee," she used to say airily, heading out the door with her tennis racquet. "Just do it your own way. That'll be fine with me."

But afterward, she would complain and blame Lee when she couldn't find anything.

"It made me understand how terrifying the prospect of marriage really is," Lee told David.

In a moment of rare friendliness, they were discussing the trials of former moves while she unpacked boxes in the kitchen and he worked on something at the table.

"Who can ever risk it?" she went on. "If I were married to a man who behaved like my sister, I'd either divorce him or kill him."

His jaw tensed. He got up and crossed the room, carrying Lee's old toaster that always burned the slice in the rear slot.

"I fixed this," he said without expression. "The element was twisted out of shape."

"Really? You are a wizard." She smiled up at him. "Thank you, David. Where should we put the first-aid supplies, do you think?"

He turned away abruptly. "One of those upper drawers will be fine. Just let me know where they are."

She watched him, chilled by his sudden change of mood as he put the toaster on the counter, plugged it in and studied it critically.

"You know, we have a lot of the same kitchen

stuff,'' she said, suddenly awkward. ''But there's no point in getting our things all mixed up together. So I thought I'd just keep yours in those boxes in the storage room, and then it'll be easy when I move out.''

David nodded absently, still peering into the toaster. ''That's a good idea,'' he said. ''You're right, it'll make your next move a whole lot easier.''

She felt an irrational wave of sadness at his ready agreement, but turned back quickly to her work so he wouldn't see.

A FULL WEEK before their jobs were scheduled to begin, they had the apartment furnished to their liking and nothing to do but enjoy Spokane in the last few days of leisure. Usually separately, they took bikes and rode the trails along the river, walked in the park or went hiking in the rugged coulees on the eastern edge of the city, close to the Idaho border.

Though she was often lonely, Lee found herself getting sun-browned and strong, falling more in love with this place every day. She liked to wake up in the morning and hear the birds chirping outside in their marble bath, smell the perfume of flowers through the open window and watch the muslin curtains lifting in the breeze.

Their stately old apartment was the nicest

place she'd ever lived. Her possessions and David's blended so well that it was soon hard to remember who owned which paintings and end tables. Overall, the effect they achieved was both cozy and rich.

Gradually he seemed to warm to her company and become less cautious, even a bit playful. In the evening, bored by summer reruns on television, they sometimes rented movies and watched them in the den, munching popcorn. Afterward they argued over the stories and the motivation of the characters.

"He was hostile toward women," Lee said after one such movie. "That's why he acted that way."

"No, he wasn't." David got up to rewind the tape. "He was just afraid of rejection, poor guy."

"Isn't it pretty much the same thing in the end?" Lee said, eating the last handful of popcorn.

"Of course not. A guy can love a woman but still be afraid of rejection."

"Well then," she said, chewing calmly, "It's his fear that makes him so hostile."

"Does not."

"Does too."

David lunged toward her and shoved her down on the couch, buffeting her with a pillow. She giggled, pulled away and grabbed another cushion to mount her own attack. Their fight spilled out into the living room, then the backyard where they ran around flailing at each other as they muffled their laughter, trying not to alarm the other tenants.

Lee darted back inside the kitchen and started to lock him out but he managed to get his foot in the door, then the rest of his body.

He sprang through and seized Lee, wrestling her to the floor as he tried to grasp her pillow. They rolled over and over on the tiles, laughing uncontrollably until Lee was too weak to resist.

"I got it!" he shouted in triumph, grabbing the pillow away from her and holding it aloft. "Stole your weapon! I'm the winner!"

Hulk watched this juvenile roughhousing from his blanket near the door, looking mildly scornful, though he growled low in his throat when they began to scuffle and wrestle.

On the floor Lee giggled again, then fell silent. They were still lying together, his leg thrown over hers, their faces almost touching. His eyes were so near that she could see the detail of each silky lash, the creases at the corners, the swimming brown depths staring into hers.

Mesmerized, she gazed back at him, overtaken by a fierce hunger she could hardly control. She remembered so vividly how it felt to be in his arms, to have his mouth on hers and his body moving and thrusting inside her, lost in passion...

Kiss me, she wanted to whisper as she edged closer to him. *Please, please David, don't you know what's happening to me? Why can't you see how much I want you, I'm dying for you....*

The moment seemed to go on forever, so silent and tense that the only sound was a scrap of birdsong drifting through the open window above the sink.

Finally he pushed her away and sat up, running a shaky hand through his hair. Lee sat up, too, and drew away from him. She was still breathing hard, hoping David believed her reddened cheeks were because of the exertion of their horseplay.

"I have to go away for a few days before I start work at the station," he said abruptly, looking down at his hands. "Will that be okay with you?"

"Of course it will," she said, more curtly than she'd intended. Her breath was still coming in ragged gasps, and she ached with a fierce sexual need. "You're free to go anywhere you want, David. You certainly don't have to ask my permission. After all, that's not part of our deal, is it?"

She got up and crossed the room to get herself a glass of water.

"Don't you want to know where I'm going?"

he asked, also standing up and leaning against the table.

"Not really." She kept her back turned, struggling to repress the memory of those sweet, shattering moments in his arms.

"Well, I'll tell you anyway," he said quietly. "I'm leaving early tomorrow and driving down to Portland to see my mother. It's about a six or seven hour trip by freeway." He hesitated, staring at the glass she held. "You're welcome to come along if you want to."

"I don't want to see your mother!" Lee said in panic, then smiled a nervous apology. "You know I'm sorry she's not feeling well, but it's just so embarrassing, this whole situation," she went on. "I don't want anybody in our families to find out what we've done. As soon as I'm able to leave and move into my own place we can forget the whole thing even happened, provided not too many people know about it."

"Everybody at the television station is going to know," he said, watching her with an unfathomable expression.

"But not our own families. I couldn't stand to deal with all their questions, and have to tell what's been going on."

"Is it okay if I leave Hulk here with you while I'm gone?" he asked. "That's a pretty long trip for him."

Lee glanced at the big dog, who met her eyes with an unwavering stare.

Just wait, he seemed to be saying. Wait until I get you alone, and then we'll see who's boss....

"All right," Lee said, swallowing hard. "I don't mind. He's like a built-in security system, right?"

David moved toward the door. "I'd better get a few things packed, then. I'll probably be gone by the time you wake up, and back on Sunday night."

"Sunday night," she repeated. "That sounds fine."

But Sunday was three days away, and the intervening time lay before her like a vast, yawning chasm. She hadn't realized how dependent she had become on the man's steady, quiet presence, even though he clearly wanted no part of her.

God, this is terrifying, she thought, hugging her arms. She had to get away from here before she made a real fool of herself.

David paused in the doorway and looked back at her. "Don't forget to call the painters," he said over his shoulder. "Find out when they plan to come, and how long it's likely going to take them. We'll have to book a couple of hotel rooms for ourselves while they're working in here."

She gave a brief, jerky nod. "Yes, I'll call

them. Have a...have a nice trip," she called behind him as he strode away.

"Thanks," he said without looking back. "I will."

Alone in the kitchen, she edged past Hulk, who lifted his upper lip in that characteristic gesture that looked like a threatening sneer.

Lee bolted from the kitchen, heading for the sanctuary of her own room, where neither David nor his dog was ever allowed to enter.

SHE WAS STILL in bed when he drove off next morning, and of course he didn't come in to say goodbye.

Alone in the dewy summer morning, she listened to his vehicle pull away from the curb. Within seconds he was swallowed up in the distant hum of traffic heading for the freeway.

She lay back with her hands folded behind her head, wondering how all this had happened to her with such dizzying speed.

One day Lee O'Connor had been happily employed, living in the same city for fourteen years, rooming with her sister who was often annoying, but at least a known quantity. Lee had enjoyed a certain life-style, a set of routines, a circle of casual friends.

And now, almost magically it seemed, she'd been transported to a different place, where the sky was an arch of turquoise and the prairie shimmered like a carpet of green and gold damask, and farmers in monstrous tractors worked fields so huge that they stretched all the way beyond the horizon.

In this new world, Lee knew nobody at all except the extraordinary man she now lived with, whose image had gradually, disconcertingly begun expanding to fill her whole world just the way it had six years ago, before her life fell apart.

When she closed her eyes, he was there, leaning back in his chair and laughing about mutual friends they'd once known, running a hand through his curls, unpacking crates with his shirt off, muscles rippling…

"Oh, God," she whispered, rolling over to bury her hot face in the pillow. "Please, please, help me not do this."

But Lee was beginning to be afraid she was beyond help. Oddly enough, David's absence now drove that fact home more than his presence seemed to.

When the man was around he was mostly withdrawn and silent, somebody to share kitchen duties and the occasional walk. On an everyday basis, she could force herself to remember the temporary nature of their arrangement, and the level of mistrust he obviously still felt for her.

But now that he was gone and she was alone

in the utter silence, all her emotions came flooding in like a tidal wave.

"I can't possibly be falling in love with him again!" she whispered aloud, turning over to kick aside the covers restlessly and stare at the ceiling again.

But it was true. Lee loved the man, adored him with a mad, hopeless passion. In fact, she knew now that she'd never stopped loving him, even through that insanely confused time when her mother's anguish had turned all of Lee's values and loyalties upside down.

Ironically, she'd also just signed a formidable legal document in which she'd sworn their relationship would remain platonic.

Of course, Lee knew the terms of their arrangement could change with just a few words.

She could say, "Look, David, so sorry but I seem to have fallen in love with you again. Now, what do you think we should do about it?"

It was possible to do that, of course. There was nothing stopping her. Lee could say those very words to him, and enjoy the huge relief of laying out her feelings instead of keeping them bottled up.

The problem was, she already knew how he'd react. He made it so very, very clear that he wanted nothing to do with her beyond the mutually beneficial terms of their arrangement.

Whenever she came close to him, David quietly withdrew. He didn't trust her, and he didn't desire her. Lee thought about their impromptu bit of horseplay when she'd practically thrown herself into his arms and he'd shoved her away.

The memory was enough to make her go hot with embarrassment.

With sudden, almost unbearable pain, she wondered if he actually was visiting his mother this weekend, or if David had a real girlfriend somewhere who was waiting for him, anxious to see him.

After all, she had no idea what he'd been doing for the past six years.

Maybe at this very moment, that unknown woman was wild with excitement because her laughing, curly-headed lover would soon be in her bed, in her arms...

Lee rolled over again, moaning, and burrowed under the covers where she began to cry softly, her face muffled against the pillow.

Gradually she became aware of a soft clicking sound, and recognized Hulk's toenails on the floor. Something cold and wet pressed hard against her bare shoulder, making her gasp. She jerked away, then realized it was the dog's nose. Hulk carried his leash in his jaws and stared at her with those penetrating yellow eyes.

But this time, for some reason, the eyes didn't

seem threatening at all. They actually looked sympathetic, even a little sad.

"Poor Hulk." Sniffling, Lee hauled herself to a sitting position. "You miss him too, don't you?" She nerved herself to pat the heavy black head, trying not to think about those massive jaws.

Hulk edged nearer and laid his muzzle on her knee, eyes drooping in pleasure as she stroked him.

"Why, you old sweetie," Lee said, astonished. "You like that, don't you? You're not so scary after all. You're just darling. Yes, you are."

She got up to gather her jogging pants and a sweatshirt while Hulk sat waiting next to the bed, still holding his leash. Lee sprinted into the bathroom, dressed and brushed her teeth, then took the leash and headed for the kitchen with Hulk galloping joyously at her heels.

She had a glass of orange juice and a bagel, filled the big dog's water dish and tied on her running shoes, then snapped his leash in position and took him off to the park for a run.

Hulk strained at the leash, pulling her along behind him. But when she began floundering and called to him sharply, he stopped at once and waited for her to catch up, looking mildly abashed.

"Good dog," Lee said, gasping for breath as

she stroked his head. "Just remember...that I'm more of a wimp...than your usual dog walker. Okay?"

They set off again. She slipped off his leash and let him run and play, then retrieve sticks until Lee's arm was tired.

Finally she lay on the grass under a spreading cottonwood tree. Hulk came to sprawl beside her, panting noisily, and rested his heavy jowls on her arm in companionable silence.

"I'll be damned," she murmured drowsily. "I would have sworn you hated me, you big lug."

Lee scratched behind his ears, then along the side of his muscular abdomen, smiling when his hind leg began to jerk rhythmically in ecstasy.

"And actually," she went on, "you were just waiting to see which one of us was going to make the first move. Maybe..." She sat up, looking earnestly at the dog. "Maybe I should be brave and not worry about getting rejected. Why not just take the bull by the horns and tell David how I feel?"

Hulk watched her sadly, and appeared to shake his head.

"Oh, hell, you're right," she muttered, hugging her knees anxiously. "The man really doesn't want to start anything with me again. He can hardly wait to get rid of me."

But Hulk was no longer listening. He suddenly

bounded off to check a squirrel chattering in a spruce tree along the path and Lee was forced to run along behind him, dragging the leash.

LATER THE SAME DAY, Edna Martlow parked her dark green Mercedes-Benz sedan outside the big apartment house where two of her new employees were living, marched up the walk and rang the doorbell.

Lee O'Connor answered, wearing red plaid shorts and a white T-shirt, carrying a peeled banana. She gazed at her visitor in obvious astonishment. A massive dog filled the doorway beside her, also staring upward.

Edna, who adored dogs, smiled at the rottweiler. He smiled back, tongue lolling, waving his whole rear quarters since he had no tail to speak of.

"My goodness," Lee said. "He must like you, Mrs. Martlow. I've never seem him this friendly with a stranger."

Edna eyed the dog, searching her memory. "Didn't you tell us you were afraid of big dogs?"

The girl flushed painfully, her fair skin reddening all the way up the roots of her hair. "This is my...it's David's dog," she murmured. "I'd never choose such a monster for myself. But he's...not so bad,'' Lee added bravely, patting the broad black head. "Quite a nice dog, really.''

Edna studied the new employee shrewdly, remembering the troubling disparity in Lee and David's respective appraisals of their marriage.

It seemed this girl would do anything to hold on to a husband she adored, even tolerate a monster dog that frightened her. David Clementi, on the other hand, wasn't concerned enough about his wife to choose a more appropriate pet.

Edna felt saddened again by the tension and obvious lack of communication in the marriage.

"I just thought I'd drop by to see how you're settling in and if there's anything I can do for you," Edna murmured smoothly. "Soon we'll all be getting to work in earnest and we'll have so little time for visiting.''

"Please come in,'' the young woman said, standing aside with a shy gesture of welcome.

She really was a very attractive girl, Edna decided, with that fiery mass of red hair, the dark green eyes and freckles.

But one of the really appealing things about Lee O'Connor, which Wilbur had noticed as well, was the impression she gave of sweet thoughtfulness, the sense that there was a great deal more to this young woman than met the eye.

She also had a kind of decency, and a winsome

vulnerability about her that made you hope no-body would ever hurt her...

"My goodness," Edna said with warm ap-proval when she stepped into the living room of the big old apartment, proudly escorted by Hulk. "The two of you have certainly made this place very cozy in such a short time, haven't you?"

"David's really good at..."

The girl's faced paled slightly when she men-tioned her husband's name and she gripped the dog's collar nervously. Again, both were telling little signs of distress that Edna's sharp eyes didn't miss.

"He's good at mechanical things," she con-cluded lamely.

"I see." Edna sat down in the living room and declined a cup of tea from her hostess. "Thank you, Lee, but I can only stay a few minutes. Where did you say your husband is now?"

"David's in Portland for a couple of days. He went to visit his mother."

"And you didn't go along?" Edna looked keenly at the young red-haired woman sitting op-posite her, noting the flush on her cheeks and the sudden look of distress. "It's such a pleasant drive over to Portland."

"I know, but...there are a lot of things to look after here before we start work on Monday," Lee

said awkwardly. "I have some unpacking left to
do, and I had to call the painters..."

"You're having the place painted?" Edna
asked, looking around.

"Yes, at the end of the week. It's going to take
two days," Lee said. "So I guess we'll have to
get hotel rooms for Friday and Saturday while
they're working in here."

"Rooms?" Edna asked.

Lee's flush deepened. "Did I say rooms? I
meant a room, of course. Could you by any
chance recommend a good hotel, not too far from
here?"

Edna named a few hotels, then went on
smoothly to other topics of conversation. But her
mind was working busily as she watched Lee's
face.

Yes, it was clearer all the time, things were
definitely not all they should be in this marriage.
Something was coming between the two young
people, and making this poor girl very unhappy.

And no matter what Wilbur said, Edna decided
as she got up to leave, something had to be done
about it.

Chapter Five

DAVID GOT HOME late on Sunday night, long after Lee had gone to bed. She heard the sound of his vehicle as he drove up and parked, the soft click of his key in the lock, the hysterical joy of Hulk's greeting and David's whispered commands to the dog for silence.

Even though it was midnight, the place seemed to fill suddenly with light and warmth. Lee lay in bed, her heart racing while she listened to the muted sounds as he moved around in the next room, had a shower, murmured to the dog, climbed into his bed.

It almost frightened her how much it meant to have him back.

So the next morning she tried to contain the feeling of contentment that floated through her as they ate breakfast together, exchanging polite conversation.

"How was your mother?" Lee asked.

He looked down at his cereal bowl. "She's going blind."

Lee stared at him, suddenly rigid with shock. "David," she whispered at last. "You never said…"

"She has diabetes. It was only diagnosed three years ago, but she's had a really rapid decline. Now she's losing her vision and she's had a serious heart attack."

Lee thought of the tall, beautiful woman she remembered, and felt tears stinging in her eyes. "I wish I'd gone with you."

"Yes, she spoke fondly of you. Maybe another time you can… Look," he added hastily, "let's talk about something else."

"Oh, David…" Lee reached out and covered his hand with her own, then was hurt at how quickly he pulled away from her.

"Edna Martlow came to visit while you were away," she said after a long, awkward pause. "Just arrived right out of the blue in a great big car."

"Did she have anything interesting to say?"

"She loved the apartment." Lee tried to keep her voice casual, though she was still shaken. "And she says the Martlows are hosting a party on Friday night for some of the new employees. We're both invited."

"Where?"

"At their mansion on the South Hill."

David smiled without humour. "Did Edna really call her house a mansion?"

"No, she just said, 'our summer home on Rockwood Boulevard.' But remember when we drove past it that day? The place looked like a medieval fortress."

"It's an impressive pile of stones, all right. Come on, let's clean up."

Working together with silent efficiency, both wrapped in their own thoughts, they washed their breakfast dishes and filled the dog's water bowl, then got into David's vehicle to head off for the first day at their new jobs.

Lee glanced cautiously at his withdrawn profile, etched with gold by the morning light. He met her gaze.

"You look nice," he said, startling her. "I like the colour of that blouse."

She gripped her briefcase on her knees. "I'm scared to death."

"There's nothing to worry about. They knew you had the qualifications or they would never have hired you."

"Yes, well, at least I told the truth about my qualifications," she said, watching as rows of houses and shops flew past the window.

He pulled into the parking lot behind the gleaming new television station, then strode around to hold her door open, an old-fashioned habit of his that Lee had always found endearing.

She passed close to him, suddenly so frightened that it was all she could do not to burrow against him for a comforting hug. Instead she forced herself to turn away casually and walk with him toward the door.

"Well, I'll probably see you at lunchtime. Have a nice day," he said when they reached the lobby.

Without another word, he vanished into the recesses of the station and the backrooms filled with technical equipment.

Lee was taken in hand by Wilbur Martlow himself, who spent the morning introducing her to copywriters, film editors and production crews. Proudly he showed her the station facilities and helped her get settled in her own office, which was amazingly spacious and had a view of a pine-covered coulee nearby.

Lee sat in the padded desk chair while Wilbur went to order coffee. She twirled experimentally a few times, punched some keys on the shining new computer keyboard and gazed out the window, still dry-mouthed with fear and tension.

At eleven o'clock Wilbur convened a meeting of the creative and production staffs, as well as himself and his wife. Working competently as a team, he and Edna outlined the philosophy of

Martlow Enterprises and their vision for the new station.

Lee sat next to one of the head writers, a young blond woman with boyishly cropped hair, languorous blue eyes and the slim, muscular body of an athlete. She wore a tight-fitting white top and miniskirt that showed off her long tanned legs.

"I'm Melanie Reeves," she said to Lee as the meeting broke up. "And I guess you're my boss."

"It's nice to meet you, Melanie." Lee smiled, wondering how a boss was supposed to act.

But at that moment, Melanie's blue eyes widened and her face was suddenly taut with interest as she looked over Lee's shoulder.

Following the young woman's gaze, Lee saw David approaching down the hallway, deep in conversation with a stocky technician in gray coveralls who carried a coil of electrical wire over his shoulder.

"Hi," David said politely when he reached them. "How's it going, Lee?"

"Fine so far."

Next to her the blonde glanced at Lee with an expectant air, waiting to be introduced.

"David Clementi, this is Melanie Reeves. She's one of the head copywriters."

"Hi, Melanie." David shook the woman's

hand and gave her a courteous smile. Melanie smiled back and held his hand longer than was strictly necessary, in Lee's opinion.

"I have to check the wiring in the sound truck," David said to Lee, turning away from the girl at last. "But if there's time I'll meet you in the cafeteria for lunch, okay?"

"Okay," Lee said, hugging an armful of file folders. David strode off with the technician through the plant-filled lobby. His shoulders seemed very broad, and he'd never looked more handsome.

"God," Melanie sighed, watching him. "What an absolute hunk. You know that guy, Lee?"

"Yes," Lee said, more harshly than she'd intended. "I know him."

"How? Did you work together somewhere else?"

"He's my husband," Lee said.

She marched back to her office, conscious of the blond woman gazing after her in astonishment.

BUT AS THE WEEK progressed, it became obvious that David's marital status meant very little to Melanie Reeves. Lee learned from bits of office gossip that the copywriter, who was also married, nevertheless had a reputation as a flirt, and so much sex appeal that she could get any man she wanted.

Apparently Melanie wanted David, even though he was married to her new boss. She took every opportunity to sit next to him in the coffee room, flattering him and making comments laced with sexual innuendo. She also annoyed Lee by going back to the technical area on every pretext, saying she needed to check out lighting and production qualities for the commercials she was working on.

Toward the weekend, Lee sat at her desk and watched as a tableau unfolded beyond the window. David was supervising a couple of other technicians while they checked the tower at the edge of the station grounds.

Melanie Reeves came out the front doors and approached the group, carrying a clipboard in her arms. She paused next to David and showed him one of the papers.

Distracted, he turned away from his examination of the tower to look down at the girl courteously, then did an obvious double take.

Melanie wore a low-cut cotton sundress that whipped in the summer breeze and clung to her body, with a skirt so short it barely cleared her thighs.

Lee continued to watch grimly as the girl said something to David, then laughed, her face glis-

tening in the sunlight. She took his arm teasingly
and held it close to her for a moment.

Suddenly Lee was conscious of another person
in the room near her desk. She turned to see Edna
Martlow, also watching the scene beyond the
window.

After a moment Edna looked back at Lee with
an expression that spoke volumes, although she'd
actually come to deliver the daily commercial
logs.

A woman should fight for her man, Edna's
shrewd eyes seemed to be saying. She shouldn't
let somebody waltz in and start flirting so out-
rageously with her husband.

Lee looked down at her desk, feeling miserable
and helpless.

She couldn't fight for the man, because she
had no claim on him.

Except that they were married, she thought,
struck by the dreadful irony. If it weren't for that
one awkward detail, maybe she'd have a chance.
But, as bizarre as it sounded, being married to
David Clementi seemed to make it impossible for
her to get close to him.

Especially when he was so deliberate and careful about holding her at arm's length all the
time...

Edna paused in the doorway. ''Don't forget the

dinner at our house tomorrow night,'' she said. ''I'm expecting you and David to be there.''

''We'll be there,'' Lee said dully, turning away from the scene beyond the window. ''Thank you, Mrs. Martlow.''

ON FRIDAY NIGHT Lee sat next to him in the van, gazing out the window as they drove over to the Martlow house. David glanced at her from time to time but said nothing.

''Do you think Hulk will be all right in that kennel?'' Lee said at last.

''No, he'll hate it. But we couldn't leave him in the apartment breathing paint fumes all weekend, and they don't take pets at the hotel.''

''I feel like I'm driving away and leaving a child alone in the hospital.''

David flashed one of the rare smiles that transformed his face. ''You and old Hulk have really bonded, haven't you?''

''He's a nice dog. I like him.''

''We'll go over tomorrow and take him out for a walk,'' David said. ''And on Sunday night when the painters are gone, we can take him home.''

Home.

How strange, that the same word could be so pleasant and comforting under other circumstances, yet nowadays seemed like a dagger to her heart.

Lee turned again to gaze out the side window so he wouldn't see the tears beginning to mist her eyes.

"You know," he said after a moment, "I don't think I've ever seen you really dressed up, except for that day when we had our job interviews."

"Those were my sister's clothes. This is the only dressy thing I own." Lee looked down at her cream silk jumpsuit. It was severely tailored, like most of her outfits, but she'd brightened it for the occasion with a wide gold belt and matching sandals.

"Well, you look nice."

"So do you," she said, feeling her sadness deepen.

In fact, he looked wonderful in pleated dress slacks, a dark T-shirt and sports jacket. No doubt Melanie would be all over him as soon as he walked in the door.

And for some reason David also seemed happier than usual today, even disposed to be pleasant and chatty. In fact, he was so much like the man she remembered that she could hardly bear to be near him.

"If you weren't stuck with me in this phoney

situation," she said at last, "would you ask Melanie out?"

He changed lanes expertly and passed a station wagon in front of them, filled with waving children.

Lee waved back automatically. "Would you?" she asked.

"Would I what?"

"Would you ask Melanie out if you were a single man?"

"Of course not. She's married."

"But if she weren't," Lee persisted.

"I don't know. Maybe," he said idly, peering at something on the street. "Look, Lee, those people have a ferret on a leash. Poor little thing."

Lee frowned at the young couple with their exotic pet, then returned to the subject that tormented her. "You would ask her out?"

"I suppose so. Why not? She's a nice-looking girl, and she likes to play tennis."

Her misery increased.

"How about you?" he asked, casting her a quick sidelong glance. "Would you go out with Jason Lane?"

"Jason Lane?" she echoed.

"Oh, come on. That muscle-bound jerk who flies the traffic helicopter. He seems to be in your office every time I go by."

"We're working on a documentary about the

station's aerial photography capabilities," Lee said. "It was Wilbur's idea."

"So, would you go out with him if you could?"

Lee tried to imagine being escorted somewhere by the young pilot, but the picture wouldn't even form in her mind. The only man she could visualize next to her was David Clementi.

"Lee?" he said.

"No. I probably wouldn't go out with him."

"Why not?"

Because I'm so much in love with you, I can't imagine being with any other man, she wanted to shout.

Instead she shook her head and clutched the beaded evening bag in her lap, biting her lip nervously.

"Look, David," she said at last, "this isn't working out."

"It isn't?" he said.

"I really hate the whole thing. It's so hard to live such a big lie all the time." Lee took a deep breath. "I think now that we're safely established at our jobs, we should start talking about going our separate ways. I'd like..." She swallowed hard. "I want to move out by the first of September."

He tapped the wheel. "That's really what you want?"

"Yes, it is."

"Okay," he said quietly. "That's entirely your right, according to our agreement. We'll start looking for a place for you to live right away, and I'll help you get your stuff packed."

"Thank you." Lee turned to look out the window again, wondering if a heart could really physically break. It certainly felt that way.

She was relieved when they pulled up to the curved driveway in front of the Martlows' stately home.

The party was in full swing when they arrived, spilling through the whole lower floor of the big house. Well-dressed people stood around holding champagne flutes, feasting on appetizers and tables of sweets, laughing and talking.

The place was brightly lit, rich and happy, filled with the sense of family warmth that the Martlows believed in so fervently. Edna and Wilbur moved among the crowd of new employees, all of whom they now knew by name, meeting spouses and pausing to exchange a few moments of warm conversation with each group.

"We've really lucked into a couple of pretty good jobs, haven't we?" David murmured as they entered the room, bending so close to Lee that his curly hair brushed her cheek.

She shivered and pulled away, wondering how much longer she could bear to live this charade.

Especially when he was looking so handsome that it was all she could do to keep her hands off him.

But as Lee had expected, Melanie Reeves monopolized David's attention almost as soon as he came in the door. She looked stunning in a little scrap of a black dress with spaghetti straps and four-inch heels that made her long legs appear even more shapely.

Her husband had been unable to attend the party, she reported. By now, Lee knew through the office grapevine that Melanie's marriage was in deep trouble. The absent husband was apparently having an affair of his own, with an elegant woman who ran a downtown clothing boutique.

Lee suspected that part of Melanie's attachment to David was simply a reaction to her own hurt. Whatever the motivation, her seductive behavior was so blatant that Edna Martlow had clearly noticed, and other workers were conjecturing how much longer the blond copywriter would be working for Martlow Enterprises.

But, Lee realized with a jolt of misery, it didn't really matter. If Melanie got fired, she could soon find another job in the city, and David would still have her phone number.

Jason Lane, the muscular helicopter pilot, appeared at Lee's elbow and began telling her a long complicated story about a traffic pileup on the freeway west of the city. Lee listened distractedly, scanning the crowded room for any sign of David and Melanie.

Suddenly Edna returned with David in tow. He offered Lee a full glass of champagne and some chocolate cherries on a napkin, then nodded to Jason.

"So, are you having a good time?" he asked Lee.

"Yes, of course." She turned and smiled politely at her hostess. "It's a lovely party."

Edna beamed in response, looking majestic in a navy blue sequined tunic. "Hello, Jason," she said to the pilot. "Would you please go and tell Wilbur that the punch bowl is almost empty? Thank you, that's a dear."

She watched in satisfaction as the young man moved reluctantly away from Lee, then smiled cozily.

"I brought David over with me," she said, "because I wanted to issue this invitation to both of you."

"An invitation?" Alarm bells sounded in Lee's head.

"Well," Edna said, "you told me your apartment was being painted this weekend, didn't you?"

"Yes, it is," Lee said.

"And I believe the two of you were going to spend a weekend at a hotel."

"I have the rooms...the room booked," David said, correcting himself hastily. "The painters started working at our apartment this morning."

"So I assume you have your luggage with you?"

"Yes, we do." Lee was increasingly afraid of where this was going. "We're planning to go straight over to the hotel after the party."

"And we have our dog in a kennel for the weekend," David said.

"Well, I simply won't have you going to a hotel," Edna told then firmly. "Wilbur and I have talked this over, and we'd like you to spend the weekend with us."

"Here?" Lee said. She and David exchanged a startled glance.

"We have a lovely guest suite." Edna put a hand through each of their arms and drew them close to her, lowering her voice significantly. "In fact," she told David, "it's very romantic. I'm sure you'd prefer it to a hotel."

Again Lee caught David's eye and shook her head frantically.

"But, Mrs. Martlow," he said, "I've already booked the hotel."

"There's a phone over there in the library."

Edna waved her hand in the direction of a paneled door. "You can call them and cancel."

Lee's mind reeled. If she had to spend a whole night in the same room with this man, she couldn't be accountable for her behavior. The thought of it was simply too much to endure.

"Please, Mrs. Martlow," she said, "we hate to impose at the last minute. We'll be fine at the hotel, really we will."

"Oh, nonsense," Edna said firmly. "I won't hear of it. You're staying with us, and that's that. As a matter of fact, come with me right now," she said to David. "We'll find somebody to get those suitcases out of your car and up to the guest room."

Before either of them could protest she swept off again, taking David with her. The last thing Lee saw was his look of dismay as he glanced back over Edna's plump sequined shoulder.

Chapter Six

THE REMAINDER OF the evening passed in a blur of panic. Only one event registered clearly on Lee's mind, a brief interlude out on the rear patio. She and David had been sitting outside quietly discussing their awkward situation, while around them the summer night was fragrant with the spicy scent of flowers, murmurous with insect noises, and illuminated by colored Chinese lanterns that fluttered overhead like glowing butterflies.

Melanie, who'd obviously had too much champagne, had joined them, trying to coax David into an impromptu tennis match on the lawn. Edna passed by at that moment and overheard their exchange. She stopped to pat his shoulder and beamed at Lee who sat tensely beside him.

"I'm afraid David has to conserve his energy," Edna said with a significant wink. "He and Lee are staying here with us tonight, and they have a very romantic evening ahead of them."

Melanie's face tightened. She turned on her

high heels and left the patio, muttering something about needing a drink.

David leaned close to Lee. "It'll be okay," he whispered. "There's sure to be a couch somewhere I can sleep on."

But, as it turned out, he was wrong.

When the party ended and the last of the guests had trickled away reluctantly, Edna showed them upstairs to their room. Lee stood thunderstruck, staring around in dismay.

The place looked like a reproduction of Sleeping Beauty's bedchamber. A huge four-poster bed stood so high that wooden steps were required to get into it, and heavy flowered curtains hung from each bedpost. Little pink-shaded lamps cast a romantic glow over the room, highlighting Persian carpets, gleaming hardwood floors and lush ferns.

Aside from an antique dresser with twin oval mirrors, and the massive bed, the only other furnishings were a pair of little upholstered chairs set cozily together in the window bay.

"There's a bathroom through that door," Edna said, "with a big whirlpool tub. We always leave a couple of terry-cloth robes in the closet. Everything else you might need is in the cabinet next to the sink. Be sure to check it out. And have fun, my dears."

With another beaming smile she was gone, marching regally toward the staircase.

Wordlessly, Lee turned away from David and went into the lavish tiled bathroom, where their overnight cases were already unpacked and stored on a bank of shelves. She bent to open the marble-topped cabinet next to the sink. It contained a vast selection of bubble baths and exotic massage oils.

"Wow," David breathed, looking over her shoulder at the colourful array of glass bottles and vials. "Look at all that stuff."

Lee got up hastily, avoiding his eyes. "I don't need anything but my toothbrush," she said.

"I'll let you have the bathroom first so you can get ready for bed, okay?"

"Thank you," she muttered stiffly, brushing past him to get her nightshirt.

Alone in the bathroom, she put on the yellow cotton shirt, which hung past her knees and had a huge screen print of a mushroom and a leprechaun on the front. Lee had a feeling Edna would heartily disapprove of the garment.

When she could delay the moment no longer, she emerged from the bathroom and looked at the bed. He'd already turned back the covers and was sitting in one of the little upholstered chairs, looking down at the moonlit trees in the yard.

"Which side should I take?" she asked.

"I like sleeping close to the window, if that's all right with you."

She nodded, about to say that she remembered his preference, but stopped herself. The last thing she wanted to bring up right now was the intimacy they'd shared in the past. She climbed the wooden steps to the bed, then waited with growing dread while David was out of sight in the bathroom.

The bed was king-sized, but his pillow still looked distressingly close to her own. She wondered if a viable bed could be created by pushing the two little armchairs together.

Or maybe they could use the chair cushions to construct some kind of barrier down the centre of the mattress…

He came out at that moment, wearing only a pair of gray boxer shorts, and gave her an awkward smile. "I didn't bring any kind of pajamas," he said. "This is what I always sleep in."

You think I don't remember what you sleep in? Or how it felt to lie beside you, holding you…

His shoulders were broad and muscular, gleaming faintly in the glow from the lamp, and his chest was matted with dark curly hair that ran down his hard flat abdomen and vanished under the waistband of the shorts.

Lee gripped the blankets tensely as he slid into bed next to her.

"This is a strange feeling," he said, glancing upward. "It's like being in a cave."

He was right, there was a sheltering, secret feeling created by curtains. The two of them seemed cozily isolated, as if they were the only people in the world. Again Lee was conscious of his pleasant male scent.

"What's that nice smell?" she said abruptly. "I've always wanted to ask. Do you wear cologne, or some kind of scented aftershave?"

He shook his curly head against the pillows. "I'm not a cologne kind of guy. It must be the soap, I guess."

Or maybe it's just you...

She leaned over abruptly to switch off the bedside lamp, and he followed suit. They lay side by side in the darkness, staring up at the swathes of fabric that glowed faintly in the moonlight.

"Well," she said at last, "this is pretty much the most embarrassing moment of my life. I swear I'll never tell another big lie as long as I live."

"Hey, come on. What's so bad about this?" he said cheerfully. "We're in a great room, we're saving all kinds of money on the hotel bill, we've just been to a really nice party.... Life could be worse, right?"

"Oh, David," she muttered in despair.

His profile was etched with silver in the moonlight, and it was all she could do not to reach out and run her fingertips along the line of his brow and nose, the firm shape of his mouth and chin.

"So you're really planning to move out?" he said at last.

"Yes." She edged a little farther toward the extreme edge of the mattress. "As soon as I can."

"Why? Don't you like the apartment?"

She stared at him in the darkness. "You're asking me *why?*"

"I had the impression we were settling in pretty comfortably."

"David, we're not roommates! If we were, this would all be completely different. But we're pretending to be *married,* and everybody believes us."

"We're not pretending," he said calmly. "We really are married."

"I know. Can't you see how much worse that makes it? We can't suddenly announce we were kidding all along. And I simply can't go on living this lie. I just hate lying to people all the time."

He shifted restlessly in the bed, flexing and stretching his long legs. "Hulk is really going to miss you."

"Oh, sure," she muttered. "Bring up the kid, and make me feel guilty."

He laughed aloud. Lee smiled back at him reluctantly, then turned away on her side to end the conversation.

"Good night, David," she murmured over her shoulder. "I'm really tired. I want to go to sleep now."

"Okay, good night." He patted her arm casually, and she trembled at his touch.

There was a long silence, so profound that she could hear crickets chirping in the moonlit stillness beyond the window.

Lee felt deeply, painfully conscious of him lying next to her in the darkness. Every nerve in her body strained toward him, reaching and seeking, though she lay still and rigid beneath the covers.

After a while he whispered, "Lee?"

"Mmm?" she murmured, pretending to be drowsy.

"Would it bother you a lot if I put on the lamp to read for a while? I usually need to read for a few minutes before I can fall asleep."

I remember that, too. I remember everything....

"That's okay," she said, keeping her back turned. "Go ahead."

She was conscious of the glow when he

switched his lamp on again, then a rummaging sound that showed he was examining the stack of books on the bedside table. Papers rustled as he turned pages.

"My God," he muttered after a few moments.

Lee rolled over to look at him again. "What is it?"

He glanced at her distractedly, then turned back to the book in his hands. "It's nothing," he said, "Go to sleep."

"What are you reading?"

He looked so embarrassed that she was intrigued. "Nothing important," he repeated. "Somebody left a pile of books here on the nightstand."

"What kind of books?" She leaned up on her elbow.

"Well, they're…"

While he struggled for a response, she took the book from his hands and switched on her own lamp, flooding the room with an additional pink glow.

"My God," Lee breathed, staring at the book.

David grinned. "That's exactly what I said."

The volume was a glossy, expensive sex manual, containing graphic photographs of a young man and woman in all kinds of loveplay and sexual positions. Lee stared at the pictures, wide-eyed and breathless, feeling her body moisten and ache with arousal.

She flipped to the opening pages and found a colored plate stating that this volume belonged to the library of Edna Martlow. Underneath, in neat black handwriting, were the words, "For my darling Edna, with love from Wilbur, Christmas 1992."

David leaned over to read the inscription, distressing her further with his nearness. He began leafing through the other books on the nightstand.

"There are six of them," he reported. "All gifts from one of the Martlows to the other. Look at this one, Lee. Wilbur got it last year for his birthday. It's a series of illustrated excerpts from the Kama Sutra."

Lee peered at the little pen-and-ink drawings, which were intensely, passionately erotic. She felt her mouth go dry.

He flipped through the book and held it out wordlessly, showing her another of the illustrations.

"I don't think..." Lee faltered and cleared her throat, staring at the page. "I don't think that's physically possible."

He grinned, his eyes sparkling in the shaded light. "Wanna find out?"

"David..." she warned.

He touched her bare arm, and she could feel his hand trembling. "Lee," he whispered.

"Come on," she said. "We can't let ourselves be seduced like this, just because we looked at some erotic pictures and got all…excited."

"Are you excited, Lee?" He gazed at her intently from the next pillow. "Tell me how you're feeling."

"I feel like I'm…"

Mesmerized, she stared back at him, then reached out involuntarily to touch his shoulder. His skin was warm and silken.

"This is ridiculous," she whispered. "We can't do this."

But he was caressing her face, stroking her cheeks, letting his fingers trail over her mouth. She wanted to pull away, to climb out of their seductive flowered cave and run away from him while she still could.

Then she was in his arms and his mouth was on hers, and she was lost. Somewhere in the depths of their kiss she realized how passionately she'd hungered for this, how much she'd yearned for him to hold her just this way, and move his lips over hers, and run his hands over her body…

"Hey," he whispered, laughing against her neck. "I like this. Let's have a look at some more of those pictures."

"But I don't want this to happen," she protested with the last of her strength. "Please, David."

He released her at once and drew away to his own side of the bed, watching her soberly. "You don't want me?"

She was so sexually aroused that having him suddenly gone from her arms was almost physically painful. Lee hugged herself and stared bleakly at the ceiling.

"I don't understand you," she said.

"What do you mean?"

"David, I've been coming on to you ever since we moved in together, and you've been pushing me away! Now all of a sudden you're..." Her voice broke.

"Completely out of my mind," he agreed. He put a hand to his forehead and shook his head. "Lee, I've been fighting my attraction to you from day one! In spite of all I suffered through six years ago, I can't shake the feelings I have for you. I know I've got to be certifiable to feel this way but I'm willing to risk that kind of hurt a second time, if it means I get to hold you."

"But I'd never hurt you like that again!" she said. "It had nothing to do with us, David. It was because of..." Lee paused, shuddering when she remembered that horrible time. "It was because of my parents, especially my mother. That divorce almost killed her, David."

"But what caused it? I always thought they were the perfect couple."

Lee twisted her hands together in the flowered coverlet, then began to pick at a ragged cuticle on her thumb.

"My father..." She took a deep breath. "He had an affair with his secretary and got her pregnant. It almost destroyed my mother. The girl was twenty-two at the time, exactly Moira's age."

David glanced at her in openmouthed astonishment. "When did all this happen?"

"Right at the same time we were...you and I..." Lee swallowed hard and forced herself to continue. "Dad told the family about his girlfriend a month before our wedding, David. Everything in my life turned upside down. It was a horrible time."

He gripped the book, frowning. "Why didn't you tell me?"

"Mom was in such a mess, utterly traumatized and humiliated. She almost went out of her mind." Lee grimaced, remembering. "She made all of us swear we wouldn't tell anybody the details."

"Okay, so you were keeping a family secret. But that still doesn't explain why you walked out on me and all our plans."

Lee watched the curtains through a brief shimmer of tears.

"I was so afraid," she whispered at last, biting her lip. "I always worshiped my father. I thought they had a really great marriage. And if he was capable of treating my mother like that…"

"Then no man could be trusted," David said flatly when her voice faltered. "Not even me."

"I guess that's how I felt."

"Do you still believe it?" he asked without looking at her.

Lee shook her head. "I got over most of the craziness soon afterward. Their lives began to settle down and Mom finally remarried. Now she's happier than she ever was with Dad. But by then it was far too late for…for you and me. You were already gone."

"Oh, Lee," he said gently, stroking her cheek. "Sweetheart, if you'd told me all this right away…"

"I wanted to. Oh God, I wanted to tell you everything! But she made us promise. She was so fragile, David. It was a scary time."

"We wasted so many years being afraid," he said in a bemused tone.

"Afraid?" Lee whispered.

"You were afraid of marriage because of your parents. And I've been afraid of the kind of pain I went through six years ago."

She took his hand and held it as understanding dawned slowly in her mind.

"You thought if we got close again, I was going to dump you again?"

"I lost you once before, and it almost killed me. To hold you again and then have to give you up…" He shuddered.

Lee put her arms around him, drawing him close.

"David, I thought you hated me for what I did and you were never going to forgive me. I wanted to leave so you could be free."

"Free! There's nowhere in the world I want to be," he whispered, "except with you. I love you, Lee. I always have."

She melted into his arms, on fire with passion.

"Look," he whispered after a moment, "I hate the way that damned leprechaun keeps watching me. Let's get rid of him."

Lee smiled and sat up in bed to take off her nightshirt. He lay propped on his elbow and watched her, reaching to cup and caress her breasts. "The most beautiful woman in the world, right here in my bed," he said in awe. "And you know what else?"

Lee slid down into his embrace again, loving the silky warmth of their naked bodies as they entwined. "What else?" she whispered.

"We're married." His lips moved against her

breasts, giving her a pleasure so intense it was almost unbearable. "You're my wife."

She drew away to stare at him, astonished. "My goodness, you're right," she breathed. "We're really, truly married."

"We sure are." He laughed in triumph and rolled closer to her, his lips still moving and seeking. "And, Mrs. Clementi," he whispered, "I think it's time we got to know each other again."

"I couldn't agree more," she told him solemnly, then watched as he reached up to pull the satin cords that held the bed curtains.

Fabric rustled and fell into place around them, completely enclosing them in a warm shell of privacy illuminated by the pink lamps beyond the bed. Lee went eagerly back into his arms.

His mouth and hands were as playful and richly satisfying as she remembered, his soft laughter mingled with her own, and she knew that after a lifetime of wandering she'd finally found her way home.

NEXT MORNING, EDNA and Wilbur Martlow sat over their coffee in the morning room, watching their young houseguests through mullioned windows as they strolled on a flagged path in the garden.

"They looked a little tired at breakfast," Wilbur said from behind his newspaper.

"Yes," Edna agreed. "They did, didn't they?"

"But very happy," Wilbur said. "Positively radiant, both of them."

Beyond the window, David Clementi stopped and plucked a yellow rose from a trellis, threading the flower into his wife's bright hair. She said something to him and he laughed, then took her face in his hands and bent to kiss her tenderly. She clung to him, her hand caressing the back of his neck as she whispered in his ear.

After a moment they moved off again among the shrubs and flowers, hand in hand, talking together quietly.

"When I went downstairs for cocoa, I heard the jets on the whirlpool tub running at about three o'clock in the morning," Wilbur commented. "Along with a good deal of muffled giggling."

"Oh, that's nice," Edna said, pleased. "I left out a nice stock of scents and relaxing oils for them."

"Well, I think they probably made use of all of them. They certainly seem relaxed, don't they?" Wilbur waved his hand at the scene in the garden.

Edna watched the young couple who now sat

on a stone bench in the sunshine, kissing again, their bodies straining toward each other. Afterward they leaned back contentedly, Lee's head resting on his shoulder while he stroked her hair with a gentle hand.

"Yes," she agreed. "They're very relaxed."

Wilbur glanced curiously at his wife. "How did you know what they needed, Eddy? You're a magician. You really are."

"Oh, pooh," she said modestly. "I could tell by the way they looked at each other that they were still in love, but there was so much tension between them, you could cut it with a knife. I thought they'd probably benefit from some time alone together to concentrate on each other, and a little…"

She paused abruptly to sip her coffee.

Wilbur lowered the newspaper and gave his wife an alert glance. "A little what?"

"Nothing," she said evasively.

"Come on, Eddy. I can always tell when you've been meddling, because you have such a cute, mischievous look. What did you do?"

"Well…" Her cheeks warmed a little. "I suspected this was a tough case because they really weren't communicating at all. I thought they might need a little push to repair their marriage. So I…helped out a bit."

"How?" He peered at her over the rims of his reading glasses.

Edna concentrated on her china coffee mug, tracing the outline of the handle so she wouldn't have to meet her husband's eyes. "I loaned them a few books from our private library," she confessed.

"You didn't!" he said, looking scandalized.

"Why not? Those books have brought us a lot of pleasure over the years, Wilbur. Haven't they?"

She glanced up and smiled, and he responded with a meaningful grin.

"Oh, yes," he agreed fervently. "They certainly have."

"Well, I thought it would be a good idea to share them with this nice young couple. Was that such a bad thing to do?"

Wilbur looked out the window at the two on the bench. They were cuddled together again, talking earnestly. Lee's hand rested on her husband's thigh, and his arm was around her shoulder.

"No, Eddy," Wilbur said at last. "It was a very wise thing to do. And you're a wonderful woman."

"Oh, pooh," she said again. But his praise was sweet and his look of warm intensity still thrilled her, even after all these years.

The other couple got up, their arms entwined, and made their way along the shaded path toward a set of French doors on the patio.

"I think," Wilbur said, "they're probably going upstairs for a little nap."

"Yes," Edna agreed placidly. "I'm sure they are. We won't see them again until lunchtime."

Her husband beamed at her, his eyes twinkling behind the spectacles. "I adore you, Edna Martlow," he said.

The young people vanished through the French doors. Distantly, Edna heard their footsteps and soft laughter as they hurried back upstairs to their room.

She sipped her coffee and smiled lovingly at her husband while the morning sun sent out gentle rainbows from the crystal serving dishes on the table.

HARLEQUIN · CELEBRATES

FIVE DECADES OF ROMANCE

Celebrate!
5 Decades of Romance.
Enjoy Harlequin superstar

DEBBIE MACOMBER

and

RENEE ROSZEL

in

the first of four 2-in-1
Harlequin 50th Anniversary
limited collections.

Available in June 1999 at your favorite retail outlet.

HARLEQUIN®
Makes any time special™

Look us up on-line at: http://www.romance.net

PH50COLL1

If you enjoyed what you just read,
then we've got an offer you can't resist!

Take 2 bestselling love stories FREE!

Plus get a FREE surprise gift!

Clip this page and mail it to Harlequin Reader Service®

IN U.S.A.	IN CANADA
3010 Walden Ave.	P.O. Box 609
P.O. Box 1867	Fort Erie, Ontario
Buffalo, N.Y. 14240-1867	L2A 5X3

YES! Please send me 2 free Harlequin Superromance® novels and my free surprise gift. Then send me 6 brand-new novels every month, which I will receive months before they're available in stores. In the U.S.A., bill me at the bargain price of $3.57 plus 25¢ delivery per book and applicable sales tax, if any*. In Canada, bill me at the bargain price of $3.96 plus 25¢ delivery per book and applicable taxes**. That's the complete price, and a saving of over 10% off the cover prices—what a great deal! I understand that accepting the 2 free books and gift places me under no obligation ever to buy any books. I can always return a shipment and cancel at any time. Even if I never buy another book from Harlequin, the 2 free books and gift are mine to keep forever.
So why not take us up on our invitation. You'll be glad you did!

135 HEN CQW6
336 HEN CQW7

Name	(PLEASE PRINT)	
Address	Apt.#	
City	State/Prov.	Zip/Postal Code

* Terms and prices subject to change without notice. Sales tax applicable in N.Y.
** Canadian residents will be charged applicable provincial taxes and GST.
All orders subject to approval. Offer limited to one per household.
® is a registered trademark of Harlequin Enterprises Limited.

6SUP99   ©1998 Harlequin Enterprises Limited

THE MACGREGORS OF OLD...

#1 *New York Times* bestselling author

NORA ROBERTS

has won readers' hearts with her enormously popular MacGregor family saga. Now read about the MacGregors' proud and passionate Scottish forebears in this romantic, tempestuous tale set against the bloody background of the historic battle of Culloden.

Coming in July 1999

REBELLION

One look at the ravishing red-haired beauty and Brigham Langston was captivated. But though Serena MacGregor had the face of an angel, she was a wildcat who spurned his advances with a rapier-sharp tongue. To hot-tempered Serena, Brigham was just another Englishman to be despised. But in the arms of the dashing and dangerous English lord, the proud Scottish beauty felt her hatred melting with the heat of their passion.

Available at your favorite retail outlet.

Look us up on-line at: http://www.romance.net   PHNRR

Harlequin is proud to introduce:

HEART OF THE WEST

...Where Every Man Has His Price!

Lost Springs Ranch was famous for turning young mavericks into good men. Word that the ranch was in financial trouble sent a herd of loyal bachelors stampeding back to Wyoming to put themselves on the auction block.

This is a brand-new 12-book continuity, which includes some of Harlequin's most talented authors.

Don't miss the first book,
Husband for Hire by Susan Wiggs.
It will be at your favorite retail outlet in July 1999.

HARLEQUIN®
Makes any time special ™

Look us up on-line at: http://www.romance.net   PHHOW

Everybody's favorite family is back—the Reeds.

HOLDING OUT FOR A HERO

Coming in June 1999
Three complete, unforgettable novels by bestselling storyteller

GINA WILKINS

You'll love these stories about how the three Reed sisters, Summer, Spring and Autumn hold out for heroes!

Available at your favorite retail outlet.

HARLEQUIN®
Makes any time special ™

Look us up on-line at: http://www.romance.net

HARLEQUIN
SUPERROMANCE

Due to popular reader demand,
Harlequin Superromance® is expanding
from 4 to 6 titles per month!

Starting May 1999, you can have more
of the kind of stories that you love!

- **Longer, more complex plots**
- **Popular themes**
- **Lots of characters**
- **A great romance!**

*Available May 1999
at your favorite retail outlet.*

HARLEQUIN®
Makes any time special ™

Look us up on-line at: http://www.romance.net   HSR4T06

Strong, seductive and eligible!

THE AUSTRALIANS

Stories of romance Australian-style, guaranteed to fulfill that sense of adventure!

This June 1999, look for

Simply Irresistible

by Miranda Lee

Ross Everton was the sexiest single guy the Outback had to offer! Vivien Roberts thought she was a streetwise Sydney girl. Neither would forget their one night together—Vivien was expecting Ross's baby. But irresistible sexual attraction was one thing...being married quite another!

The Wonder from Down Under: where spirited women win the hearts of Australia's most independent men!

Available June 1999
at your favorite retail outlet.

HARLEQUIN®
Makes any time special ™

Look us up on-line at: http://www.romance.net

PHAUS12

**Show Mom you care this Mother's Day
with gifts from
Harlequin and Silhouette.**

Marriage FOR KEEPS and **BABY** *Fever*

With the purchase of either *Marriage for Keeps* or *Baby Fever*, receive a set of three cookbooks featuring delicious desserts. With the purchase of both *Marriage for Keeps* and *Baby Fever* receive the set of desserts cookbooks plus a set of three cookbooks featuring main courses.

**EXCLUSIVE OFFER!
ACT NOW TO RECEIVE
YOUR COOKBOOKS TODAY!**

To receive the set of desserts cookbooks send in one (1) proof of purchase plus 40¢ U.S./65¢ CAN. for postage and handling (check or money order—please do not send cash); to receive the set of desserts cookbooks plus the set of main courses cookbooks send in two (2) proofs of purchase plus 80¢ U.S./$1.25 CAN. for postage and handling (check or money order—please do not send cash) to COOKBOOKS, In the U.S.: 3010 Walden Avenue, P.O. Box 9071, Buffalo, N.Y. 14269; In Canada: P.O. Box 609, Fort Erie, Ontario L2A 5X3. Please allow 4-6 weeks for delivery. Quantities are limited. Offer for Desserts and Main Courses cookbooks expires July 31, 1999.

Marriage for Keeps and *Baby Fever*
cookbooks offer!
OFFICIAL PROOF OF PURCHASE

Name: _____

Address: _____

City: _____

State/Prov.: _____ Zip/Postal Code: _____

Account Number: _____ (if applicable)

HARLEQUIN®
Makes any time special ™

Silhouette ®
097 KHH CSGU

PMFKBFPOP